FAREWELL,
MY QUEEN

Chantal Thomas

Translated by Moishe Black

D0815408

Weidenfeld & Nicolson

LONDON

First published in Great Britain in 2004
by Weidenfeld & Nicolson

First published in France in 2002 as *Les Adieux à la Reine*
by Editions du Seuil

© 2002 Editions du Seuil
Translation © 2003 George Braziller Inc.

A CIP catalogue record for this book
is available from the British Library.

ISBN 0 297 64550 1

Typeset at The Spartan Press Ltd,
Lymington, Hants

Printed in Great Britain by
Clays Ltd, St Ives plc

Weidenfeld & Nicolson

The Orion Publishing Group Ltd
Orion House
5 Upper Saint Martin's Lane
London, WC2H 9EA

FAREWELL, MY QUEEN

Also by Chantal Thomas
in English

Coping with Freedom: Reflections on Ephemeral Happiness
The Wicked Queen: The Origins of the Myth of Marie-Antoinette

Contents

Prologue: Vienna, 12 February 1810   1

Versailles, 14 July 1789   19

15 July 1789   51

16 July 1789   113

Vienna, January 1811   241

Prologue

Vienna, 12 February 1810

My name is Agathe-Sidonie Laborde, a name rarely spoken, almost a secret. I live in the émigré quarter of Vienna, in an apartment on Grashof Street. Its windows open above a paved inner courtyard surrounded at ground level by a number of shops: a second-hand bookshop, a wig maker's, a small print-shop, a violin maker's. There is also a spice seller's stall, just at the foot of my apartment building. A lively neighbourhood, but not too noisy. In the summertime, along with Eastern aromas, there are always notes of music floating in the air. The rose bushes winding their way up the building fronts add a garden charm to this little corner of Vienna. But in the dead of winter, which is what we have at present, the rose bushes have ceased to bloom and the sounds of life from the shops no longer reach me. But for me, the sounds of life are well and truly stilled whatever the season. It's as though the terrible winter around me, this unending snow and the feeling it gives of being buried, were a symptom of my advanced age, the outward sign of that deeper, permanent winter creeping over me.

Today, 12 February 1810, I celebrated my sixty-fifth birthday. 'Celebrate' is not an apt term for the mood of those assembled in my room, a few French exiles of my own vintage, fellow survivors from the collapse of that world commonly called 'the Ancien Régime'. The snow never stops. When my faithful friends arrived, they were wet through, for (I regret to say) when one requires a cane in order to walk, one cannot then use an umbrella. If only old age held no greater misfortune! I set their sodden garments to dry before the fire. The ladies fixed their hair and redid their faces, and then my guests offered me their presents: flowers of wild silk, a fan, and a tiny oval-shaped box that I was asked not to open until after the others had left. I kept the flowers and fan on my lap while we drank coffee and ate pastries. As usual, and like the whole of Europe, we talked about Napoleon – with hatred, naturally, only ours was restrained, not the genuinely raging hatred that inspires a large segment of Viennese society. We saw the conqueror's triumphant arrival here last July, after the battles of Essling and Wagram. We endured the bombardments, the pestilence of blood, death, heaped-up bodies, the horror of those thousands of wounded to be encountered in virtually every part of the city, their death rattles and cries of pain forming a backdrop of sound to our regular daily lives. We also endured the spying and plundering, the violence that is the lot of an occupied city. But this army had come from France and was difficult for us to hate. Though exposed to the arrogance of its soldiers, we could not consider them as enemies. At the same time, we found these young men – who spoke our language and might have been our children's sons – foreign, painfully foreign. It was not just their attitude of hostility towards us, it was their deportment. 'They walk like him,' someone had pointed out to me. And it was true: they all walked too fast. Stiffly upright, heels striking the ground, they looked like so many automata. Napoleon's officers copy his manner of walking, and his manner of speaking, too, his abrupt way of addressing people (the only thing no one has so far attempted to imitate is his accent). With no preamble, the Emperor will suddenly ask the bluntest question. He does not converse; he fires at point-blank range. Our conversational ideal was the dialogue of the polite salon, with its sense of allusion and innuendo, its ability to place the speaker in a brilliant light, never making a vulgar show of knowledge, playing delicately with trifles, and, for the space of a verbal encounter, drawing out from those trifles pearls of intelligence and felicitous expression. Napoleon's model of discourse, by contrast, is the police interrogation. I expect he has the most delightful memory of his 'conversation' with Friedrich Staps, the student armed with a kitchen knife who tried to kill him at Schönbrunn last October.

'Do you regret your action?'

'No.'

'Would you do it again?'

'Yes.'

Had he not been obliged to condemn Staps to death, he would gladly have pursued this conversation a little longer. The young man was very like him, as Charlotte Corday was like Marat. Terrorists attract terrorists . . . A civilisation based on the dagger, the bayonet, and the cannon. In former times a man prided himself on being the perfect embodiment of polite behaviour. When he had occasion to make war or engage in military activities, he did not boast of it. Thus, for instance, no soldier would ever have presented himself in uniform at court. First he would change his raiment, even if he had news of a victory to bring, and a flag wrested from the enemy to lay at the King's feet. Similarly, given the choice of wearing the blue cordon of knighthood in the Order of the Holy Spirit and the red cordon of the Order of Saint-Louis, honouring a military exploit, what well-born man would have hesitated? The blue was undoubtedly a source of greater pride.

During my birthday celebration, even as we warmed ourselves at the flames of a generous fire and listened to the satisfying sound of the logs crackling between the andirons, we lamented the Emperor's latest plans, which, pacific though they were, did not lessen the already colossal list of his crimes. Some said that he proposed to live for a month every summer in the palace of Versailles, though he found it small and misshapen, 'a horrible aberration', and an aberration, what's more, that cost him a fortune to keep up. He had decided to stay there occasionally, after having the impudence to declare: 'The Revolution destroyed so much; why did it not demolish Versailles?' But other reports claimed that Napoleon planned to cut down the trees, take away the statues, and replace them all with monuments commemorating his victories . . .

We had another serving of cake – absolutely delicious – and continued our lamentations . . . Monuments to his victories . . . It is not enough for him to contemplate marriage with Queen

Marie-Antoinette's great-niece Marie-Louise – *the Austrian woman*, as he so elegantly calls her – he must needs take over the palace as well. And he puts his 'N' everywhere: this man, who cannot tell the difference between hunting to hounds and hunting rabbits, has commanded that all Louis XVI's hunting guns be engraved with his initial. 'You cannot hunt stags when you are hounding kings,' as the Prince de Ligne mockingly observes . . . In the event that he fails to get the Tsar's sister, I wonder whether Vienna will tolerate such an abomination, whether Metternich will hand the poor archduchess over to her country's oppressor. In all this hellish warfare, with its threat of armed gangs and looting, its reduction of rape and murder to commonplace events, Napoleon's pretensions to legitimacy are very nearly the thing I find most offensive. I say very nearly, for what really offends me, what saddens and distresses me, is something that is not to be found in our professions of indignation; nor is it part of those choruses of loathing in which we habitually join. No, the thing that appals me derives rather from what we do *not* say, from our hypocritical acceptance of the rule that Louis XVI and Marie-Antoinette are never to be mentioned. The prohibition applies at all foreign courts, but the place where it is most strictly observed is certainly here, in Vienna. To pronounce those forbidden names in defiance of the interdict causes fearful embarrassment. If it involves Louis XVI, the social blunder, though serious, can be overcome; but to name Marie-Antoinette is unforgivable. Her memory is suppressed more viciously in her own home, family, and city than anywhere else. For this, her second death, Napoleon cannot be held accountable. If anything, the reverse is true . . . And we, with our noisy jeremiads, contribute to the work of obliteration. Noisy? I much overstate the case. I only wish we were still capable of making noise.

Around the fire, earlier today, our chairs so close together that we were almost elbow to elbow, we were saying how wretched it is to survive in the midst of ruins. 'If you survive, it means you're alive,' said one of my friends, but she uttered these words

so inaudibly that it was hard to put much faith in them . . .
Though the afternoon had barely ended, darkness was falling.
It was time for my guests to make their way home. And
just then, a group of schoolchildren came into the courtyard to
sing. Their voices were extraordinarily clear, rising up with the
same strength and joy that they put into their running, their ice-
skating . . .

Alone once more, I opened my last present. It was wrapped in so
many layers that at first I thought there was nothing else: just
coloured papers laid one on top of the other. But when I came to
the little silver box, it opened up to reveal a marvel. I had been
given a miracle: a pendant set in enamel, on which was painted
in miniature an eye of blue: blazing blue, almost turquoise,
of gem-like brilliance, the pupil seemingly bedewed with the
merest hint of moistness. I closed the palm of my hand over
the treasure, and let the blue of her eyes bring back the Queen's
entire face, her face as I knew it . . .

This ban on names is one of the pacts binding our society of
survivors, and when I am with others I respect the pact. But
when I am alone with myself, why should I be afraid of words,
or of the ghosts they summon up, or of the unknown with
which they sometimes bring us face to face? True, in my case
the ghosts fill the entire stage, during my waking life as they do
in my dreams, whether these be changing or recurrent. Thus, for
example, what I call my 'Dream of the Grand Staircase'. It has
variations – in particular, sometimes the faces are farther away
than at other times – but for the most part, it's always the same
dream: stationed at intervals, on broad steps, stand various
members of the royal court. Their magnificent apparel has a
kind of still quality that hampers movement. Some are leaning
on canes, others not. There are no groups. Each individual is
isolated, set slightly apart from the next. All, however, are outlined with perfect clarity. They stand there, on the rim of
nothing. 'The Dream of the Grand Staircase' haunts me. I feel

as though the people in the dream are waiting for me; mute, invisible, never very far away – that *they* are my truth, whereas the handful of survivors with whom I associate are merely illusion. Under their scrutiny I become uncomfortable. I seek distractions: embroidery work, writing letters, reading newspapers, books, every sort of publication in French that comes my way, but they will not loosen their vice-like grip. They press down upon me with all the weight of their non-being. I have become accustomed to 'the Dream of the Grand Staircase', but the dissatisfied feeling that it brings with it remains unappeased, for the faces in the dream, while recognisable, are not completely so. I am quite sure that I have known them but am unable to put names to them.

I lived for a time at Versailles, where I was a reader to Queen Marie-Antoinette – deputy reader, I should say. It was a very minor office, made even less significant by the fact that the Queen had little taste for reading. My patron, Monsieur de Montdragon, Steward Ordinary to the Court, had been careful to make that clear, though he welcomed me with the greatest kindness. It was a late December day, a midwinter day like today, but with no snow. The daylight had a sharp, almost metallic quality. The trees with their dark trunks stood out against a very blue sky. At the palace, to venture into the gaps separating the fireplaces – and the smoke-filled, blinding, choking zones their fires produced – was to become paralysed inside a block of ice. You had to keep moving; otherwise you might well perish.

Swathed in his wolfskin pelisse, Monsieur de Montdragon was putting me through an examination. From my first response, though I spoke timidly and could not help moving my fingers to keep them from going numb with cold, he had judged me fit for my duties. 'You have a fine voice,' he had said to me, 'rather low-pitched and not obtrusive.' And a bit later, observing my discomfort, he had added: 'Go to it, my dear madam, clap your hands together; that's a more straightforward, effective way to get them warm.' So after our interview, noiselessly, I had applauded. My patron had informed me what my duties would be, in my capacity as deputy reader to the Queen. 'To sum up, I would say that, by and large, there aren't any.' Then, in sudden anxiety, he had asked me: 'But you *can* read, I trust? Mind you, when I consider how long it may be before the Queen ever sends for you, there is ample time for you to learn; and even should she discover you to be unlettered, I am sure she would not take it amiss. Her Majesty's benevolence to all her familiars is boundless. You cannot conceive how far, in her household, she carries the virtue of patience. As for the precise details of your obligations, Madame de Neuilly, Reader to the Queen, will explain them to you . . . if it occurs to her, for when she comes to Versailles, she is, as you can well imagine, taken up with visits, solicitations . . .'

I could well imagine nothing whatsoever. My eyes and mind were quite dazzled with all the riches that surrounded me. I felt as though I had stepped into the kingdom of Beauty. I thanked Monsieur de Montdragon; he brought the interview to an end, and without pausing to reflect what an utterly unfamiliar world Versailles might be for a newcomer, he left me there in that little private room hung with yellow silk. Overcome by timidity and at the same time exhilarated by the unbelievable splendour that I sensed all about me, I remained for a time, seated on a couch, waiting. Finally, I found the courage to leave the little room and walk a few steps; I stopped at a glass door that opened on to an immense gallery. My earlier impression, of having been transported into a palace all of gold and precious stones, persisted. If someone had told me that the slate roof tiles of the palace of Versailles were in reality slabs of onyx, I would have believed it . . .

I arrived in 1778, the year of Queen Marie-Antoinette's first pregnancy, a blessing she had hoped for through eight years of waiting, the gift for which prayers had been said in all the parishes and convents of France, down to the remotest monastery.

In the eyes of the populace, that was the year of her true accession to royalty: the pregnancy provided the only possible justification for the position she occupied. Like everyone else, I knew the glad tidings; knew, too, that December, the month of my arrival, was the ninth of the Queen's term. All this I knew, and was aware that as reader, I would one day have occasion to be in her presence. And yet my first sight of Her Majesty threw me into an unbelievable state of rapture, as though it had been a sight afforded me by purest chance, against all reasonable expectation.

The Queen, towering, huge, clad in a very full robe of white woollen stuff, on her head a bizarre cameo-embroidered turban of bright blue silk with several peacock feathers pinned to it forming an aigrette, was striding rapidly along at the head of a group of women who were wearing themselves out in their efforts to keep up with her. She was walking as though she were abroad in the open countryside, when in fact she was in an enclosed gallery and at that walking speed – which, I later learned, had been recommended by her doctor – she reached the end after a few paces, only to wheel about and cover the course again, still with that same greedy, space-devouring stride . . . Surprise left me reeling. My legs were unsteady, my face was burning. There was something unbelievable about this apparition, a fantastical element that would forever mark all the images that followed. I thought I was seeing fire in motion.

I dwelt eleven years at the palace – 'in these parts', as people said, referring to the court – and never became accustomed to it, but assimilated its strangeness as a vital need. Eleven years . . . when I think about it now, it seems very remote, taking into consideration the line that separates me from that period of my life: the bloody slash mark of the Revolution. But also very near, probably because life in that place bore no resemblance to anything else. Time at Versailles was purely ceremonial; it was spent differently, marked off by curious signposts. The unit from which the divisions were calculated was not the year, or the month, or even the week, but the day. There was a Perfect Day, whose programme had been set more than a century earlier by Louis XIV: Prayers, Petty Levee, Grand Levee, Mass, Dinner, Hunt, Vespers, Supper, Grand Couchee, Petty Couchee, Prayers, Petty Levee, Grand Levee . . . Every day since that time was supposed to reenact the Perfect Day. Life at Versailles was a succession of identical days. Such at any rate was the rule, in theory. But reality never ceased to throw up obstacles. The reenactment was never completely successful. We were doomed to wither and decline. Life at Versailles could only degenerate . . . Tiny modifications became snags, reforms became upheavals, and so on, leading down to the days in July 1789 that saw the King capitulate and the court disperse – the collapse, in less than a week, of a ritual system that I had assumed was fixed for all time. For me, though, that first view of the Queen, which no painting or sculpture of a goddess has subsequently dimmed, had entrenched me from the outset in a timeless world. Life at Versailles was a succession of like days. That was the rule, and I believed in it.

I was not the only one to be obsessed in this way. When people said 'the court', they meant the Court of Versailles. Ours was the model par excellence, toward which the eyes of every capital city – St Petersburg, Rome, London, Madrid, Warsaw, Vienna, and the rest – were turned. This did not mean that people were unaware that despite ruinous attempts to drain the swamps, the palace of Versailles had been built on an unwholesome site, and unwholesome it remained. People were not unaware, either, of the epidemics and fevers, and the tremendous stench, which spread through all the rooms in warm weather. 'The perfectly natural result of exudation from the commodes' – so the casual visitor, on the verge of feeling ill, would be informed. And the women would prettily shake their heads like goats trying to shake free of their tethers. To drive away the fetid smell, they would wave their fans a little faster. Exudation indeed! . . . People choked! And it was terrifying to behold, against the white skin of some fashionable lady, the blisters dotted across her neck by insect bites.

Marie-Thérèse, wife of Louis XIV, would swallow spiders that had fallen into her bowl of chocolate.

Marie Leszczynska, wife of Louis XV, besieged by mice, would utter cries of distress. And in the early days of their marriage, the Queen's little cries (from her perch on an armchair whence she refused to come down), charmed Louis XV . . . till the day he wearied of poor Marie and her fears, saying with a shrug: 'I keep telling you, madam, that nothing can be done.'

Marie-Antoinette had a particular aversion to fleas and bedbugs. With the help of chemicals sent at her request from Vienna in boxes she treated as so many treasure chests, she had launched a systematic campaign. Her abhorrence of fleas was simply regarded as another of those peculiarities to be expected from a foreigner, along with her odd habit of washing before applying make-up . . .

All this we bore without a word: the stings and bites, the pimples and sickly humours, the strange swellings and suspicious growths. We endured without complaining the numerous bodily discomforts, including – I found this especially repellent (but it left most of the courtiers quite unmoved) – an unimaginable swarming of rats, for there was food left lying about more or less everywhere in the apartments, food that had fallen under the furniture, been forgotten between the sheets or quite simply left to spoil in the food closets or in the warming ovens that were installed in window nooks, on landings, and under staircases. The rats thought Versailles was wonderful. By night they conducted a witches' sabbath there, taking complete control in some of the living quarters, where floor and furniture were reduced to ruin . . . We might also have complained of finding it difficult to breathe, outdoors because of exhalations from what remained of the swamps, indoors because of the crowds squeezed into spaces that were too small. And if ever there was a place where one might die of asphyxiation, it was the palace of

Versailles. Yet none of these evils had any importance for us, nor for the rest of the world; our position was envied.

For we were at Versailles.

Versailles, where Fortune reigned and where a word from a minister, or from a courtier with the ear of those in power, might alter your fate totally from one day to the next. For better, as well as for worse.

Where the best tone prevailed, and men bowed themselves out of a chamber with greater style than anywhere else.

Where Fashion was decided. Never mind that sometimes you wore lace chewed by mice: the cunning little creatures sometimes invented new stitches.

Where, even in the least frequented sections of the park, at the farthest end of an avenue, at the entrance to a wood, some small detail of great beauty might always appear: the equivocal beckoning of a statue, the goblet of fruit and flowers carved into the stone and set against the sky.

Where, above all, there dwelt the Queen.

And on certain mornings, in the half-consciousness that precedes waking, when I can let the state of pleasant confusion persist awhile, I make believe I am still back there, I imagine my fingers are touching the wall of the room I had there, that I am turning over in my bed, that once again I feel my hair lying in thick abundance against my pillow, and I tell myself that a few rooms away from mine, She lives and breathes.

Versailles held me under its spell. And I was not the only one. To be sure, it was no longer the sacred place it had once been, under the dominion of Louis XIV. But Versailles continued to exercise its fascination. Wherever you went in society, you had but to pronounce these opening words: 'I was at the court . . .' and those around you held their breath, looked at you differently. It is hard now to imagine how deep were the wounds inflicted on self-esteem 'in these parts', how humiliating it was for a courtier, after hours spent waiting in an anteroom, to confront the fact that he would not be summoned to the King's Privy Supper. His shame was palpable; I could read it in people's faces, in the bearing of those who had been ushered out and were returning to their carriages by way of the inner courtyard to avoid scrutiny. What I did not see was the joy of the chosen as they slipped through the half-opened door and proceeded to the sanctuary. But I could imagine it . . . And even later, during the Directoire, when court was held at the residence of Joséphine de Beauharnais, and Bonaparte was posing as a model republican, even then the passion for Versailles still burned. As soon as one of the official soirées ended, they made sure the doors were properly shut and said to one another: 'Let's talk about the old court, let's spend some time at Versailles; Monsieur de Montesquiou, tell us how they used to . . . Monsieur de Talleyrand, tell us about . . .' And the younger ones would draw their chairs up closer to hear the stories . . . They were doing what we do, here in Vienna.

I am determined to set this down in writing, to recall the magic, in today's climate, when a campaign of propaganda is tending to stigmatise Versailles as a bottomless pit of needless expense, or else speak of it as an empty stage, a landscape of dust and ashes, already dimmed by an awareness that the end was near. Marionettes with powdered perukes, men and women old before their time, puppets doomed to disappear . . . From the winners' standpoint, those whom they had beaten and outstripped had in any event no existence worthy of the name, no future. The arrogance of young people would be touching, but for the fact that it so often leads to brutality.

I am convinced – and my most recent impressions of the world we live in do not encourage me to change my mind – that humanity does not progress. It rearranges things in other ways, to accord with altered social standards and reflect different aspirations. The system based on a hierarchy of castes had its faults, but the one based on oppression through money does not strike me as preferable. This obsession with getting rich . . . Now there are things called banks. These, so I am told, are little fortresses located in the centres of certain capital cities which, seen from outside, cannot be distinguished from normal houses. It is very odd to try and imagine such places. I have probably seen banks without realising . . . My parents were poor. Whenever my mother, speaking with no hint of acrimony and motivated solely by the desire to keep some of her children alive, ventured to point out to him the destitution in which our family lived, my father, who was very pious and loved us dearly, would smile in response. Averting his gaze from our wretched circumstances, he would lift up his eyes towards an attic window and say: 'Is not life more than meat and the body more than raiment? Behold the birds of the air: they sow not, neither do they reap, nor gather into barns; yet your heavenly Father feedeth them. Are ye not much better than they? And wherefore should you have a care to clothing? Consider the lilies of the field, how they grow; they toil not, neither do they spin.' My mother's glance would follow his towards the window with its missing panes. She would smile with the same smile as his . . . The lilies of the field are trampled and trampled again by the soldiers. If there is progress, in our day, it can only be in weaponry. We kill more quickly now, and in greater numbers . . . At the battle of Essling alone there were forty thousand deaths, forty thousand deaths in thirty hours of combat . . . The mind recoils. Yes, machines for killing are improving. Aside from that, I do not see . . .

The palace of Versailles, sacred symbol, focus of so many desires, was abandoned at the first signs of impending danger, in July 1789. The whole drama played out very swiftly. Louis Sébastien Mercier, a democrat, a Parisian, and what is worse a man of the theatre, but with an honest mind illuminated by intuitive flashes of truth, has written: 'The Revolution could have stopped on 18 July after Louis XVI had taken in his hand the national emblem – the cockade – and kissed it, on the balcony of City Hall.' I cannot but agree. The entire outcome was decided between Saturday 11 July, the day Jacques Necker, Controller General of Finance, was dismissed, and Friday the 17th, the day that the King was stripped of his title in Paris and royalty was repudiated. The 16 July saw the Breteuil government dismissed and Necker recalled. That same day, the court was in flight. Defeat was now inevitable and irreversible; Louis XVI grasped this fact, but too late. In 1792 he would admit to Count de Fersen: 'I ought to have left on 14 July. I missed my chance and was not granted another.' Indeed, he was not granted another; whereas in his and the Queen's entourage, on the other hand, the chance was grasped all too quickly. Court, friends, relatives dispersed in the twinkling of an eye. Princes and courtiers made off for London, Turin, Rome, Basle, Lausanne, Luxembourg, Brussels . . . And I myself was swept along in the flood tide of that disaster. I left without stopping to consider, without questioning what I was doing. Rather than act, I simply obeyed . . . I suppose . . . Ought I to feel consoled by that thought? 'The King's Couchees have been quite deserted,' the Queen had complained. All at once, not just the Couchees but the entire palace answered that description. We abandoned ship the moment the timbers began to creak. We fled.

I would like to give an account of that defeat; it happened so quickly, it was so total and complete, but in some sense it has remained a secret, a tale never told. A stealthy defeat one might almost say . . . a moment of silent consternation, a few words so exchanged as not to be overheard, orders given, great lords disguising themselves as servants, and carriages moving at a gallop along the roads. There was no moonlight on that night of 16 July 1789, and when I turned around to look back at Versailles, the palace, hidden by forest darker even than the sky, had disappeared . . . I would like to tell the story of that desertion, thus appeasing the intruders who invade my dreams and mitigating the isolation of days spent in this enclosed space composed of silence, wakefulness and writing: my room, which I now rarely leave and which, when the fancy takes me, I call 'my castle of solitude'. I shall find a place for everything that comes back to me, all the remembered fragments of a wrecked world; I shall not be so heartless as to kill that world a second time by striking things out. My mind takes up the same facts again and again, changing them to fit my changing daydreams, while other, possibly more essential facts have been obliterated. I do have this excuse: I speak of a time long ago, a time leading nowhere, certainly not to our grim nineteenth century, even if some people, naive in their use of numbers and fooled by hindsight, see in that earlier century no more than the prelude to this one.

Versailles, 14 July 1789

Early Mass: 6 a.m.

It was a rather cool morning for July; that, I guess, is what I was thinking as I stood on a stool in my attic room, head thrust out of the window, peering at a rainy sky. Quickly, I got into my clothes, pulling winter stockings on to my legs and slipping a dark-violet, nearly black dress over the heavy cotton petticoat I had worn in bed. I added a woollen jacket and a neckerchief, then snatched up a large umbrella. No need to snatch up the missal, however: it was always in my dress pocket, and I transferred it whenever I changed dresses. I set off hurriedly for Saint-Louis Church to hear early Mass there. I knew the way by heart, but that did not prevent me from getting it wrong and going too far along the rue de la Chancellerie, instead of immediately turning right, on to the rue des Récollets. A minor error, certainly, considered in terms of distance, but the gravity of my mistake was brought home to me when I reached the fringes of the market. Clusters of poor wretches eked out an existence in the filth and corruption there. They would do anything to improve their regular fare, which consisted of the worst leavings, bits of refuse that dogs would not have eaten; occasionally they would fight one another for the privilege of drinking the oil that fed the wicks of the streetlamps. I could not see these people, but I could tell they were there, huddled together beside rows of hovels, scattered about in the hidden protection of anything that might serve as a shelter or simply lying dead-drunk in the gutters. I was walking as fast as I could. I slid on what I took to be some vegetable peelings and let go of my dress, which was a bit too long, with the result that its hem got soaked in the mud, the horrible mixture of blood and filth in which that collection of huts was mired. Very close to me, things were stirring, shady dealings were going on, men's voices could be heard. I ought to have taken greater care and not have crossed this ill-famed Parc-aux-Cerfs quarter alone in the grey light of a day that refused to break.

When I reached Saint-Louis Church, my heart was pounding and I became absorbed at once in fervent prayer. We were enjoined to pray very hard for the preservation of the kingdom and for the soul of the Dauphin, poor child, who had died on 4 June. At the King's behest, a thousand masses were to be said for the soul of his son. I prayed passionately, with the uneasy feeling that there was a link between the death of the King's oldest son and some nameless threat to France. Early-morning hour notwithstanding, the church was full. Along the rows of seats, sombrely clad, kneeling, silhouetted figures were whispering. The bit of light we had came from holy candles forming a border around the congregation, not from the stained-glass windows. The priest who climbed the steps up to his pulpit was not Father Jean-Henri Gruyer, curate of Saint-Louis, but Father Bergier, confessor to the Queen, to the King's brother the Count de Provence, and to the Count's wife. This priest must surely know a great deal that he was keeping to himself! I tried to make out, through the words he spoke, some other, subtle message, informed by facts gleaned in the secrecy of the confessional, that he might indirectly be revealing to us. Father Bergier, needless to say, let nothing escape his lips. In his customary dry, extremely unassuming voice, he eulogised Saint Bonaventure, whose feast day – 14 July – it was.

I made my way back to the palace following the approved route, along the royal kitchen garden, then the rue de la Surintendance. This itinerary might appear safer, judged from outside; in fact, it disturbed me even more deeply. In this old quarter, which had once been the village of Versailles, many delegates of the Third Estate had taken up residence. The prospect of encountering these drearily garbed men, who talked to each other the way most people hit each other, was most unalluring. I overcame my misgivings, however, and managed to walk the full length of the street without seeing anything. Not till I was almost at the first gate of the palace did I feel safe enough to recover the gift of sight. In the royal courtyard, the changing of the guard was under way. I hummed an accompaniment to the music of the drums and trumpets; as I went by, I took a pitcher of water from the cupboard under the stairs at little Alice's – she was chambermaid to Madame de Bargue (who was lucky enough to have an apartment with a fountain) – and went back to my room to don formal wear. I changed my wool stockings for ones made of floss silk, and replaced my neckerchief with a black-and-white tartan shawl. I did my hair very carefully. I also wanted to get in order the readings I had chosen for the Queen. For I had been notified yesterday: this would be one of the days when she sent for me.

Reading session at the Petit Trianon – *Félicie* by
Marivaux; summer flowers and light; the Queen
and her *Notebook of Ladies' Attire*: 10 to 11 a.m.

———————

The Queen had slept at the Petit Trianon, although traditionally
Tuesdays were reserved for ambassadorial visits, which involved
her being present at the palace. Apparently, however, either
there would not be any visits from ambassadors, or the Queen
would not be obliged to receive them . . . I was to present
myself to her not merely at the Trianon but actually in her
bedchamber. I looked forward eagerly to that moment. When
she was in her own realm, I could hope to capture her attention.
It was obvious that she was much happier at the Petit Trianon
than at the palace of Versailles. On each occasion, at the
Trianon, in the very gesture that she used when inviting me to
be seated, I could detect a special sort of inner peace and outward kindness.

At the palace, the morning sessions of reading took place just
before the beginning of the Grand Levee. I would find the
Queen still in dishabille, sitting on the great theatrical bed in
the ceremonial bedchamber. She would beckon me to pass
through the ornamental railing, I would open the little gate and
proceed to seat myself on a narrow stool to the right of her bed. I
could tell that she was perturbed, fuddled with sleep, and totally
inattentive. In her mind, she was already being subjected to the
first ritual of her day. And something of the stiff formality, the
self-assured, remote, and purposeful image that it would be her
duty to project, had begun to come over her. It was as though
the rows of chairs and folding stools, set out ahead of time for
the ladies who were going to attend her Levee, were watching
her; as though the public already had its collective gaze fastened
on her and was making her feel the weight of its constraints,

through the intermediary of those chairs. The reading sessions at the palace were always hastily conducted, official, submitted to rather than enjoyed. They antagonised the Queen and left me inwardly wretched.

But at the Petit Trianon, that 'bouquet of flowers' given her by the King, the entire performance was quite different. What Monsieur de Montdragon had told me was true: the characteristic aura you encountered, on coming into the Queen's presence, indeed, as soon as you stepped into the atmosphere of her household, was one of gentle kindness. And to anyone who was also familiar with the households of Monsieur the King's eldest brother, or that of Madame his wife, or those of his other brother, the Count d'Artois or his wife, the difference was quite remarkable. At home in her own place, the Queen avoided giving orders. She would suggest, mention, ask for each thing as a favour that someone might care to do for her and for which she would be ever so grateful. She was absolutely polite to the humblest of her servants and never evinced the slightest impatience or brusqueness in her dealings with them. She was maternal and deliberately playful with her pageboys, and she addressed her female attendants in accents not just of friendship but of mutual understanding. Was it an appeal for closer affection? Did the Queen forget who she was? By no means; nor, moreover, did anyone have illusions on that score, but the atmosphere I have described was the affecting, affectionate harmony in which she desired to live. The gentleness that distinguished her gestures, her tone of voice, and her dealings with other people were an extension of the tremendous elegance possessed by everything that came within her orbit – clothing, furniture, decor. Entering Versailles itself, I had thought I was entering the kingdom of Beauty. My introduction to those domains where the Queen ruled taught me that the beauty I so admired could assume a more personal, subtle, delicate hue.

My visit was expected. I went up the marble stairway leading to the second storey where her bedchamber was. I can still see the curve of the stairway, the blue-and-white porcelain pots that were set on the steps (the sight of them always made me long to go to Holland; I am exceedingly fond of windmills), the somewhat narrow corridor, built to allow two people to brush past one another, the doors on which were chalked the names of those few friends considered worthy to spend the night at the Petit Trianon – the same thing was done during country sojourns at Marly, Fontainebleau, or Saint-Cloud, when lodgings were requisitioned from local residents to accommodate those who had not been found room for at the château. There were also, in various corners, little improvised rooms for the servants, removable boards on which they would lay a thin mattress that they rolled up immediately on awakening and stowed out of sight. At the Petit Trianon, as at the Trianon and the palace, day erased the traces of night. But not in her special place, no, not in her bedchamber, not in the private territory that she marked with her gentle sweetness, with her scent. There, night and day commingled, prolonged each other, met, and intertwined. And this was especially true in that bedchamber at the Petit Trianon, which was so dear to her because it could not be confused in any respect with an official setting. The room looked out on to an ornamental pond and the Temple of Love, partly hidden from view by a little forest of reeds. Forest? That at any rate was how she referred to the ten or dozen reeds whose rustling, when the window was open, was part of the enchantment I found in that bedchamber at the Petit Trianon. Sounds of water and reeds, voices of the lace makers, seamstresses, spinners, and ironers, whose songs the Queen liked to hear as they went about their work in the washhouse. That, in my memory, is the music of the Petit Trianon, and not the succession of concerts held there, numerous though they were. It is the music of the garden and of women's voices. And the fragrances? Like the music, these come in the first instance from outdoors. They are delicate, and they change, in the spring, with the changing garden blossoms. But one there is that persists, identical across the seasons: the smell of the coffee brought to the Queen for her breakfast. If I chanced to arrive just when she was having her coffee, she would ask her attendants to bring another cup for me. And the instant it touched my throat, the savour of the strong black brew, that to her was the taste of her daily awakening, became part of the very flavour of my life. If I search my memory, there is one other fragrance, more fraught with meaning, with a very strong, smooth odour to it, that I smelled only when I came to the Petit Trianon. But I was afraid to breathe it in, because it was too closely involved with the Queen's body and the care she lavished on it. This was a jasmine-flower salve that she had her women smear around the roots of her hair. The salve prevented hair from falling out and could even make it grow. All the women longed to get some for themselves, but Monsieur Fargeon, of The Scented Swan in Montpellier, jealously guarded it for the Queen's exclusive use.

When her attendants showed me in, the Queen was drinking her coffee. The flowered white background of the hangings in her bedchamber, the huge bouquets of dahlias in their crystal vases, the transparency of the finely embroidered net curtains, all conspired, that morning, to make you forget the dull weather. But nothing would have had any effect on me had it not been for the charm of her smile, dawning when I appeared, then, when I stood up after my curtsey, shedding a joyful, golden warmth over everything; drapes, partitions, rugs, mirrors, writing stand, and harpsichord, even the hollyhocks that stood in bright sprays around the half-opened curtains of her bed.

'How good of you to have walked all this way in order to come and read to me here at the Trianon. And so early in the morning, too . . . I don't know how to thank you.'

'I would walk much farther, and with the utmost willingness, should Your Majesty so desire.'

'I know, I know, you are entirely devoted to me. And it is a great comfort to me to think of all these willing people ready to offer me their services.'

A chambermaid handed me a cup of coffee. I was so flustered

that I swallowed it too hot. The table stood ready, as did the stool on which, when she signalled to me that I might do so, I took my seat. My throat was on fire. I got off to a bad start, in a voice that probably sounded hoarser to me than it actually was and made me uncomfortable. I had intended, by way of light reading, to start with *La Vie de Marianne*, for the Queen enjoyed Marivaux, then continue with a travel narrative, and finally conclude with the few pages of pious reading (extracts from Bossuet's sermons or Fléchier's funeral orations) that the Queen was supposed to hear every day since arriving at Versailles, in accordance with the expressed wishes of her mother, Empress Marie-Thérèse. The Empress had been dead for nine years now, but I observed that with the passage of time her precepts, so far from losing potency, had steadily gained it; and though in a way the Queen seemed to comply against her will, she no longer sought to avoid doing so.

While praising me for my excellent choice of readings, the Queen said in the same sentence that, nevertheless, and since it was most surely all the same to me, she would prefer passages from a play. Marivaux by all means, only not *La Vie de Marianne*, but rather *Félicie*, a very short, amusing, dramatised fairy tale. She appreciated theatre more readily than novels. For her, stage characters had a level of ready existence that characters in novels did not attain.

It was not all the same to me. Nothing that had to do with her was all the same to me. I did not dare to tell her so. Blushing and embarrassed, I went to the bookshelves and fetched down the volume she wished for. She had rejected the passages I had prepared: my feelings were hurt. At the same time, I felt flattered to join her in reading a play, to be giving her the cue to her lines. It was one way of gaining access to that temple of intimacy, that most secret of secret places: her theatre at the Petit Trianon. I tried to visualise the blue of the velvet chairs, the fragility of the blue and gold papier-mâché ornaments. I imagined it as a doll's house proportioned to the Queen's taste for whatever was very tiny, suited to the passion she had for scaled-down objects, miniatures, anything small. Small, *petit* – her pronunciation of this word was a delight; she made the first consonant too hard, then let the remainder of the word melt away in a sigh as though her mouth was kissing the ambient air. *Petit*, little – everything to do with Marianne is little (for instance, the Queen loved hearing me read aloud: 'I omit entirely the period of my early childhood years, when my instruction consisted of learning to make innumerable little items of feminine apparel . . .'), but she had rejected *La Vie de Marianne*. There we were in *Félicie*. The Queen was the fairy. I was playing Félicie, the young girl.

I began:

FÉLICIE One cannot but agree that the weather today is fine.

HORTENSE (the fairy) And as a result we have been walking for a long while.

FÉLICIE And as a result, though my pleasure in being with you is always very great, I have never been more aware of it than today.

HORTENSE I do believe that you love me, Félicie.

And I responded with all my soul, trying to restrain my fervour when I realised that unlike me, the Queen was reading tonelessly. She was delivering her lines without putting the least expression into them. She was reciting passages with her eyes shut, wearing a look of concentration as though she were reciting irregular verbs. She had completely forgotten that I was there. Totally absorbed in the effort of memorisation, she was muttering the words for her own benefit. I would come to a stop, whereupon she would go back to speaking audibly, and the fairy tale would resume its course . . .

The fairy asks the girl what gift she desires to have bestowed on her, and the girl replies: 'Beauty.' At once the fairy grants her wish and Félicie is overjoyed.

HORTENSE You rejoice at my gift; I wonder if it should not make you uneasy instead.

FÉLICIE Be assured, Madam. You shall have no cause to repent.

HORTENSE So I hope; but I mean to add one thing more to this present I have just given you. You are going out into the world; I want you to be happy out in the world, and for that I need to be perfectly informed of your inclinations, in order to ensure that the sort of happiness you find will be the one most suited to you. Do you see the place where we now are? This is the world.

FÉLICIE The world! And I thought I was still quite close to home.

At this point the Queen had had enough. Among the books I had put on the table, she had espied the latest issue of the *Magazine of New French and English Fashions*. That was what she wanted to hear: it was all about bonnets, the ornaments for grand court apparel, and trimmings for ladies' dresses.

'Dresses are commonly trimmed with a webbing of gold or silver, but the ornaments preferred today are tulle or net trim, accompanied by garlands of various flowers mingled with clasps fashioned into love knots.' A questioning note must have crept into my voice, for the Queen, her manner unpleasantly troubled, firmly directed me to continue . . . 'To these are added acorns in the Chinese manner, or horns of plenty scattering flowers and berries over the background of the fabric. When the background is plain, a dress may also be adorned with flowers and plants in imitation of nature, such as sunflowers, lilies, hyacinth, lily of the valley, hawthorn . . .' She was entranced. But it was when I embarked on the topic of embroidery work that she truly listened to me with bated breath: 'From lawn camisoles embroidered in a variety of colours, our ladies of fashion have rapidly moved on to dresses likewise embroidered. This vogue for embroidery is so pleasing that they are bound to put forth their best efforts in the perfecting of it.'

Embroidery work was the great innovation of that July. The Queen, as though gripped by inspiration, sat suddenly erect amid her pillows with a surge of energy such as I had not seen her display of late. She called for her *Notebook of Ladies' Attire*. The reading session was at an end; what followed was the responsibility of Rose Bertin. By the time I had retrieved the books I had brought with me and arranged them in my big cloth bag, the Queen was already absorbed in contemplation of her precious *Notebook*. Eyes fixed on the samples of fabric glued to the *Notebook*'s pages, she was withdrawn from the world. She was choosing her gowns. And, as though the sense of sight alone did not satisfy her insatiable desire for those stuffs – those silks and velvets, those goffered materials and fabulous weaves created to please her – she was stroking the samples with her fingers, wanting to feel them against her skin as she sat there and gazed pensively off into space. Absent-mindedly, she removed her nightcap. Soft and very fair, her hair spread cloud-like over the pillow, while at the same time a powerful smell of jasmine filled the room. One shoulder was bared. I sat motionless, enthralled . . . I could not make up my mind to leave. I do not know what I wanted from the Queen, but I wanted more and more.

At last I contrived to come away, but before I withdrew, I looked at her one last time; she was passionately examining those bits of fabric. At that moment she was fifteen years old, the age she was when she first arrived in France. Fifteen . . . at most.

Lunch at 'Little Venice': 1 p.m.

I went to have lunch by the water's edge, at one of the cafés set up along the north traverse of the Grand Canal, in those sham fishing villages that had continued to exist since the time of King Louis XIV and that were called 'Little Venice'. Country folk dressed as sailors (when they were not play-acting life at sea, they tilled the fields) served fish, conveyed at top speed from the ports on the Channel. I asked my waiter whether there had been a good catch. He launched into an account of dangerous moments at sea, shifting winds, shipwrecks narrowly avoided. There were a few other customers in the outdoor section of the café, including some I knew by sight. They enjoyed the account of a storm out on the open sea, and with the characteristic ability of the palace dwellers to abandon reality in a split second and leap on to a playhouse stage, they joined in the game.

'And right now,' I asked when I had done with my meal and was getting ready to leave, 'would it not be imprudent to put out to sea?'

I pointed to the dead calm of the Canal's surface.

'A little, but I'm going to fetch you an experienced sailor, an old sea dog who has been through many a squall.'

A gondolier appeared, and I took my place in his boat, on the damp fabric covering the seat. This young lad belonged to a Venetian family established in 'Little Venice' for more than a century, the Palmerini. He knew the entire history of the flotilla that plied the Grand Canal, but I had no wish to hear it. 'I would rather you sang me a song.' He began singing in Italian, and at once the sad, sad grey of that near-wintry sky turned clear and bright. And so I was carried away from the Trianon to find myself on the other side of that branch of the Canal, over towards the Menagerie Pavilion. I had not really planned to go there, but I was glad rather than vexed. Monsieur de Laroche, Captain-Custodian of the Menagerie, was a colourful personality. Beyond that, for me, he was a friendly soul, and on that free afternoon I was quite in the mood to pay a friendly call.

Visit to Captain de Laroche, Captain-Custodian
of the Menagerie – 'Enough of that':
from 2 to 4 p.m.

The like of Captain de Laroche was nowhere to be found. The most spectacular phenomenon in the Captain's Menagerie was no doubt the man himself, an individual such that I cannot resist the urge to pen his portrait. People pretended they were observing the animals but in fact what they came to see was him . . . only not from too close a distance. His company was best enjoyed out of doors.

Tall, swarthy, imposing, with military stripes and ribbons aplenty, as lavishly adorned in rings and diamonds as any financier, Laroche was the most fetid creature imaginable. At a distance of several paces, you could detect his presence with your eyes shut. He stank like a herd of billy goats, or like heaving masses of sows rolling around in the mire, or wild boars in their own muck. Compared to his aura, the air by the lake known as the 'stinking pond', in the park at Versailles, was sweetly scented. He was connected by birth to the rich and ancient Provençal branch of the Moizades and, following family tradition, had first been destined for a diplomatic career, but he would have cost France all her allies. The stink of Laroche struck like a bomb. Your choice was either to exit in great haste or to vomit. With the passing of the years, a problem that had already been extremely trying in his youth came to assume almost supernatural proportions. On the day of his presentation at court, a plan to seize him bodily and cast him by force into a bath having failed (he had broken one valet's arm and smashed another's teeth to smithereens), his household had been obliged to settle for dousing him with casks of perfume and putting two pairs of shoes on his feet in the forlorn hope of containing the man's stench. The combined effect of his personal odour and those perfumes was overwhelming. When the 'debutant' made his entrance, the King (at that time Louis XV) had recoiled, and when the moment came for the young man, still heated from the violent scuffles he had just been involved in, to proffer his right cheek for the ritual salutation, the King had turned away. His hands clasped Laroche's handsome face in a gesture he employed regularly but which on this particular day heralded not only a particularly tenacious bout of the royal melancholia but a fearful migraine as well.

In order that there might be no recurrence of the incident, and to avoid giving offence to a family that enjoyed royal favour, someone had the inspired idea of giving the new courtier a post at the Menagerie, where, it was hoped, his bodily emanations would commingle with those of the lions, tigers, and other big cats. He had been appointed 'Captain-Custodian of the Versailles Menagerie', a coveted position, for, aside from the fact that the duties it involved were not demanding, it included the right, nay, the duty to reside in the little octagonal château built to order by Mansart for Louis XIV. The Menagerie, erected at the end of one branch of the Canal on the farther side of the Grand Trianon, was by all accounts a most superior place before the Captain arrived. On the ground floor there was a large salon done in rocaille, kept permanently cool by fountains, and by rivulets that ran among ferns. It was an ideal meeting place in hot weather and on those stormy late afternoons so common at Versailles. People engaged in conversation there; they played at charades or at word portraits; and it was commonly said that with the murmur of the water in their ears and the softness of the moss around them, forming a tapestry over the uneven walls, wit flowed more freely in that place and was more happily infectious than anywhere else. Under Laroche these wellsprings of sociability had dried up at the source. Still, as Versailles was constantly overpopulated, there were always individuals housed at the Menagerie. But sojourners would only accept this arrangement for a limited duration, and would also contrive to occupy not the Menagerie château but its little adjoining lodges – in short, to reside as far away as possible from the Captain's evil-smelling lair.

If memory serves me correctly, in July of that year Monsieur de Lally, Madame de Gouvernet and her aunt were in residence there. Upon my arrival, as I stepped out of the boat on to dry land, I could not see any of these people. I could see only the Captain-Custodian. He stood at the entrance to his domain, under a boxwood arch. He was smoking a pipe. As ever, the Captain was full of energy – energy deriving, so he claimed, from his principles of hygiene, since, as he put it, 'every time you take a bath, you lose a bit of yourself'. His rings sent out glimmers of light much more luminous than the dreary colours of the sky. In his own way, Laroche was a sun. He was firmly convinced this was so, but without falling into the sin of pride, for he was in all sincerity and with fanatical affection the faithful vassal of Louis XVI, whose Couchees he had enlivened over many years.

'Good day to you, my pretty'; thus he greeted me from afar. 'Have you come to enquire after the ostriches? The ducks are none too well either . . . but that's normal for them: the water at Versailles kills them.'

Even in 1789, I was already past the age for being addressed as 'my pretty', but Laroche and I were on those sorts of terms. I knew his gallantry was quite innocent, and – why not admit it? – though it cannot be said that I ever precisely encouraged him, neither can it be claimed that I dissuaded him from it.

The same period of time that saw the rocaille salon dry up, and the spirit of those indoor gatherings wither and die in sympathy, also witnessed the decline and death of the Menagerie's outdoor residents. Laroche may have been a sun, but he was also a liability. First the elephant had drowned in a little pond. Barely a puddle. As the accident was such as to occasion surprise, there had been a brief inquiry, from which it emerged that at the time of falling down to rise no more, the victim was drunk. The elephant, Laroche had explained as he wept bitter tears over the loss of one of his favourite animals, needed its five daily litres of Burgundy wine. On that particular day, the beast had downed its quota somewhat quickly and in direct sunlight. Laroche had wept harder. What he had failed to mention was that he had granted himself the right to succeed to the privilege of the five bottles of wine! The elephant, that oh so affectionate, friendly, intelligent, gentle giant, was dead . . . An animal that wore 'its nose on its sleeve', as the Captain liked to repeat, quoting Comte de Buffon, whom he admired. Indeed the reason he was often seen loitering near the entrance to the King's private study was that he liked to glimpse the statue of Buffon that stood there (he had thought at first that it was not a statue, but the great naturalist himself, stuffed and mounted!).

After the elephant came the lion, who began to lose the hair of his mane and to appear unwell. The lion was not as sweet-tempered as the elephant, but he was a prestigious possession. He had been delivered to us with great pomp and ceremony as a gift from His Most Heathen Majesty the King of Senegal to His Most Christian counterpart. He was treated concurrently as ambassador and prisoner. A red carpet was rolled out for him, tracing its crimson pathway from the great marble staircase to the Apollo Salon where the King sat in state for the occasion. The lion had arrived, confined in a cage inlaid with precious stones and drawn by three slave girls, blacker than ebony. Stuck like a curling paper into the complex structure of her plaited hair, the first of the trio bore a little note from her country's king. That monarch informed Louis XVI that the young women were henceforth his property and that he could, at his pleasure, keep them for his own use, give them away as gifts, or feed them to the lion. Louis XVI had consigned them to the Menagerie. There the three of them lived, arms constantly intertwined, spending their time doing and undoing one another's hair, and speaking a language punctuated by shrill bursts of laughter that made you shiver. Their gestures were sharp and enigmatic. They had contrived to communicate with our world only in order to have sumptuous fabrics brought to them. They draped the material over their bodies without sewing it. Their dressing-up sessions were also the few quiet periods in their existence: they would only whisper or gaze at each other in silence. They would appear so deeply lost in thought, that if, without blaspheming, you could have attributed souls to those creatures, you would have said they were at prayer . . . There was one other quiet time for them; that was when they stood on the shore and watched the boats set off for the Trianon. They looked in solemn concentration at the big gondola-shaped craft, the yachts, frigates, and feluccas laden with courtiers. Under the unwavering stare of those eyes, haunted by vistas unknown to us, the courtiers would fall silent and return the stare. So that something resembling a wind of petrification passed between the three Africans and the Queen's Trianon-bound guests . . . And what of the Africans and the Queen? I was convinced that nothing could pass between them, and my opinion has not changed. For it was not so much a matter of passing, but rather something else, something indefinable, a tiny point of similarity in the mutual passion for fabrics, in the rapture engendered by contact with material. An unlikely point . . . a point of love?

Yes, if I think now of the Queen as I saw her that morning, with her wide lace sleeves, she all pink and delicate, motionless, her lips parted, while her eyes were fixed on those little pieces of fabric, those swatches of her finest gowns, the word that comes to my mind is *love* . . .

The lion, too, had died. Laroche experienced a terrible feeling of helplessness, and had asked the King for an audience. A very young Louis XVI, who was known at that time as *Louis the Virtuous* and wanted to earn the title *Louis the Stern* (I never did find out whether this was 'instead of' or 'as well as'), heard Laroche's petition: for an end to the slaughter at the Menagerie. Though well disposed, Louis XVI had not been much comfort. His manner had been evasive. At Versailles, the hot weather brought maladies with it. At such times, a goodly number of humans were unwell, too, and some died. He mentioned a certain Monsieur de Las, who had suffered an open fracture when he fell off his horse. Presently he lay dying in a hunting lodge, where family members had had him conveyed so they didn't have to hear his howls of pain.

'But the humans can say what's bothering them. Whereas my animals implore me with their dying eyes and can't give me the least hint of what is tormenting them. I'm about to lose the polar bear,' Monsieur de Laroche had moaned, twisting his handkerchief. 'Can His Majesty conceive of my suffering?'

'No,' the King had said. 'No, I cannot.'

Then, perhaps to punish himself for his lack of feeling, Louis XVI had cast aside the bunch of thyme he was holding under his nose, had bent over towards the despairing man and, breathing deeply, inhaled him to the full. And – oh, wondrous working of divine royal essence – the King, so far from being indisposed by what he smelled, drew strength from it. He had squared his shoulders, which he normally held somewhat stooped atop his longish, flabby arms, and smiled.

'I hold you in great affection, Laroche,' he had stated, speaking in his choppy manner. 'Let me see you occasionally at my Couchees, I shall be most pleased. As for the animals in the Menagerie, stop tormenting yourself on that score. There are hordes of animals here on earth. God provides for their existence, in vast quantities, nor is He ungenerous about replenishing their numbers. Polar bears, for instance, abound in the Far North.'

'I will resign myself to the inevitable. My polar bear is ill, very ill, and I can do nothing about it. Well, never mind! Enough of that!'

From then on, Monsieur de Laroche stopped talking about the health of his animals when at court. He discussed it only at the Menagerie. But he carried away from his conversation with the King a mania for saying 'Enough of that', on any and every possible occasion. And the words had become a catchphrase among the courtiers, who, initially to make fun of Laroche, then later for no good reason, punctuated their conversations with the ritual formula. There were days when it seemed to me that all I heard anyone say was 'Enough of that'.

Laroche drew near; I was submerged in his smell. (Silently, I recited the prayer of the dying: 'I beseech you, O Lord, to forgive me the pleasure I have taken in seeking out perfumes and good smells and for having allowed myself to become fastidious in the avoidance of bad ones . . .') Moderating his voice, he asked me the reason for my visit. Really, the ostrich? No, not the ostrich . . . It was a long time since we had seen each other, I missed him . . . He was delighted and paid me some compliment or other in return. He, too, was glad to have a companion during the idle hours of this July afternoon.

'Is all well up there?' he said, pointing to the palace.

'I haven't noticed anything out of the ordinary. Two thirds of the courtiers have colds, and the rest of them sneeze and wipe their noses to be in tune with the group. But you aren't putting your question to the best-informed person. I'm scarcely ever away from my books and am not invited to the Royal Council Meetings.'

'I should hope not. A lot of good they do! Those meetings are merely so many traps laid for our King, with his natural inclination to justice. The Royal Council Meetings indeed! Even thinking about them makes my blood boil with indignation. The very idea of *daring* to advise so wise a king as ours is a piece of insolence. Take Master Necker, for instance, can you imagine a more pretentious individual? The man's obsessed with figures! I heard his opening speech at the meeting of the Estates-General. I could have climbed the wall with boredom! Figures, figures, and more figures! For two hours. Finally, even he couldn't go on. After half an hour, he had to get a reader to take his place. I'd never seen anything like it: a speaker in the middle of inflicting a punishing schoolroom assignment on his listeners and giving up on it before they do!'

'And you'll never see anything like it again. At any rate not involving Necker.'

'Why so? Don't tell me he's learned how to be interesting.'

'That, I doubt, but in any case, there is no more Necker. He's been dismissed. Had you not heard? He was dismissed on Saturday. That's the big news of the moment.'

'My animals are very ill informed. And so, as a result, am I. But, my word, Necker dismissed! Now that *is* good news. Tell me all about it.'

'All I know is that on the eleventh – Saturday, then – at three in the afternoon, his friend, Count de La Luzerne, Secretary of State for Naval Affairs, came to him bringing a letter in the King's name. His Majesty requested that he resign and discreetly leave the country.'

'If it had been me, I would have thrown him in prison.'

'That's exactly what Baron de Breteuil says. He wanted Necker arrested.'

'That opening session of the Estates-General was sheer torture. A two-hour speech, and from that lout! Hundreds and hundreds of figures. A crashing bore should never be forgiven. But, my dear friend, you are obviously far too modest. The truth is that you are magnificently well informed. You didn't find that kind of news in the novels of Madame de La Fayette, Marivaux or Madame de Tencin.'

'You flatter me, sir. Everyone knows about Necker. Nobody is talking about anything else. For my part, it all makes my head spin. Fortunately, Monsieur Moreau quite likes to sit me down and explain what is happening. As far as I can follow it, at any rate, for he contemplates History from such a height that he can distinguish neither trifles nor anecdotes. He embraces only the essential.'

'And what does our gentleman Historiographer of France have to say about the dismissal of that jackass?'

'Like everyone else, he ardently desired it. He continues, however, to say: "There's going to be trouble." But he's been saying that for many a day.'

Laroche's face clouded over momentarily; just long enough for a great idea to come to him.

'If they've dismissed Necker, then his post is vacant! I'll be a first-rate Minister of Finance. I'll retrench in fine style, frills and essentials alike will have to go. I''ll start with the essentials; by the time I get around to doing away with the frills, the French will long since have lost the strength to protest.'

'Take care. If you go too far in your attempt to cut expenditure, you're likely to get cut from the cabinet yourself. That's what led to Necker's downfall. His tendency to economise, his excessive concern about matters of food supplies, and his timidity when faced with the disruptive influences so prevalent in Paris, his reluctance to strike hard and strike fast. He gave the impression of wavering, of tacking and turning . . .'

Laroche began to laugh – with that abrupt laugh of his that did not allow others to join in. (He had that in common with his king: not, as he liked to think, the same good judgement, but the same laugh.)

'Look how green it is hereabouts; those days of rain are what did the trick,' he added, turning toward the meadows that bordered the Menagerie.

Close by, there was a vast farm; its tenants exploited that part of the grounds, and its splendid herds grazed indiscriminately among the fallow deer and the roe deer, supplying some of the dairy products needed by the court. The remaining part was provided by the farm at the Petit Trianon. This side of the grounds gave an impression of lush green abundance. It made one think of Switzerland, if Monsieur de Besenval, who came from Switzerland, was to be believed. For my part, I was born beside the sea, so it didn't remind me of anything at all.

The Captain turned his attention away from this rural scene. He likewise ignored the Pheasantry lying next to the farm and turned to face the Saint-Cyr road, at one end of the Menagerie.

'No one goes along that road. What purpose does it serve? The convicts from the prison repair it regularly. They bring a bit of life to the place for a few weeks. They certainly sing well, those fellows! And then they vanish. And there's nobody there any more.'

'And don't people on horseback use the road?'

'Small chance of that! If they're gentry, they consider a road as a restraint on their freedom. They simply ride cross-country. Just like at the customs house when you come to enter Paris: a young man of good birth doesn't slow down. He whips up his team, and any customs employee who has the nerve to try and stop him gets sent flying. That's how it was when I was a young fellow, and I'm sure it's still the same.'

'I never go to Paris. Heaven forfend I ever should!'

'Nor do I. What would take me there? That's why I'm telling you about my younger days.'

'And did you behave like a young man of good birth?'

'Of course. I always drove into Paris at a gallop. I can still hear the shouts of the passers-by. The watch didn't dare to stop me. He took it out on the ones who looked poor and needy. He would vent his fury by thrusting his pike into wagonloads of hay to fish out any stowaways.'

'Fish them out?'

'Or finish them off! . . . The King is too benevolent . . . He sacrifices himself for the sake of his people. A pack of good-for-nothings who don't deserve his benevolence. He builds roads for them, and cities, orders the ports to be fortified and sends ships out to sea. The wiser course is not to do anything. Not build, not repair. Just let everything fall to bits . . . I shall be Minister of Ignorance. Minister of Abysmal Ignorance. "When all the mixed-up atoms have been separated out and returned to their original place, God will cover the whole world in absolute ignorance, so that all the creatures who now make up the world shall stay within the limits of their nature and not desire anything foreign to them nor anything better; for, in the lower echelons of the world, there shall be neither mention nor knowledge of what is to be had in the upper echelons, so that no souls can desire that which they cannot possess, and such desire cannot become a source of torment to them." Basilides, my dear. Greater even than Buffon . . . So that all the creatures that now make up the world shall stay within the limits of their nature and not desire anything foreign to them nor anything better . . . They're going to have a hard time up there finding a replacement for Necker . . . Still, if you assure me that everything is peaceful, I'll take your word for it.'

'Better than peaceful, serene.'

'In that case, everything is the best it can be, and the only dark spot left on my horizon (and it concerns no one but me) is the ailment afflicting my ostrich . . . But, you know, I haven't heard the royal hunt, not yesterday and not today. All is well, but the King isn't hunting . . . Well, enough of that!'

'No, not enough of that; let's talk about it,' I said, for I felt once again a vague uneasiness – the sense of strangeness I had had early that morning in the streets of Versailles.

But Monsieur de Laroche had moved on to another subject.

'And what are the King's Couchees like, these days?'

'Dismal, I'm told. Poorly attended.'

A triumphant expression lit the Captain's face. He blamed this disaffection on the ban that had excluded him from the Couchees. He harboured no resentment towards the King himself – obviously it was all a plot at some lower level. Louis XVI had yielded to pressure from the other Couchee participants. Especially the pageboys, for whom there was no possibility of stealthily opening a window and staying there, hidden from sight. There had been a universal complaint brought to the royal ears by the King's First Valet for the trimester. Louis XVI had bowed to the inevitable; in any case, he had lost his taste for merriment. Laroche's madcap behaviour, which occasionally involved pulling off other men's wigs and tossing them up on to the bed canopy or, like the King himself, laughing fit to burst as he tickled the ticklish, was not missed . . .

'The fun we had at those Couchees!' said Laroche.

And he dragged me off to the monkey enclosure. Then, as though suffering an attack of delirium, he rolled on the ground uttering cries. The monkeys leapt from end to end of their cage, hung by one arm, spun round and round. When his fit had passed, the Captain-Custodian got to his feet, as though nothing out of the ordinary had occurred, and solemnly declared:

'I have a great regard for you, Madam, because most of the time you are *you*, which is a rare and remarkable quality. When is a king a king? He is always King, of course. But in some situations he is more so than in others. Situations in which he is very much the king he was created to be. The king that no one else, standing in his place, could have been. In the case of our King Louis XVI – I realised this at once and have confirmed my first opinion many times – his special moment is in the evening, before they undress him for his Couchee, when he empties his pockets and sets his knife on the bedside table. At that moment, in that gesture, he is tremendously royal.'

I went and sat on a bench, close to the water. All the various craft had docked. 'Enough of that' had lifted my spirits. I was no longer uneasy. I had a feeling of perfect calm and of an immense stretch of time lying before me.

Chatting and embroidering with Honorine:
late in the day, before supper

At Versailles, even in dull weather, the sky clears as the day draws to a close, and is breathtakingly beautiful every time. It struck me so again that evening. I was sitting with my friend Honorine Aubert, First Chambermaid to Madame de La Tour du Pin. We were comfortably settled in a little room that was part of her mistress's quarters; Madame de La Tour du Pin, a neighbour to Princess de Hénin, resided in a large apartment above the Galerie des Princes, high up in the buildings that formed the South Wing of the palace. On one side, this apartment opened on to the rue de la Surintendance, and, opposite, on to the terrace of the Orangerie. I especially liked being there, out of friendship for Honorine, and also because my own room on the slope-roofed upper floor of that South Wing, though it allowed me to experience the full glory of the heavens, was cut off from any view of the palace grounds or the city. To sit in that handsome apartment, then, meant having a panoramic wholeness restored to me.

Together Honorine and I were completing a tapestry begun and then abandoned by Madame de La Tour du Pin. I have always liked embroidering. I was less skilful at it than Honorine, but as she was by nature slower-moving than I, we went along at the same pace. Through the open window we heard sounds of music coming up from the apartments of young Princess Marie-Thérèse. We were exchanging accounts of how we had each spent our day. I told her that the Queen seemed to be in a more tranquil humour, one might almost say happy, despite the depth of her grief, and that it warmed my heart to see this change. Honorine was very glad. Needles held aloft, at our feet the reels of silk, we were progressively creating a wooded landscape, stitch by stitch. Chattering all the while, we were doing our best to achieve a gradation of greens.

For amusement, I told her about my afternoon at the Menagerie, and the African women. 'I don't believe it,' said she. I beg pardon? She didn't believe it? But I had seen them, in fact more than once. Heard them, too: they were cackling louder than a henhouse. 'I don't believe it, that's all. There are no African women at Versailles. Or in Africa, for that matter, because Africa doesn't exist. Travellers come back and say whatever crosses their mind. Who's going to go and see if what they say is right?'

When Honorine started playing the sceptic, it always put me in a temper: I became stiff and disapproving. Not for long, however, as there was an unexpected diversion: three timid knocks at the door, a man stuck his head in, could we tell him where to find the Queen, he had something to show her. What might that be, pray? He hesitated, then came all the way in so we could see his whole person. 'This', he said, 'is what I should like to show her.' And he stood before us, very straight, feet slightly apart. We looked the fellow over. He would have been unremarkable, were it not for his attire: he was dressed like Harlequin, in a multicoloured garment all of one piece. Only instead of lozenges, he had stripes, and the stripes were blue, white, and red. 'I'm looking for the Queen,' he said again, 'so I can model this design for her; I am proposing it as a national costume.'

An evening in the Great Hall

The rest of the evening, which we spent in the Great Hall, had been gay and cheerful. And the supper simply royal: we were served what was left over from the King's Table. I remember that quail featured, as did fresh cod from Newfoundland. Towards nine o'clock, some priests had come to sit with us. They were not hungry, because they had just been at the feast given by Cardinal de Montmorency: this was the day when he had taken his oath of loyalty to the King. They described the desserts for us: more than a hundred kinds, not counting the preserved fruit, compotes, ices, and nougatines. Father Hérissé had brought along several bottles of quince ratafia liqueur and cherry wine that he insisted we try. Honorine and I, as neither of us was accustomed to alcoholic drink, couldn't stop laughing at the least thing that was said, and we laughed even harder when the speaker was being serious. Thus when the diners at our table talked about the latest decree issued by Louis XVI, forbidding gentlemen in the army to strike common soldiers with the flat of a sword, we gave a great guffaw, with our noses in our drinking glasses. I am a little ashamed when I think back over it, but that is how things were at the time. There may not have been any children at Versailles, but there was plenty of childlike heedlessness in the air, and that was the air I was breathing.

The strong drink continued to circulate freely, and the merriment of the assembled company grew accordingly, though all was perfectly decent. Someone produced a fiddle, and we danced.

At about eleven in the evening, I went back to the palace, which stood a few yards away from the enormous structure of the Great Hall. Darkness was just beginning to descend. I was holding Honorine's arm. Our lodgings were a few rooms apart. There was still coming and going in the underground passage linking the palace to the kitchens of the Great Hall. In the palace itself, this was the hour when the lantern men, armed with their pikes, were lighting the torchères on the corridor walls – a sight so familiar that we no longer bothered to take notice. What did surprise us, on the other hand, was to see the windows still lit up along one wing of the government Ministries building.

'Good heavens, is the new government already in session? Or still in session? At this hour of the night? The energy of his lordship Baron de Breteuil is most impressive.'

'If his capacity for work is on a par with his sense of rank, we are in good hands,' added someone who greatly admired the de Breteuil family.

'I doubt whether at so late an hour the government is sitting; rather, it is settling in. The gentlemen are sharing out the offices among themselves.'

'But who are they, exactly? Have all posts now been filled?' asked my friend, somewhat sobered by the cold air. Living in the sphere of the de La Tour du Pin family, a very political family, she followed what went on at court closely.

I heard a list of names recited, which pleased me. I like lists. I like things that are numerous without necessarily requiring to be counted, things that fall naturally into ritual order.

Names can also be recited like a lullaby, when eyes are closing in sleep. And that night, in spite of the excitement of a reading session, despite my long walk early in the day, and the Captain of the Menagerie, and the knitted Harlequin, the dancing, the quince ratafia, and the cherry wine, I had difficulty closing mine. Stretched out on the bed, I stared up at the sombre sky. The calls of nocturnal birds came from the woods. The ululating hoot of the screech owl, that strange sound verging on a sob, gave me the shivers. And outside there was a continuous noise of car- riages, horses, a hubbub of voices. This time, too, however, it was the names that finally prevailed:

The Duke d'Argile

Monsieur de Sainte-Colombe

Monsieur Desantelle, *Intendant des Menus Plaisirs*

Countess Ossun, Mistress of the Robes

The Duchess de Polignac, Governess of the Children of France

The Ladies of the Bedchamber

The Ladies-in-Waiting

The Queen's Trainbearer

The Princess de Lamballe, Superintendent of the Queen's Household

The Duke de Penthièvre, Master of the Horse

Count Vaudreuil, Master Falconer

Count Hausonville, Master Wolfer

Count Zizendorf, from the land of Greater Tartarie

The Prince de Lambesc, Grand Equerry

The First Equerry

The quarterly equerries, the equerries in ordinary, Equerry Cavalcadour

The equerries, all of them . . .

15 July 1789

DAY

Someone dares to interrupt the King's slumber

The news spread with the dawn of day, shattering news that left me dumbfounded: the King had been awakened in the middle of the night. How could that be? Access to the King was impossible at night. The gates were shut, watch was kept over entrances and main staircases. Who could have got past the first line of protection, the guards stationed at the entrance to the Royal Courtyard, and then the second obstacle of the sentries in the Louvre Courtyard? After that, how could any person make his way into the palace? Or go all the way to the Royal Apartments and reach the actual door to the King's Bedchamber? Bodyguards were on duty there. After the guards, there were the Gentlemen of the Bedchamber, awake and watchful in the next room. And supposing that some unheard-of, supernatural being, some sylph or creature-who-walked-through-walls, had somehow got past all these obstacles, there remained the final obstacle, the presence of the trimestrial King's First Valet, who slept right there at the foot of the King's bed. And yet, against all plausibility, that is what people were saying: someone had awakened the King.

On the floor where we lived, high up under the eaves, unable to believe it ourselves, we ran from room to room, knocking at doors and spreading the wild rumour. I ventured a suggestion: indigestion, perhaps? Louis XVI was subject to terrible attacks that left him almost lifeless . . . I was roundly taken to task. The King had been awakened by someone. Someone who had something to tell him.

★

A fine rain was falling. The paving stones were black and glistening. The small shops set up along the metal fences looked shabby. Walking into the kitchen of the Great Hall, I was overwhelmed by a smell of wine and food and the unattractive remains of our previous night's supper . . . Gradually, not immediately perceptible, a feeling of cold and nausea crept over me. The soup I was served had a sharp, sour taste. The bread that came with it had gone stale and was hard to swallow. We sat together again, much the same group as the night before, minus the priests.

Honorine was not there either. She had gone down to Madame de La Tour du Pin's apartment. I expected to learn more from her about the events of the previous night. So did the others: our information bureau, that's what Honorine was. She arrived at last, dishevelled and unkempt. She was wrapped round in a greenish cape (that she had had from her mistress, a tall, rather thinnish, fair-haired woman, where Honorine was short, plump, and brunette). Every face turned in her direction. Well? Tell us. That outlandish business of waking the King in the middle of the night? Who was it? What did he have to tell? Actually in the King's Bedchamber?

Normally Honorine was chatty, quick-tongued, and inclined to put on airs: her verbal agility, which made her so attractive, she owed to her lively Southern temperament; as for the air of superiority, that reflected the haughtiness of the Marquise de La Tour du Pin, who was very intelligent and used this natural gift to hold the rest of the human race in contempt. On this occasion, however, Honorine was silent. Then, in a piteous voice, she confessed that she was at a loss to answer our questions. Yes, this morning there was much animated discussion between Monsieur and Madame de La Tour du Pin; but, as was their frequent practice – whether spontaneously or so as not to be understood by the servants – they were speaking English.

'Mind you,' said Honorine, 'one word I did hear several times was *Bastille*.'

*

Not till mid-morning, after several people had arrived in great haste from Paris, did an assertion vouched for by a few individuals begin to gain general credence: it was said that the Duke de La Rochefoucauld-Liancourt, Grand Master of the Wardrobe, was the person who had awakened His Majesty at two in the morning. To tell him something concerning the Bastille. An escape? A fire? There was time enough for me to hear any number of stories and memories involving the citadel-prison ('The Bastille!' one old gentleman had exclaimed. 'Why, my entire youth is bound up with it!'), before the incredible news broke: the people of Paris had seized the Bastille. I can hear to this day the sarcastic jibes, the outcries, the hoots of derision that greeted those words. Words uttered by whom, incidentally? From whose mouth did I hear them? I don't remember now. Probably I paid them no heed, for I certainly put no faith in them whatsoever. I had seen the Bastille; no more was required to convince me that it was an impregnable fortress. Its huge bulk dominated the ill-famed Faubourg Saint-Antoine – a quarter that anyone was ill-advised to traverse, even in a carriage with locked doors and surrounded by armed manservants.

There came a succession of messengers. We accosted them; we asked them whether this impossible thing could be true. Most of them doubted it, as did we. Some of them were quite positive: 'The Bastille, seized by the common people? You're not serious? It's a lie, anti-royalist propaganda, invented by those who preach sedition.' If we persisted in our questioning, they would finally say that nothing special was taking place in the capital. I concluded that the Parisians were still stirred up by what had occurred on the previous Sunday, but that was all . . . And the deeply entrenched notion, a sort of *basso continuo* of the convictions I held at that time, a notion common to the greater part of the palace's residents at every level in the hierarchy, on every floor of the building, still reigned intact: there was no need for undue concern; we were going through a bad patch, to be sure, but not for the first time. This wind of rebellion was no worse than the one the King had confronted in the first year of his reign. Since he had subdued it successfully at the age of twenty, surely he would more easily emerge triumphant now, in the prime of his maturity.

To remove any lingering doubts I might have on this score, I walked over to where the Ministry apartments were located. The activity there showed no signs of abating (had they been working all night?); on all sides, orders were being passed along, furniture was being moved: desks, tables, armchairs, pedestal tables, went speeding past me as though self-propelled. It seemed to me that there was something very promising about this feverish haste to settle in. I did not catch sight of any government minister in person. Nothing surprising about that; I was told that they were meeting in consultation. From this point on, everything could be expected to return to normal very quickly, since the only discordant voice, that of Necker of Geneva, had been excluded.

My peace of mind was further strengthened by another certainty: the conviction, widely held in the palace, that the whole affair was a fabrication invented by journalists. Nothing was happening, or almost nothing, but they had their pages to fill. And meanwhile, what did the King think? How had he reacted, always supposing such a thing could really have happened, to Monsieur de La Rochefoucauld-Liancourt's intrusion into his sleep? Had the Master of the Wardrobe parted the alcove curtains himself, or had he, at least on that one point, respected court etiquette? In which case the trimestrial King's First Valet would have been the one to open the curtains . . . And what about the Guards of the Royal Bedchamber; where was their captain now? I didn't know what to think about any of it. No one around me had the smallest piece of definite information to contribute. Monsieur de La Rochefoucauld-Liancout himself was nowhere to be seen. And did our new government have an opinion? 'The government is settling in,' someone said. 'It cannot do everything at once.' The same individual stated his own opinion: 'There is no such thing as the people, it's just an abstraction. What *I* propose, and we have here a very concrete proposal, is that the populace, I mean the entire populace, be placed under arrest and locked up in the Bastille.' There was no immediate support for his proposal; at last someone more conciliatory suggested: 'Or we could lock up just the leaders . . .'

Strangely, for she was generally the chief topic of conversation, no one made any reference to the Queen. But I carried her smile of the previous day with me; the image of her smooth, radiant face bowed over her *Notebook of Ladies' Attire* stayed with me as I moved from one group to another. I was curious, of course, but not alarmed. A rumour, however extraordinary it might be, did not constitute an event.

The King and his brothers go to the Tennis Court
Hall: 11 a.m.
The Queen on the Balcony

Something that did, beyond a doubt, constitute an unprecedented event, was the little group of men who suddenly
emerged to the right of me. They were coming out of the Petit
Théâtre, known as the Hubert Robert Theatre, which had been
fitted out at the Queen's wishes, halfway along the unfinished
wing of the building. The little group walked out to find themselves in among the Swiss Guards keeping watch at the entrance
to the theatre. Honorine had joined me. We were inside the
Royal Courtyard, leaning against its fence.

The group – but surely I was dreaming – consisted of the King
and his two brothers, the Count de Provence and the Count
d'Artois. They had no guard, no escort, none of the usual trap-
pings. All three were making their way out of the palace on foot,
trying to pass unnoticed. A few gentlemen were around them, but
the scene did not resemble a procession; it was more like a group
of friends. Honorine climbed up on to the fence's supporting wall
for a clearer view. 'The King does not have his plumed hat,' she
informed me. He was wearing a velvet one, broad-brimmed
but unassuming. It was a truly surprising sight to see the three
brothers walking along together, over uneven paving stones that
were slippery with the damp. At eleven o'clock in the morning –
which could by no stretch of the imagination be called a prome-
nade hour! And moreover, they were walking not towards the
grounds but towards the town! Only the King appeared to forge
ahead; the Count de Provence and the Count d'Artois were more
reluctant. The King, tall and of sturdy build, was treading heavily,
with that uncouth rolling gait of his and the impression he always
conveyed of doing whatever it was against his will.

For the Count de Provence, the walk was not just drudgery, it was torture: Monsieur was dragging himself along. Short, obese, with swollen lower limbs, he had trouble moving. Ill-natured folk called the Count de Provence 'His Heaviness', and without being mean, one had to admit that the nickname was appropriate, just as 'Her Heaviness' aptly described their married sister Clotilde, living in Italy. As usual, straw and manure were scattered on the paving stones so the horses would not slip: Monsieur, whose shoes sparkled owing to the jewels on their buckles, contemplated this arrangement with distaste. Probably he had never encountered it before. The same was true of the wretched soldiers' huts on the Place d'Armes.

As for the Count d'Artois, who was slender, stately, fascinating to look at, his displeasure was not so obvious, for his slightest gesture was always a study in elegance. At first, it was apparent that he did not want to set forward, but once they were outside the palace and he made up his mind, he had to hold himself back to avoid taking the lead in this strange delegation.

We followed them, Honorine and I. We soon found ourselves mingling with the townsfolk of Versailles; they were as astonished as we were to recognise these simple pedestrians as the King and his brothers, and they began to walk along beside them. Women were laughing and conversing with one another from their windows. Their small children went and stood four-square in the path of the King and the Counts till their mothers called them to come away. Everyone was very curious to know where the trio were going.

Not very far, as it turned out. They were only going to the Tennis Court Hall, where the National Assembly now met. It was a place all three of them knew quite well, having played any number of tennis matches there when they were young. But in the circumstances, the place had presumably lost something of its familiarity. The King was walking faster and faster, head down while the crowd acclaimed him. The Count d'Artois, keeping almost abreast of him, was being heartily booed. The

Count de Provence, left hopelessly behind, perspiring freely and out of breath, was looking around for a chair to rest on.

We went with them as far as the doorway. There we would be obliged to stop, and we watched enviously as Monsieur de La Tour du Pin, in his capacity as a representative of the nobility, went on into the Hall. We remained outside, while round us the ranks of the crowd were swelling. After a few minutes, during which we could not hear anything, there was applause, then shouts, then once again nothing audible, and finally roars of joy.

'That bodes well,' Honorine whispered. And already, before the King and his brothers had come back out, some highly excited young men appeared to pass on the news. So that bit by bit, we were able to piece together everything that had transpired.

The King had declared before the National Assembly: 'There are no matters more pressing or that touch my heart more deeply than the fearful disorders that reign in the capital city . . .' At the start, he had been listened to attentively, but with hostility. The public was expecting a new edition of his earlier declarations and his reiterated determination not to yield. Then, when he had announced the reason for his presence, there was endless applause. It was difficult to hear him over the uproar triggered by his announcement. And the King, who had been listened to in glum silence on those previous occasions, was moved by the enthusiasm of the representatives. He could not go on speaking. After several attempts, he had finally managed to conclude: '. . . and relying upon the love and faithfulness of my subjects, I have ordered the troops to withdraw from Paris and Versailles. I authorise you and even urge you to make my intentions known throughout the capital city.' In the Assembly the tears and transports of delight had risen to fever pitch. And even after the formal response from Bailly, President of the Assembly, reminding everyone present that the dismissal of Ministers dear to the Nation was chiefly responsible for the troubles, the ovations went on undiminished.

*

When the King emerged, nothing could have equalled the happiness of his demeanour. His words had produced a triumph – to the best of my knowledge, it was the first time they had generated anything other than discouragement. He was intoxicated by this oratorical success. Along his path, the shouts and tears went on unceasingly. Some, in the excess of their enthusiasm, lay down on the ground so he would walk on them.

Whereas the King's departure had been unobtrusive, his return almost caused mass delirium. It took him more than an hour to cover the short distance from Tennis Court Hall to the palace. His brothers, this time, walked ahead of him. They were surrounded, or followed, by all the Representatives. The King walked on, to uninterrupted acclaim from the crowd, with shouts of: *Long live the King, Long live the Nation, Long live Liberty*. The Representatives of the three Orders had joined hands, to form a chain, an enclosure in the middle of which the King, the Count de Provence, and the Count d'Artois moved onward. The King was going along with the same heavy, ungainly walk, but his head was no longer bowed. Very close to him the Count de Provence showed every sign of exhaustion; he was virtually being carried by the gentlemen whose arms supported him. The Count d'Artois, meanwhile, driven by a crude streak in his nature that all too often got the better of him, was insulting any Representative who came close enough to touch his person.

The King was not affected by his brothers' ill humour. He was savouring his triumph, greedily drinking in the expressions of his people's love, and becoming intoxicated with both. The Representatives, hands linked, were endeavouring to keep the crowd at a distance, but the crowd was hard to keep in check. People wanted to come close to the King; they wanted to touch him. A woman from the crowd had tried to kiss him: 'Let her come to me,' he said. She threw her arms around his neck with an impetus that sent him staggering. The King seemed utterly bewitched by the ecstatic sense of communion with the multitude. So often, over the past several days, he had felt inclined to 'scold' his people; now he could love them again, and his sternness melted in the joy of this reconciliation.

When the King returned to the palace, he soon reappeared on the second-storey front balcony, with the Queen, the Dauphin, and the royal princes and princesses. But what metamorphosis was this? On the King's countenance was no lingering sign of joy. Beside him the Queen stood quite rigid, not waving. Instead, she took the Dauphin's little hand, where he stood in front of her, and waved that at the crowd. It was she who gave the signal for retiring into the palace. She was the first to leave, with her son His Royal Highness the Dauphin, while Madame the King's daughter, Marie-Thérèse, the little girl whom the Queen dubbed 'Little Miss Sobersides', clung to her father's hand and would not leave the balcony. She looked down with great curiosity at all these people gathered below her, shouting of their love for her father. The King now looked quite dejected. He followed his wife, as did the Count and Countess de Provence, the Count and Countess d'Artois, and their children.

Gabrielle de Polignac, Governess of the Children of France, had not appeared on the balcony. 'The Duchess is like a mole,' someone said. 'She burrows beneath the surface, but a pickaxe will force her up into the open; we'll find her.'

Enthusiasm of the crowd; I am confident of victory: afternoon

The people's love and gratitude continued to find expression in loud acclamations. These became more strident when the King attended Mass, where the motet *Plaudite Regem manibus* was sung: there were rounds of applause, promises of fidelity, tears. An entire crowd caught up in a frenzied show of love. They were all stamping their feet and clapping so hard that the noise drowned out the singers of the King's Choir.

Since that time I have learned about crowds, about mobs. The mob will shout acclaim or hurl insults at anyone, or anything. The object of their emotion is of no account. The mob is roused by the feeling of being a mob. Its hysteria mounts in proportion to the strange phenomenon of its self-consciousness, or consciousness without self. 'I am no one,' says the mob. Multiplied by thousands, this non-personhood is an irresistible force. And I surrendered myself to it, for the space of an emotional outburst, which I could grasp because I seemed to hear, to have within reach of my senses, tangible proof of the people's love for their King. And I really did have the proof, but what I did not know, then, was that there could exist a people as changeable as the French, as quick to pass from tears of compassion to cries for murder . . . In my naivety, I, too, began to applaud, along with everyone else. I was shouting *Long live the King, Long live the Nation, Long live Liberty.* Honorine was dancing where she stood and hugging the people next to her. She kept saying that she ought to leave, that Madame de La Tour du Pin might be needing her services, but she made no move to go. At last she made up her mind and pushed her way through the densely packed crowd. I stayed. Soon there was no further sound from the chapel, whether of singing or prayer.

The members of the royal family had no doubt dispersed and gone their several ways back to their respective apartments. Unless perhaps the three brothers, after their unplanned walk and as a result of its spectacular success, had chosen not to part, but to take their meal together with their wives, at the apartment of the Countess de Provence, as quite often happened . . .

The crowd – which extended well beyond the Place d'Armes and as far as the entrances to the avenues of Saint-Cloud, Paris, and Sceaux – continued to wander about, but the bursts of applause were subsiding. We needed some sort of sign or signal to get us fired up again. None came. I felt as I did at the theatre, when the actors had taken their final bow and I desperately waited for them to come back one more time . . . waited in vain. I could see that, on the contrary, most of the palace windows were shut and their curtains drawn. And suddenly I felt sad – just as I had felt cold and discouraged that morning. I had witnessed the erecting of something like an immense and perfect monument to the glory of the King, and now I was conscious only of the cracks already splitting it and the weakness of its foundations. I went back to the South Wing, where my living quarters were.

The thing I have failed to report, which probably inspired my questionable image of a monument, is that with the gradual fading of the applause, discussions started up again. Beside me, the townspeople of Versailles (one of them worked at La Belle Image tavern; I had seen him before, making his regular deliveries of lemon drink to the palace) were arguing about the latest events in the capital city. Not only did they have no doubt that the supposed taking of the Bastille was an irrelevance, they were already making gleeful remarks about the plan for what would happen next: the people were proposing to erect, on the spot where the Bastille had stood, a monument dedicated 'To King Louis XVI, who Restored Liberty'.

'On the spot where the Bastille stood?' I asked.

There was silence; distrustful glances were sent in my direction. The group of townsfolk moved away from me. The tavern keeper turned around to look at me and whispered something to his cronies.

NIGHT

I have a character trait that has not improved with the years: I
find it difficult to face reality squarely. I had heard someone say:
'The people have seized the Bastille.' I had noticed the hard,
withdrawn expression on the face of the Queen when she appeared on the balcony and that motion of her body when,
instead of presenting her son, showing him to the public, she
had sought rather to conceal him. She had kept him in front of
her for barely a few minutes, then moved him so that he was at
her side, and little by little the child had been hidden by her dress
(a manoeuvre that had drawn spiteful remarks from those
around me). Several times the Queen had turned around as
though someone had been supposed to come and fetch her
son – her only surviving son – and was slow in coming. Someone . . . the Governess of the Children of France, of course. All
this I had seen, and it would have been worth my while to pause
for a moment and let my mind take in the implications, but 'it'
couldn't, 'it' does not function that way. With me, Captain de
Laroche's catchphrase 'Enough of that' is an irresistible tendency
– or almost irresistible, for that same mind has a strength of
obstinacy, or a latent anxiety, that reacts to signals coming from
outside and more or less forces me to see them.

Besides, was the King's air of triumph really convincing? If
that had truly been the case, some part of his joy would have
spread through the court, whereas what took place was quite the
reverse. Indeed, the contrast was strange, between the delirious
ovations from the crowd and the rigid stance of the princes and

princesses – and the King himself – on the balcony. As though they had been replaced by wax dummies.

When is the King a king? Captain de Laroche had pondered. Certainly not when he came and stood on the balcony. And the Queen even less so.

I ate supper alone in my room, having brought back with me, on a tray, a small trout pâté, an artichoke, and some strawberries, given me by a woman friend in the service of a marquess who enjoyed the privilege of 'eating at court', that is, of being boarded at the palace by courtesy of the King. Afterwards, I made my way to the study of Jacob-Nicolas Moreau. I was sure I would find him there. And even in the exceptional event of his not being there, I would have gone to the little library adjoining his study and taken one or two books for the night.

My friend the Historiographer of France was very inadequately housed. Truth to tell, he was not housed at all. He had for his use, in his study that was entirely blackened by candle smoke, only a great free-standing wardrobe, on whose floor he had spread a straw mattress. When overtaken by excessive fatigue, he would rest there for an hour or two. So going to see him meant going into that dark, dusty cubbyhole, completely lined with books, situated on the topmost floor but one – that is to say the fourth floor, in the North Wing, not far from one of the five or six royal libraries, the Attic Library, which expanded, but only via narrow corridors, into a first and then a second library annexe plus several physics and chemistry rooms. Rather unsettling places to have so close by, making the Historiographer feel as though he were living in an extension of the fields of study that were the King's particular passion. Jacob-Nicolas Moreau worked unceasingly. He was obsessively conscious of the importance of his task. No less strong was the torment of knowing with certainty that he must, by his efforts alone, wipe out the stain that the name of that disbeliever Voltaire represented in the long, virtuous succession of historiographers of France.

The idea that I might be disturbing him never bothered me, for we were on such close terms that he would simply have told me if I was. But this time, when I went in, I immediately became aware that the Historiographer was not doing anything, which was most exceptional. He was sitting not at his work table but in a low armchair, among piles of books. He stood up at once, offered me the armchair, and sat down on a footstool that was even lower. Both of us were now totally hemmed in by the high and labyrinthine piles of books. Above this chaotic scene hung an immense crucifix. The small amount of light that found its way into the room, from a window on sufferance, illuminated the crucified Christ. My friend took my hands in his and said in a lifeless voice (indeed, it seemed to me he had been crying):

'We are doomed. The King has sent away the army of foreign soldiers that Monsieur de Puységur brought in. Only the presence of that army gave him the self-confidence to dismiss Necker – assuming the decision came from him and not from the Count d'Artois or the Queen, but we've reached a point where it makes no difference. That army was his sole support. He gave in to pressure from the so-called National Assembly. He has given in on that point. He'll give in on everything. Just think of it, my dear, when he gave his speech to the representatives, he was standing up and hatless. This is the end. I'd been predicting it for a long time, but no one could be more shocked or devastated than I.'

I was speechless.

'All we can hope for now is that the regular troops won't be won over. They say that in Paris the French Guards cannot be counted on. Here, they still can be, but for how long?'

'What about the Bastille? Everyone says it has been seized and is going to be destroyed. What do you think of so preposterous a notion?'

'I think what you said yourself: the whole idea is outrageous. I had already been told of this by others. But there I draw the line, and I say "You are WRONG. What you are telling me is simply not possible." I do not deny that we are in a bad situation, but that is no reason for believing every wild tale you hear. Let us think it through, my dear. Can such an enterprise be undertaken without an order from the King?'

'N . . . n . . . no.'

'And to your knowledge, has the King given such an order? Remembering that one of the projects he has had in mind for a long time is, as it happens, to have the Bastille demolished.'

I hesitated.

'Not that I am aware, no . . .'

'Then why would you expect it to be destroyed?'

It began to rain hard. Monsieur Moreau stood up. He was of average build, rather short, pale-complexioned, round-faced, with sagging cheeks. He sat down at his table, lit a candle. I felt cast into outer darkness, buried beneath the books. And even when I was once again on a level with him, the feeling of being *underneath* persisted. He said again:

'The Bastille cannot be seized, it would be a superhuman endeavour, you might as well set out to smash the Alps or dry up the ocean. But we are still doomed, for all that; *outsmarted*, as Monsieur the King's brother said.

'Odd,' the Historiographer added, 'that someone so refined and demanding in matters of speech should have used such an expression. *Outsmarted* – a hateful word. The King is well spoken, though I have never been able to form a personal judge-ment in the matter, as he has not so far done me the honour of addressing me personally, but there is no comparison with the sense of style shown by His Lordship the Count de Provence. Monsieur is a poet. *Outsmarted* must have been the result of fatigue, the physical and mental fatigue of the morning's events. Just imagine: requiring Monsieur to go from the palace to Tennis Court Hall and back, on foot. Even asking him to go one way on foot would have been cruel.'

'We are doomed . . .' I thought about the Queen, standing so stiffly up there on the balcony; about her pallor, emphasised by the dark-coloured dress. I thought of her as an ivory statuette outlined clearly against a background of mourning garb, or a silver teardrop set against a black sheet. I thought of her . . . What would she do now? What about the King? If he no longer had an army, if he was left with no means of asserting his mastery over the National Assembly . . .

'The King is sorely tried by this defeat – a defeat that may have the outward appearance of a triumph, but a defeat nonetheless. His immediate plans are not known. He has shut himself up alone in his apartments. He is considering . . . This morning, before his visit to the Tennis Court, he spoke vaguely of transferring the National Assembly to Noyon or Soissons, while he himself removed with the royal family to the château of Compiègne. In that way he could remain in communication with the Assembly without living in the same place. This close proximity is unhealthy.'

At that moment we heard the scraping of footsteps on the other side of the wall. Rapid footsteps. Someone had been eavesdropping.

We sat there silently for a moment, listening intently. Then each of us became absorbed in our separate unhappy thoughts. Mechanically, I picked out the titles of the books published by Jacob-Nicolas Moreau. They sat imposingly on the shelves above his head, and at the very sight of them I was filled with veneration.

Those suspicious noises had terrified me. I was afraid to leave
the room. My friend sensed my panic and offered to walk back
to my room with me. Then he would come back into his study,
he said, and try to pick up his work, his *Lessons in Moral
Behaviour*. No sooner had we set foot in the long, winding
corridor leading above the Grand Gallery, than I noticed something out of the ordinary. The corridor, usually bustling with life
at that time of the evening (that floor also housed part of the
kitchens, and work went on there day and night), was empty.
The third storey, on the other hand, which had apartments and
so should have been quiet at this hour, surprised us with the
great number of people who were heading, as we were, in the
direction of the Royal Apartments. We were at a loss to interpret
this circumstance. It could not be some night-time festivity; the
Royal Entertainments were not much sought after these days.
And there was nothing festive about the facial expressions or the
attire we were encountering. Indeed, it seemed to me that some
individuals were wearing nightcaps and dressing gowns.

The closer we came to the Royal Apartments, the greater the
press of people. They all appeared disoriented, a little shame-
faced at having heeded the urge to leave their living quarters and
seek out the Royal Apartments and the Gallery, plunged in semi-
darkness at the time, for the sole purpose of being 'closer to the
news', as Lady Olderness said to us. There had been no prior
consultation, but as the evening wore on, those who had come
back to sup in their apartments (the caterers had condescended
to come with their trays of food as usual that evening), and who
had started a game of backgammon after their meal, had perceived that it could not be helped: they were not in a mood for

pleasant pastimes. Then they had begun paying courtesy calls on one another. At last, since no one managed to sit still at anyone else's apartment, since no conversation took lasting hold, since it seemed to all of them that while they were sitting there in a polite circle possibly vital decisions were being made, anxiety finally swept social convention aside. They cut the visits short and stepped out of doors; and, like the Historiographer and me, they had been astonished to find that everyone else was out of doors as well, in the strange out of doors that was unique to the palace and meant 'outside one's own living quarters', in any space intended for public foot traffic, where you might always expect the King or Queen to come by, and you had a chance to show your presence and be seen.

This was not the reason for being abroad on that night. So great was the agitation that, perhaps for the first time in the annals of Versailles, the perpetual, anxious torment of wanting to be noticed no longer operated. Shadowy figures crossed paths on the stairways, in the corridors, in the anterooms. No one was talking. All were disheartened; none could foresee anything but calamities. I soon fell prey to the ambient mood and became disheartened like the others.

The Historiographer had been reluctant to go back to his work. He was torn between his duty to bear witness – he was the person who was supposed to set down on paper the events of the reign – and his duty as a moral philosopher: if the will of God expressed itself through history, then his task was to make that will as manifest as possible. At last the urgent need to write his *Lessons in Moral Behaviour* had got the upper hand. He had gone back to his book of magic spells, leaving me to wander . . .

I was not at ease. I would have been glad to encounter a close friend or acquaintance. Occasionally there was a low-voiced exchange of news. What I heard did nothing to reassure me. It was all about town houses, owned by the nobility, being destroyed, and their inhabitants put to death. It was also rumoured that armed bands assembling in Paris were going to attack the palace. They were on their way even now. How long would it take them to get to Versailles from Paris? Twelve hours? Fifteen? They would be here by morning. I had that much of a reprieve. I remember realising that I had forgotten to take any books away for the night.

We were going around in circles. The least sound made us jump. The clock had struck eleven. 'Going out' had not calmed our nerves. Quite the opposite: our fears had increased at the sight of the haggard appearance we presented to each other; they were gaining ground, along with insomnia and a sensation of suffocating. In the circumstances, with the terrible awareness of how vulnerable we were, all the windows were closed. So were the curtains. And in certain public rooms, even the wooden shutters, and the metal shutters on the outside. The air around us was heavy and murky, as we moved from place to place. For fear of making the palace too easy to find, everyone had lit the smallest possible number of 'tapers', as they said at court – copying the parlance of the King who had struck the word 'candle' from his vocabulary. There were a few rooms where candlesticks lit earlier had been put out, and it was as dark as in a forest. We brushed against other people or accidentally jostled them. Eyes would suddenly shine with an eerie light.

People began to get thirsty. They wanted wine, beer, fruit. They called, they rang. No one came. They could not believe it and rang again. They shouted, confidently at first, then in voices that betrayed growing uncertainty. The person who had called would stand there, hand still on the bell pull, uncomprehending. A crowd would gather round: 'Well, but, what are they doing? Have they stopped hearing when we ring for them? Where are they? What has become of our domestics?' Many servants lived in Versailles, in private town houses, brand-new dwellings, while their masters preferred lodgings, however uncomfortable, at the palace, so they would not have to go back to their houses every time they needed a change of attire and could always be somewhere close by, near enough to be seen. But those who had made that choice suddenly had the impression that their own dwellings were occupied by the enemy and they could never go home again. They pictured themselves standing in front of their barricaded mansions, with cries of rage raining down upon them along with bottles thrown directly into the yards. Into *their* yards. Here at Versailles, the domestics had vanished, the ante-rooms had emptied. But when, when exactly had it started? Before supper? A little earlier? In the Gallery, I noticed the absence of the guards who set up camp beds there every night. Were they busily plotting with the domestics? Had they all turned against the palace together? Had they gone to guide the brigands now marching on Versailles?

Night, filling the Grand Gallery and the apartments with broad expanses of darkness, and melding the corridors, ante-rooms, and halls into a uniform pitch-black, intensified my feeling of being in the midst of total destruction. A few tapers were lit; it gave me some physical relief, but that was all. It was now easier to walk around, but emotionally, it was just as taxing as before. Mental anguish was not uniting us. We kept peering stealthily at one another. We *logeants* – 'lodgers', as those who were privileged to live at the palace used to be called (I loved saying the word over to myself: he's a *logeant*, I'm a *logeante* . . .) – were experiencing the negative side of our cruel isolation. How nice, how wonderful, to live apart like this, in sublime unawareness. How frightening, how terrifying, to know noth-ing, or almost nothing, when the rest of the country was joining in league against us. For the fact is we knew very little. And what information we were getting was so hard to believe . . . Maybe it was just me; maybe I had gauged the value of my time so completely in terms of my reading sessions with the Queen that I had completely drifted away from reality. Perhaps I had carried the cocooning of 'these parts' farther than the others had, but I had the feeling that everyone around me, each person staggering to and fro in his separate darkness, shared the same plight.

I was keeping away from the windows. I preferred the corners of the rooms, the bends in the corridors, all those undefined spaces with temporary uses and variable designations, which the palace had in abundance. If there was any sort of opening to the outside, I crept along the opposite wall. For it was from outside that THE EVENT had burst upon us. A word that was quite new at court, where everyone adored 'the anecdote', or 'today's vignette'; these were required to be trivial, minute, so that people could exercise their ingenuity at fleshing them out from one telling to the next, till they became fabulous narratives, for a few hours, if a sufficiently talented storyteller picked them up. An *event*, on the other hand, had scope and import from the start, leaving no room for invention. The thing itself frightened me, the word repelled me. I uttered it as unintelligibly as I could, running the syllables together. I said *ev* . . . , but could not hide from myself the fact that something was trying to break through.

The 'List of the 286 heads that have to fall in order to effect the necessary Reforms'

Night very quickly produced terrible fatigue. Endurance at staying on one's feet, hitherto a major qualification for living at court, no longer prevailed. Everyone was looking for somewhere to sit. People were falling asleep here, there, and everywhere. Some were lying right on the floor, on the carpets. I took care not to step on their hands. I went into the Study Leading to the Terraces, a room (although it no longer led to any of the terraces) where I always liked to be, for its very name enabled me to imagine the Versailles of Louis XV, consisting entirely of aviaries, salons of vines and trellises, terraces with borders of bougainvillea . . . but on this occasion all I found there was a dismal gathering, into which, in a manner of speaking, I stumbled. Facing a bench pushed against the wall, a few folding chairs stood in a line. A small group of people were using this arrangement to talk to one another, sitting in the dark, each one sunk in her or his private torment. Nonetheless, for the first time in a long while I was hearing at least a semblance of conversation, and the result was that little by little I began to feel more cheerful. Indeed I believed – without formulating the thought clearly in my own mind – that if we could talk to each other again, if we succeeded in rescuing, like some sacred fire, the eternal conversation that had been kept up ever since the court was established at Versailles, then the palace would live on, and royalty with it.

The listless phrases uttered first by one person then by another, in weary tones sustained by a fierce determination to keep talking, brought me out of my lethargy. I have no clear memory of what was discussed . . . Subjects of no moment . . . Possibly the new heating system that His Majesty was having installed in the royal gallery of the chapel for next winter; or *The*

Malabar Widow, playing to full houses at the Ambigu-Comique in Paris. Finally old Father Noslin, Superintendent of the Royal Tree Nurseries, had courage enough to face the situation squarely. 'It's as though a coalition was operating,' he said, in the same measured tones that, more than ten years earlier, had succeeded in convincing a young Louis XVI to have the old trees uprooted. It must have looked a bit sparse at first, but by 1789 it was splendid. The grounds, though certain groves looked uncared for, had achieved perfect equilibrium. I loved those trees. On my favourite walks, I had the feeling that I knew them each individually and that they in turn knew me. One day they had arrived at Versailles and taken root there. I would talk to them, and they had things to say to me as well . . .

Shortly after my arrival at the palace, when I was still settling in, Monsieur de Montdragon had taken me on a tour of the grounds. When I started going into raptures over the glory of nature, he had at once informed me that everything at Versailles was artificial; everything there had been deliberately planned, even the trees. The first ones to be transplanted had been taken from the château of Vaux-le-Vicomte. Whenever he looked at the trees in the grounds of his palace, what Louis XIV saw before him was the trophies physically wrested from Fouquet, the symbols of his victory over a Superintendent of Finance too fond of lavish display for his own good. Nothing at Versailles had originated there, save the nobility. And they were what mattered. Everything else was a setting for them . . .

'Is that perfectly clear, madam?' Monsieur de Montdragon had added. I had said yes, which was not entirely true, but I was sure that as time went by it would become perfectly clear . . . At present, however, we were no longer concerned with trees or banks of foliage.

'It's as though a coalition was operating,' the old priest said again.

Silence followed. Monsieur de Goulas, a man of strong character, a notable gambler and fine trencherman, was the first to react:

'A coalition operating. I will grant you that, Father, but a coalition of whom with whom?'

Father Noslin was not in a position to be more specific. But Monsieur de Feutry responded for him. 'It is a coalition of malcontents,' he said. And he described an incident he had just witnessed, in the palace itself. At about six o'clock on the previous evening, he had been going into the Grand Gallery. At the entrance, on the same side as the Salon de la Guerre, hence very close to the Royal Apartments, he had noticed a group behaving suspiciously. Four or five people were giving out tracts. Servants, common people, were eagerly reaching for the printed sheets. Monsieur de Feutry had told his lackey to get a few for him. The lackey had managed to get his hands on a number of copies and had spent a good while – despite the fact that his master was waiting – talking to the people who were handing them out. Monsieur de Feutry had refrained from comment, being impatient to read what the tract contained. It was a pamphlet entitled 'List of the 286 heads that have to fall in order to effect the necessary Reforms'. 286 heads! There was a slight shrinking movement along the velvet bench.

'Do you remember the names of the people they wish to behead?' asked Father Noslin.

'Certainly not you, Father. Nor me, nor, I believe, any of us here. Although there has been so little etiquette observed tonight that I am not quite sure in whose presence I have the honour to find myself . . . The first two names are those of the Queen and the Count d'Artois, of that much I am certain.'

I shuddered.

'Cutting off people's heads in order to effect reforms; I don't understand,' said a lady I had never seen before.

She had a clear, childish voice. She received no answer.

A man asked Monsieur de Feutry: 'Who were they, I mean the people distributing the pamphlets; who do you think they were?'

'I don't know. What I can say positively is that they looked like *very* ugly customers.'

A coalition of malcontents, a group of individuals who looked like *very* ugly customers – it all left my head in a whirl. But where had they been till now? Why were they suddenly appearing out of nowhere? They had always looked happy before. All I had ever read in the gazettes was: 'The people were loud in their expressions of happiness,' or 'The shouts and applause of the people betrayed the joy they felt at seeing their Sovereigns.'

That's just it, I was told. The people are not the people any more. They've been bought. Bought by mercenaries, foreigners, mustachioed ruffians with big staves. They mingle with the populace, make inflammatory speeches, give out liquor and money. And suddenly the talk was all of prisons spilling forth their entire contingents of criminals. Crazed with freedom, killing for the pleasure of killing, they were suddenly in their element, fighting each other with stones and iron bars.

I was near to fainting. I wondered fearfully: What will happen in the hospitals? Who is to stop the lepers or those afflicted with the pox from going out into the streets, raping us, infecting us? And they would gag us, using bandages stiff with blood and pus . . . O dear God, I would rather die right now! And for a few moments I was so distressed that I wished the court would commit suicide. So that when the brigands came they would find only corpses. How horrible! Lord God! How horrible!

I next heard: 'In Dijon, the butchers have committed unspeakable acts of violence. And in Vizille, Lyons and Marseilles, all the guilds are taking that behaviour as their cue. It isn't just the butchers, the other trades will follow their example. The pork sellers, the cobblers, the masons, the joiners, the ironmongers and farriers. They all have tools and know how to use them.'

The palace, too, was full of masons, plasterers, nail makers . . . We had only moments left to live . . . My neighbours were talking back and forth over my head. Each one had predictions to offer, of atrocities hitherto unknown. Our little chamber of anguish, there in the Study Leading to the Terraces, was ready to explode.

'Why this delirium?' piped up the same clear, childish voice, now with a moaning quality to it. 'His Majesty emerges from his private office in tears, because, he says, referring to his people, "his children are wounding him grievously". Meanwhile, in Paris, the people march through the streets shouting: "Give us back Mister Necker, he is our father!" Which is the father? The King or Mister Necker? And what do the children want?'

Once again, she received no answer. I wished she had. I, too, would have liked to understand. Then someone said: 'The children want to choose their father. That is the new Gospel, Your Ladyship.' I do not know why, but I was seized with a fit of shaking.

Earlier, in that time we all remember so
happily . . .

It was too cramped and gloomy there in the study; we were
being driven crazy. I made my way toward rooms that were not
quite so dark, and as I soon became aware, everyone behaved
better if a few candles were lit. One such room was the Dispatch
Office. I recognised Monsieur de Pujol and Monsieur de Chèv-
reloup. They were engrossed in a discussion (periods of exhaustion alternated with renewed surges of energy, as always when
people stay awake). They were wondering how the court had
collectively contrived to end up in such a sorry predicament.
They tried first to lay the blame on the English, who were
always ready to rejoice in the misfortunes of France and consequently even willing to contribute to them; then they incrimi-
nated the Illuminists and Freemasons; and finally, with greater
conviction, the Philosophes . . . The Philosophes? I was all ears.
In the bag I carried back and forth to the Trianon there was scant
place for books by writers of that ilk. But my two gentlemen,
while not approving of them, had apparently read them. Their
systematic attempts to undermine society, said the pair, their
determined efforts to propagate religious disbelief, their mania
for defending work as an instrument of liberation, the fact that
they dared to hold out the promise of happiness, had taken over
people's minds. Capital punishment was what those fellows
deserved. They were fuzzy-minded, dyed-in-the-wool intriguers.
The right to happiness – could there ever be a more disastrous
notion?

The Philosophes soon monopolised the discussion. Everyone
had something to say about them. The tone rapidly became as
heated as in the little corner I had just abandoned. Monsieur de
Pujol spoke up again: what was more, all these Philosophes,

badgering us incessantly with their talk of equality, were ambitious individuals. They had but one wish: to outdo their colleagues. They were consumed with ambition. They were poor specimens of humanity, tormented by megalomania. They could not tolerate kings because they considered themselves to be kings. Gods, rather! The Philosophes believed they should be an object of worship.

'We must put them back in their place; remember, it was not so long ago . . . Think back; under the previous reign, even someone as passionately fond of literature as the Prince de Conti would never have let a Philosophe sit down at his table. Not even away from court, on his own estates.'

Whether it was 'the previous reign' or 'on his own estates' that set Monsieur de Pujol's mind on a different course I do not know, but a wave of nostalgia swept over him. And he began to intone; I can still hear the chanting rhythm, the languid dipping-of-oars effect permeating the Southern accent that coloured his words.

'Under King Louis XV, that time we all remember so happily, every prince kept an author who became part of his household. Thus Collé belonged to the ageing Duke d'Orléans, Laujon to the Prince de Condé. When festivities were held, these fine minds were much in demand. They composed couplets and kept us amused with their set-rhyme poems. We treated them courteously, and I must even confess that I often derived pleasure from conversing with them. But there was never any question of allowing them to step outside the understood limits. They took their meals at a table set aside for them, among the equerries and the stewards ordinary. As for dining with princes . . .' (Monsieur de Pujol suppressed a nervous giggle) 'let us not descend to absurdities! Never would a man of letters have taken his seat at the table of a prince. After lunch, they had leave to consume an ice in the salon. Occasionally, at the prince's pleasure, they might return to the billiard room to watch the play, but always standing up, as was the case when they consumed ices. They would remain for half an hour, forty-five minutes at most.' (And he tapped his cane in time with these last words, for added emphasis.)

Though the speaker was recalling things everyone already knew, he was heard in blissful contentment. But suddenly, perhaps because thinking about those vanished times was too cruel to be borne, an unappeasable awareness of the present moment forced its way back to the surface. The reign of Louis XV was over. Talented individuals now ate ices at any hour of the day. They could enjoy them lying down if they felt like it . . . Around the table, gentlemen were dozing with their heads on their arms, like lazy schoolboys. I would have been glad if I, too, could have sat down, but all the chairs were taken. I was about to go elsewhere (I had in mind the room called Cabinet des Chiens, which had a wide couch), when a hard, cold voice echoed in the doorway.

A commanding voice; was it a man's voice? A woman's? It was hard to judge. What was not hard to judge was the provocative intent of the speaker and the tremendous energy behind the voice. We had reached a level of despondency where no one had the least desire to resume a debate on any subject what-soever, and especially the subject of the Philosophes. But the newcomer seemed quite ready to prolong the discussion. The authoritarian voice rapped out:

'Not all the Philosophes are witty conversationalists and court jesters. The real Philosophes are independent. They work. They think.' (Those last words were underlined with an emphasis meant to be insulting . . .) 'There are good things, in fact excel-lent things to be found in the writings of the Philosophes. Anyone who has not read Helvétius's book *On the Human Mind* or Jean-Jacques Rousseau's *Social Contract* cannot hope to grasp the dynamic of our times.'

Diane de Polignac

This pronouncement told me the speaker's identity: Diane de Polignac. The discovery made me still more anxious to slip quietly away, but I did not dare: I always went numb in that woman's presence. It certainly had to be her; who else would talk about dynamic at the very moment when we were all crashing down? Her way, in any situation, was to find the current that would carry her where she wished to go . . .

She took up a position in the middle of the room. The men immediately stood up. They were vexed at themselves for unguardedly dropping off to sleep in the presence of so eminent a personality. Heavily built, lacking in beauty, Diane de Polignac crushed other people with her intelligence and haughtiness. To these 'qualities' she added an ill-concealed natural violence. In her presence, you felt as if you were facing a military commander, and when she desired a man, she wasted no time or effort on roundabout manoeuvres, but simply took him. But at a deeper level, the man with whom she truly formed a couple was her brother.

The Duke de Polignac had pleasing manners, and his career had progressed with unbelievable speed. After obtaining right of reversion to the post of First Royal Equerry, he had been appointed as General of the Posts and Director of the Royal Stud. Finally, to crown this series of achievements, he had recently been ennobled and risen from the rank of count to that of duke. He owed his prosperity, as can well be imagined, not just to his own abilities, but to the complete confidence he placed in his sister. Having no illusions about the fact that her political acumen was immeasurably greater than his own, he had placed himself in her hands, and he carried out her every instruction to the letter. Besides boldness, and strength of purpose, Diane had an instinctive flair for calculation, so that she would instantly detect anything that might work to her advantage.

Thanks to this gift, she had sensed immediately, at the very first signs of the Queen's friendship for Gabrielle de Polignac, that here was the key to unlimited power. Diane and her brother reigned supreme at Versailles, but the bait they used to capture influence was Gabrielle. So it came about that the entire Polignac clan, with Diane at its helm manipulating and making decisions, depended on a tenuous, sentimental, emotional bond: the Queen's friendship for her favourite. From one day to the next, the conspicuous preferment granted to this family might end. The Queen need only, just once, remain impervious to Gabrielle's smile, her graceful gestures, her apparent total unawareness of the fact that she was at the Court of Versailles. Gabrielle had a way of walking through the Royal Apartments as though they were a private garden, so calmly that it took your breath away. To watch her, you could easily believe that she had no idea how fortunate she was: she had been singled out by the Queen, had become her friend, and more particularly had remained her friend, despite the schemes that other people were forever devising to cause a rift between them. Ladies of fashion were brought into Marie-Antoinette's apartments to capture her attention: she was blind to their presence . . .

More than once, Diane had spoiled a drive the Queen was taking with her friend. Gabrielle, gifted with the faculty of not hearing, and accustomed to her sister-in-law's intellectual enthusiasms, was not bothered. But the Queen was in agony. She did not succeed in turning a deaf ear, perhaps because she could not imagine a conversation centred on anything other than herself, or else from a habit going back to a time when she was not too sure of her French, and so listened with extreme attention for fear of missing a word. During Diane's monologues on Jean-Jacques Rousseau, the Queen would turn her head away and have recourse to her fan. Diane, eyes alight, sitting erect on her short stocky body, would expound a theory. By the time they arrived at the château of Saint-Cloud, the Queen was so depressed she no longer cared to alight. Her carriage would make the return trip along the broad Belvédère avenue. She preferred to go back to Versailles, with never a glance for the fountains, the rose gardens, and the tangled growth of jasmine. Gabrielle, leaning back so her head rested against a cushion, would sit there smiling. Diane took advantage of her silence to pursue her own disquisition. The Queen would stifle a moan. To her, abstract ideas were physically painful. Intelligence, too openly displayed, horrified her. She appreciated intellect only if it was softly blended into a temperament . . .

Leaning against a mantelpiece, the Countess was taking snuff. Her harsh-voiced delivery was punctuated with powerful sniffs. Standing very close to her, my eyes were riveted to the voracious mouth below the down that shaded her upper lip. Diane was holding forth in her usual manner. Shreds of tobacco were accumulating on her chest. In the presence of the imperious Countess, people were acting like children caught misbehaving. Diane watched their grovelling antics in some amusement. As for me, I was hypnotised by her thick painted lips, the growing pile of debris on her chest, her stubby hands. I was falling asleep on my feet . . . I did not start listening again to what was being said until Monsieur de Feutry, another refugee from the Study Leading to the Terraces, repeated his story of the pamphlet incident. As with the earlier telling, all his hearers were frantic to know whether their names were on the list. A list . . . not something that could be chanted like a nursery rhyme. By now it was surely posted on the walls of Paris.

Diane occupied a prominent position in the list. Not at the top, since that spot rightfully belonged to the Queen, but not far down. She had begun by joking about it, but after a particularly resonant sniff, her manner changed abruptly. Such sudden shifts were customary with her, but this one, because of its timing and on account of the unmistakable accents of conviction and sincerity in which Diane was suddenly expressing herself, has remained, as if engraved in my memory.

Abandoning mockery, Diane began to castigate all this pointless chatter. She saw us, herself included, as wasting in general considerations the little time we had left, in which to mobilise our forces and offer our services to the royal family. She spoke with great effect about fidelity and about our urgent need to save the King and Queen, putting our duty above our interest. She went on and on. Standing very close to her, enveloped in her tobacco smell, stupefied to hear such noble utterances issuing from that mouth, I hung my head. Fidelity, Sacrifice, Saving the King and Queen . . . Getting ready to die for them, we who were their subjects, their vassals . . . Her voice became increasingly sonorous, irresistible; it drilled into our conscience . . . By this time, Diane was thundering: 'Everything proves, everything bears witness to the existence of systematic, organised insubordination and contempt for law. The rights of the throne have been challenged . . . Already we have heard proposals for an end to feudal rights as though this meant abolishing a system of oppression . . . But even were His Majesty to encounter no obstacle to the execution of his will, could that fount of justice and benevolence bring itself to sacrifice and humiliate the good, ancient, respectable nobility that has shed so much blood for king and country? . . . When they speak of the nobility, the princes of your blood are speaking for themselves . . . Their first claim to consideration is that they are of gentle birth . . .'

Carried away by her own eloquence, Diane went on speaking. I was no longer seeing her lips move; I could only hear the reproaches of my heart. When the words *Mémoire des Princes* were declaimed, silhouetted figures appeared, converging on the twin doors to the Dispatch Office. Were the besieged about to unite, take up arms? Reject the helpless resignation of condemned men and instead die fighting? I was tense with excitement. Visions of crusades, spontaneous heroism, and courtly love flashed through my mind. I could see the Queen, in armour and on horseback. Behind her, standards unfurled, the

King and princes of the blood . . . Diane had at once stricken me with guilt and worked me up to a height of emotion. I walked through some of the other rooms, expecting to find all the 'lodgers' on a war footing . . . Sire, we beseech you, hear the wishes of your children . . . motivated by a desire to have peace in the realm and uphold the power of a king who is most worthy to be loved and obeyed insofar as he seeks only the welfare of his subjects . . . The princes of the blood . . . the Count d'Artois, the Prince de Condé, the Duke de Bourbon, and the Prince de Conti . . . all signing in blood . . . and I wanted to shed my blood with the others . . .

I was perfectly well aware of Diane de Polignac's cynicism, but that had not prevented her from making me feel guilty. I thought she had experienced a change of heart, had suddenly come to appreciate how great a debt she owed her sovereigns. I had been wasting my time listening to idle chatter instead of hurrying to the Queen's side. I told myself that what I should do was go back to my room. Vegetating here did not make any sense. Did not help matters. Did not help her. I must also have realised belatedly that if the Queen should happen to send for me, no one knew where to find me. That thought alone was decisive. This was horrible! It was as if I had shirked my duties on the one occasion when my presence might have been of some real help. I must go back up to my room and await her call.

But alas! I was too exhausted to move a muscle. I would have liked a cup of hot chocolate to comfort me. I set out to beg one from Honorine, whom I thought I recognised in one of the groups. She was wearing the same long greenish cape as this morning. Her dark curls made little horns around her head. Before I had time to speak, she guessed what I wanted: 'Of course, Agathe, you shall have your cup of hot chocolate at once. I'll just ring for a servant and he'll bring it to you.' She shook her curls and tugged with all her might on a bell pull.

I started to cry out to her not to do that, but it was too late. Honorine had disappeared, and instead of one servant there was a whole army of them standing before me, and they were not bringing hot chocolate. There they were, huge and unbearably visible, almost glowing. They wore every colour of livery – the blue of the Gentlemen of Versailles, the Queen's red, the Count d'Artois's green, the Prince de Ligne's pink – but the colour of the servants' livery, normally the only thing to which anyone paid attention, had become an affair of secondary importance. It was outmatched by the sense of their sheer numbers and their monumental presence. They were unbelievably big and strong, with broad faces and terrifying red, bony hands. Everything about them was threatening, but especially those hands, dangling in front of them like billhooks. Don't look, I kept saying to myself. Turn your eyes away. And a sentence came back to me from the *Manual of Correct Behaviour*: 'Do not demean yourself by looking at a lackey; do not demean yourself by looking at a dog.' But I couldn't help it; I could not take my eyes away from them. In the conquering advance of the lackeys, in the scandal of those bare hands and those suddenly very visible faces, there was something exciting – something at once fearsome and powerfully attractive.

When I regained consciousness, a man sat dozing on the couch where I lay stretched out. He had closed his hand over my ankle. His breathing was rapid and laboured. I did not dare to budge. Very close by, two men were attempting to raise each other's spirits.

'For my part,' one of them was saying, 'I place the fullest confidence in Baron de Breteuil; it is splendid that he should be the minister of our new government.'

'A Catholic, royalist, French minister. Which, coming after a banker who was Protestant, republican, and Swiss, makes a pleasant change.'

'That Jacques Necker, moreover, came to us out of nowhere. Who is he? Who ever heard of the fellow's father? We've heard of his daughter, of course, but of his ancestors, never a word . . . I believe there is wisdom to be found in proverbs . . . Blood will tell. His Lordship Baron de Breteuil, like his grandfather, whose skill at presenting ambassadors remains unequalled to this day, has a superlative sense of what is socially correct. That may suffice to see us out of the present . . . er . . . awkwardness.'

'Monsieur de Breteuil has contrived to place men of solid worth around him.'

'I would add that his programme of action is faultless. He has asked the King for a hundred million écus and a hundred thousand men to put down the rebellion. Clear, concise, admirable in every way.'

(The man holding my ankle stirred in his sleep. The impropriety of what he was doing had me paralysed. I wondered whether I was destined to spend the rest of the night with my foot at the mercy of a stranger.)

'He has my full approval. A hundred millions and a hundred thousand men. There, now, is a man who does not mouth elegant phrases, who does not write treatises, but goes straight to the goal. The King, for once, must pay no heed to his own pathetic, cheese-paring, thrifty bourgeois instincts (a descendant of Saint Louis with the soul of a shopkeeper!); instead, he must let Monsieur de Breteuil have money and soldiers. And then we can move on to other things. This state of turmoil has gone on much too long.'

The sleeper had woken up. When he took in the enormity of where his hand was and the extent of my shame and embarrassment – I had exposed my limb up to the ankle in pulling away – he was overcome by confusion, and repeatedly craved my pardon.

With the Queen, in the gilded Great Study; her
preparations for departure: midnight to 2 a.m.

My head was buzzing, my temples throbbing; I wanted a fountain, to splash myself with water. Or simply my bed, to snatch a
bit of rest. But just as I was starting to cross the Cour des Princes,
I was stopped by one of the Queen's valets. He had a note
for me, with a message; I recognised the hand of Madame
Campan, First Lady of the Bedchamber. The mere sight of
her rounded, careful, servile writing, as civil and stupid as the
woman herself, made the weight of my fatigue twice as crush-
ing. But knowing where the message came from, I would not
have dreamed of trying to avoid complying with its instructions.
On the contrary, I was filled with gratitude for the order summoning me abruptly to her apartments. It was an absurd time of
day for a regular reading session, but, very early on, the Queen
had introduced the custom of sending for me at all hours,
whenever an attack of insomnia was likely, even if she put off
going to bed for as long as possible. In that voice of mine, which
my sponsor Monsieur de Montdragon had rated as merely 'subdued' and conveniently unobtrusive, the Queen had discovered
a soothing quality. I could skip a passage, or read the same one
twice, and the Queen would not notice. She desperately needed
to forget her cares and respond to the invitation which my voice
conveyed, beneath the words themselves: 'Close your eyes; rest
a while.' I would come running, half asleep, barely decent, a
dress pulled on hastily over my nightgown. I would arrive to
find a little table standing ready, with four lit candles. I would
slip into the shadowy bedside space and open the book. Sometimes, in the draughts of air, the flickering flames would carry
the words away in a rolling movement of waves. There were
heavy seas around my printed pages, as the Queen, stretched out

on a reclining bed, listened to me the way one might listen to a nocturne. The words followed lazily, one upon the other, reduced almost to a murmur in the troughs of the waves. Deep depression would descend upon me, soon shaken off as my voice rose once again with a strength I thought could save both of us from the agony of those hours for which no one at Versailles had ever found the appropriate ritual.

Both of us; I dared to say those words, but only to myself. I blushed at my own secret immodesty. I would cast a rapid glance in the Queen's direction, as though she might have read the thoughts I dared to harbour. She appeared to be in the greatest physical discomfort. She would stretch, sit up, take her head in her hands. Then she would lie down again and close her eyes. My function was not performed at a set time; it was tied to the phase when the sea of night was at low tide. It was dependent on that dreaded zone where the worst that has happened to you resurfaces to assail you once again and drag you to the bottom. The zone where you drown. I was the boat girl, ferrying across the water those things that have thus far refused to make the crossing.

'Put me to sleep, madam,' the Queen would sometimes request with a sigh.

In his white-gloved hand, the valet held a torch aloft. I followed him. As we walked past the Quarters of the Queen's Watch, I heard a confused sound of men's voices, glasses being smashed, weapons falling on the floor. I also caught choruses being sung in dialects so totally incomprehensible that I mistook them for foreign languages. I actually thought that these were soldiers from the army of foreign troops, come despite the King's counter-orders that they should offer their support to the Queen. Their noise filled the antechamber of the Royal Dining Room, which stood quite empty; but immediately beyond, a small padded door lined with heavy dark green Tours cloth, set into a corner of the Peers' Salon, only needed to open before me, and I was in the peace and quiet of the library, and the even greater tranquillity of a little adjoining room called the Library

Annexe. The impression of shelter and isolation culminated when I reached the heart of the Queen's Little Apartments, a group of tiny ill-lit spaces in what was known as the Great Interior Study, or Gilt Study.

Great it was not, but gilded it was. And all that gold, applied over the white wainscoting and around the mirrors, in garlands, ribbons, delicate friezes, profiled sphinxes, over the ledges of the mantelpiece, the elbow rests of the armchairs, the table legs and harp strings, was like a wondrous curtain of rain through which, as I looked, the Queen appeared, herself covered in droplets of gold. Bent over a writing desk, she was reading letters or papers. She turned her eyes in my direction but did not seem to notice me. She no longer looked anything like the very young girl, almost a child, whom I had left the previous day, nor like the ivory statuette glimpsed on the balcony. Madame Campan was parading her own importance. Puffed up, acting the soul of discretion, she kept shoving me to one side. I was edging my way forward at an angle, curtseying deeply as I went. And she, a big, fat hen in her heavy corpulence, repeatedly obtruded her person between the Queen and me. The woman nudged me away into the Bathing Room and from there into the Bath Compartment. Why does she not just shut me up in the Commode Room? I wondered. Madame Campan handed me several sheets of paper and pointed to a table covered with flacons of perfume. I made as though to touch them with my fingertips.

'You will not handle Her Majesty's perfumes, I trust,' she hissed angrily. And she added: 'Her Majesty is busy with reading and sorting personal papers. There is not the least need for *you* to read to her.'

Giving me no time to protest, she went on to explain: 'The only thing required of you is to take a sheet of paper and write down a few titles, ten, perhaps, that you consider indispensable in the event of a removal from Versailles. Monsieur Campan' (her father-in-law, whose name was constantly on her lips) 'would gladly have assumed this task, but has been called upon to perform a more essential service.'

I immediately envisioned the transfer of the National Assembly to Soissons or Noyon, and a royal departure for Compiègne. I liked the idea. The request, however, struck me as illogical: in every château where the Queen stayed for any length of time, there were several libraries. But I did not argue the point; the only reservations I expressed had to do with where I was to carry out my assignment: I would have preferred to work in the library.

'The Library, as also the Library Annexe and the Méridienne Room, will soon be crammed full of baggage. With the best will in the world, you would be in our way, Madame Laborde,' replied the Queen's First Lady of the Bedchamber, and it was as though she had punched me in the stomach with her elbow.

So I set to work there in the Bath Compartment. I concentrated as best I could, given all the whispering going on in the next room, whose door stood ajar. The whisperers were Madame Campan and her subordinate Madame de Rochereuil, Commode-Bearer to the Queen. They were sorting undergarments. Anything not selected for the move was appropriated by Madame de Rochereuil, who, it was common knowledge, would then sell it as dearly as she could. She had fingers like talons, long, pointed fingers that seized and held whatever they touched, fingers whose fearful nails made holes in the tips of her gloves. At the name Rochereuil, I could not repress a shudder. Some day, I thought, she will gouge the Queen's eyes out.

For the time being, not daring to do that, she was conspiring. She was doing her best to draw the First Lady of the Bedchamber over into the enemy camp. Madame Campan resisted, but Madame de Rochereuil did not lack for arguments.

'You and I are scorned and belittled and it has to stop. We have to say "No more!" We are human beings, just as *she* is. We have our dignity. Why did she demand to have a close-stool of lacquer and gilded bronze? Even when she's doing that, even sitting in that posture, she has to feel superior to the rest of the world. Does that strike you as fair or just, Henriette?'

Henriette was sick with embarrassment. She gestured at the

Rochereuil woman to be quiet. She was mortally afraid that the
Queen might hear. But Madame de Rochereuil took perverse
delight in making fun of her friend's natural timidity.

'Believe me, I'm in a good position to know what she really is.
When kings come closest to nature, that's the time when a
person can best see for herself how fraudulent it is to try and
set them apart from the rest of the human race. They were not
born to command us. No one was born to command us. There
should be no masters but those we choose. We ourselves.
Freely. Knowingly.'

'Hush, oh, hush! We'll discuss it all later, at more leisure.'

'Come on, now, you're already convinced; you just don't
want to admit it, even to yourself; you're held back by a bunch
of old prejudices. Listen to what your brother Monsieur Genêt
says . . .'

'Oh, don't even mention that lad's name to me; he's a good-
hearted man, but he's . . . how can I put it? . . .'

'He's a republican instead of a monarchist. He sees things as
they are and he's made the right choice. Listen to what he says;
he's showing you the way you should go.'

'That scamp?'

'That scamp. You should be proud of him. He's a decent,
intelligent young man. He goes around proclaiming: "The very
sight of a king is repugnant to me." That's the kind of young
person we need.'

Madame Campan was trying to escape from the evil counsels
of the Commode-Bearer. I suspected her of not being quite so
upright when there were no witnesses and the Queen was not
within hearing. She came to see how I was progressing. I gave
her some titles. 'I shall see to it those books are packed,' she said.
Shortly afterwards – and in my memory this scene is strange
because it bears absolutely no relationship to any of the other
reading sessions – Madame Campan and I were sent for. The
Queen needed us in the Great Gilt Study.

My task, I discovered, was to leaf rapidly through a number of books on eastern France, or maps if any were to be had ('*detailed* maps,' the Queen insisted), in order to determine the best possible itinerary between Versailles and Metz.

So the Queen was leaving Versailles and going to Metz! This was something new. All the papers were gone from her table. A burning smell suggested that she had not stopped at reading or rereading. Her gestures were quick and nervous. The expression on her face was one of strain, beyond weariness. Her complexion was muddy, her skin covered with red spots. And the celebrated grimace, the downturn of the lips, that so often made her look odiously contemputous, when in fact she was perhaps feeling no particular emotion: the grimace was very marked. But in her eyes, enlarged by the leaden circles spreading all the way to her cheeks, was a hardness I had not seen before. Despondent she was not, or not completely. Or else she had been despondent earlier, but was not now. Now she radiated determination and vigour.

I liked looking at her. I had acquired a sixth sense that alerted me to her unguarded moments, when she was busy either doing something or daydreaming, so that she was mentally absent but had left behind what one might call an effigy of herself that I could contemplate at will. Only rarely did I look directly at her – the way I had been lucky enough to do on the previous day, in her bedchamber at the Petit Trianon. Most often, what she made me free of was her reflected image. From the corner where I stood in the Great Gilt Study, all the mirrors favoured my wishes.

That haggard face, prematurely aged, with no remaining hint of careless adolescent grace, was still attractive. In fact, in its own way, more attractive. Between then and now, the Queen had been hard hit, beaten. Though endeavouring to give my thoughts a different direction, I could not put from my mind the Historiographer's words: 'We are doomed.' But the keenness of her gaze, the cold, hard brightness of her eyes, defied anyone to think she was prepared to accept defeat.

The Queen had ordered her servants to fetch what she called her 'travel table'. It was inlaid and the workmanship was very fine. It had a movable top with double doors that swung open. The table was hollowed out to provide a deep drawer containing her jewel casket. Not all her jewels were stowed in it, only the ones she wore regularly. Seated at this table, she was trying to sort them into two lots, the ones she wanted to take away with her, and the others. She found it impossible to choose.

'I shall take them all . . . and I am asking you, Madame Campan, to remove the settings. You are to assemble the stones in a travel case that I shall keep with me in the carriage. Count Esterhazy is waiting for us along the way with his regiment. At Metz we will mobilise troops and come back to Paris in strength. It is criminal for that city to think it can impose its will on the King. And on France. Paris is not France. And the Parisians are going to understand that fact, before we are done. Get up, Madame Campan . . . As for the itinerary from here to Metz, if you find you are unable to draw me a map' (she had just cast a quick glance at the improbable wavy line I had traced) 'I shall ask my coiffeur, Léonard, to do it instead; he is a resource-ful man, with a variety of talents. You, madam, have talents as well' (she must have noticed how crestfallen I looked) 'but geo-graphy does not lie within your sphere of competence. The King, thank heaven, has a passion for geography, and that may just give me my chance in this decision to leave Versailles and reconquer the country. What do you think, Madame Campan? Please, do get up on your feet; you cannot crawl around under that commode chair for the rest of your life. You can find that pearl later on, when we have returned!'

At that precise moment, the Campan woman gave a little crow of delight: she had spied the object of her search. She slithered farther under, then reappeared, somewhat flushed, dis-hevelled but very happy. I loathed her.

I had proved to be incompetent at mapping out a travel route (I suspected Madame Campan of having deliberately suggested to the Queen that this was something I could do, so she could rejoice at my humiliation). Aside from that, there was, so it seemed, no need whatever for the special soothing effects of my voice; and so I waited in trembling expectation of being sent back to join the shadows wandering about in the dark. That this did not happen was probably due to the Queen's haste to see the jewels prised out of their settings: she preferred to put me to work with the others. And from that point on, in the prevailing confusion, the Queen's treatment of me made no distinction between reader and chambermaid.

Obediently, I went and sat beside Madame Campan. She had finished doing the 'travel table'; now she was taking other jewels out of a tall, carved cabinet. There were so very many of them. It was fantastic: rings, bracelets, necklaces, pendant earrings, pins, brooches, lockets, tiaras . . . I would separate out one ring, bend aside the claws holding the stone in place, extract the stone and set it carefully in the travel case. Will the Queen, when she is away in Metz, simply wear her jewels loose? I wondered. Fortunately, I did not ask this aloud. My stupidity, my obstinate refusal to understand, would have drawn Madame Campan's sarcastic fire. We were working very vast, as fast as we could. Our fingers played nimbly over the emeralds and topazes, the rubies and carnelians, over sets of sapphires and diamonds. With a couple of deft movements, we freed the stones.

'I want to leave,' the Queen said again. 'For royalty, for us, it is a matter of life or death. The King must not stay one more day in a country he no longer controls.'

But then, oddly, instead of urging us to be quick, she stood up, as though ensnared by the sparkle of her jewels, and came over to look at them. Finally, unable to resist, she began sliding a ring over her finger, then another; she put several strings of precious stones round her neck, one atop the other; she covered her forearms with heavy bracelets. Transfixed, she stared at the mirror of her dressing table to see its reflected vision of her, all aglitter. Madame Campan and I dared not stir, but eventually it fell to the First Lady of the Bedchamber (who always firmly believed she was right, and on this occasion actually was) to break the spell. With infinite respect and ever so gently, Madame Campan reminded Her Majesty that if she wished to set off on her journey the next day there was a need for haste. The Queen tore herself away from her dream.

'*Wish* is an inadequate term to express what I feel. We *must* leave Versailles. Not to do so is equivalent to signing our own defeat – which is already a fact – our defeat and possibly worse . . . I want to go away from here. I want to leave this palace. I have done everything to try and make it mine. I have not succeeded. All I feel about the palace is the cold, the damp, the uninhabitable spaces . . . the neglect and disrepair. When I think that the King almost perished in his bed, crushed by a section of ceiling . . . I have really tried everything . . . I divided it into smaller and smaller rooms. I have had drapes installed, tapestries, mirrors. I increased the number of stairways so people could visit their friends' apartments more easily and find comfort in being with them. From the very outset, Versailles rejected me. Versailles was already occupied, by the Great King, who never left. No matter what room I went into, he was there, as a young man, or an old man, or a dancer, or a lover, or a warrior, always in majesty. The palace is under his surveillance. It will never be my home. Nor is it the King's home. Any more than it was home to Louis XV.'

A woman came to remove the accumulated jewels that had transformed her into a barbarian princess. The Queen, distraught, did not move away but stood facing her mirror. There were things she wanted to know.

'Where are my travel clothes? Are they ready? What about the little sailor suit for my son, the straw hat for my daughter? And what about teapots, coffee pots, chocolate pots? Hot-water bottles, chafing dishes, drawing materials, my paintboxes, my paintbrushes, my knitting needles, a spinning wheel? What do *I* know of evenings in Metz?'

Now she made a strange motion. She raised a protective arm and swayed on her feet, as if blinded by her own face. Then she said, slowly, groping for the right words:

'Louis XIV tolerates the King and me, because we are entrusted with the preservation of his Mausoleum, but he is dissatisfied with our services. I take refuge at the Petit Trianon and in the rustic cabins of my hamlet. The King, too, has his places of refuge. He shuts himself up in his dining room and sits in front of his portrait in hunting costume, by Oudry. Or rather in front of the portrait of Louis XV in hunting costume – the King ordered another artist to alter it so that it looked like him. But in a dining room, people you have no wish to see are always apt to appear. So the King goes to hide in his Most Private Office. There the paintings are not of royal hunters but of nymphs. No matter; the King, hidden away in his Most Private Office, has no eyes for the nymphs: he counts. And in his diary he makes note of everything he has counted, the number of curtseys and bows for the visits of condolence upon the death of my mother the Empress, the number of baths he has taken in the course of the month, the number of horses he has ridden since the age of eight, the number of animals killed in hunts, the number killed per day, per month, the total for the first six months, the yearly total, stag hunts, boar hunts, hundreds and thousands of animals killed . . . And the inkblot on our wedding day, did he count that, I wonder? I made only a single blot but it could not be erased. That inkblot was more ignominious than tripping over a rug . . . I have gone over the scene in my mind a thousand times: I am bending over to sign, using the given name that is still foreign to me. Because I do not see well, I have almost to hold my face against the paper. Ma-rie-An . . . toi . . . I am pressing down hard, too hard. The pen scrapes. I have ink spattered all over me, even on my cheek.'

A moment earlier, the Queen had shone like a heathen idol. Now she wore a single garment: a plain grey dress. She was rubbing her cheek to try to erase the inkblot. A big lock of hair had fallen across her forehead. How beautiful she was, rambling on like that!

Madame Campan was becoming frustrated over a piece of jewellery that refused to be prised apart. I looked at that big heaving bosom. I could hear her rapid breathing. It was a minuscule room. I was too hot. And her dress, crushed against mine, made me think of a faded flower clinging to its neighbour and mingling its petals with hers as it died.

'And what about me; will I be going with you?' proclaimed the turmoil oozing from her very pores. 'And what about me; will you forget me?' quavered the unspeakable distress that overwhelmed my very soul.

Exhaustion; ominous dawn: 2 to 4 a.m.

How did the time pass after that? I don't really remember . . . I plunged back in among the wanderers, and the night-time round continued. More uncertain than before, more scattered, increasingly eroded by the conviction that it was futile. In my case, holding as I did the secret of the royal family's departure and believing I was virtually the only person in possession of that secret, the futility of this night watch struck me even more cruelly than it did others. And there was also the isolation imprisoning each of us, with its deep uncertainty, the mixture of wanting to learn more about the King's decisions and fearing what they would be. In the Queen's Gaming Room, some women had stretched out on the tables. Others, settled snugly in the window recesses, were talking in whispers, exchanging the latest news: 'They kidnap our children, and demand huge ransoms in exchange.' I was back among ravaged faces, poor creatures wavering between flat despair and morbid, irrational excitement. Somnolent bodies here and there. In the room where sedan chairs were stacked, people had taken the chairs down and climbed inside. Some had drawn the curtains.

I left the Gaming Room and the Grand Gallery for the Lower Gallery. The apartments all along it had their doors shut. No sound came from them. Then I went back up, the way one would go to the Opera Theatre, and crept along a corridor at the level of the *loges*. I could make out the surface of the reservoirs, visible above the far end of the North Wing, the rather frightening ink-black mirror of their watery expanse. I lingered a moment to look. The desolation of that dark pond, strangely suspended in space with the sky behind it, chilled me to the bone. Was it to get away from that image and from the gloomy forebodings it filled me with, that I walked aimlessly, taking the first stairway I chanced upon, a narrow, dank, smelly one, leading to other twists and turns that were darker still? For a while I met no one. Then a disconcerting company of inhabitants began to emerge. People such as I had never seen in the palace until now. Were they climbing up out of the hold, driven by instinctive knowledge that over these and the next few hours the fate of the ship was being decided? I had never ventured into these regions before. As I looked, implausible beings came into view. Worn-out figures like threadbare garments, with yellowish, shrunken faces. Deformed creatures were appearing as well, individuals who were hunchbacked, one-eyed, lame, swollen with goitre, much too fat or skeletally thin. I was revolted by their lacklustre eyes, their sickly masses of flesh, their blackened teeth. Others assailed my nostrils with a rancid, sticky smell. They were swathed like mummies in their old lacewear, and only with slow, deliberate care did they manage to put one foot before the other. There were also a number of women – some sort of farmworkers – who looked and moved like birds, and inspired real fear. I hastily drew aside, for I remembered, as I watched them sidling past, girded in fierce odours, amulets clinking round their necks, pockets bulging on their long aprons – I remembered, as I was saying, the suspicious deaths, the rumours of poisonings which at the time I had refused to believe. I was afraid that, without having to lift a hand, they would shove a cold, slimy toad into the hollow of my back. My pointless roaming had taken me too far. I summoned up enough strength to run. I escaped them, at any rate temporarily, for if they should decide to hold their evil sabbath beneath the chandeliers of the Grand Gallery, it would be up to us to make way for them . . .

Breathless, sweating, I returned to my point of departure. A night such as this was no time to wander away from the vicinity of the Royal Apartments. We must remain on familiar ground as much as possible – assuming those words still had any meaning, of course. I found it reassuring to be back where I could hear the usual hum of conversation. And I gained still greater comfort from recognising a person who was dear to me and who, oblivious to hints that he should exercise discretion, was making no effort to keep his voice down. This was a large man who was obviously trying to convince a much smaller one of something. Convince him or smother him: the smaller man was struggling to break free of the giant, who, almost half as tall as him again, pressed against his chest.

'The alliance we formed four hundred years ago with the royal house is prejudicial neither to them nor to us . . . Monsieur de Noailles has been used quite unfairly; the suddenness of their recent favour has provoked a paroxysm of envy; the next thing you know they are yesterday's men, while in fact they are persons of rank and condition all the more for being connected to our family.'

I did not need to see his face – a face remarkable for its distinguishing feature, a kind of great pimple or fleshy growth on its nose – in order to recognise the Marquess de La Chesnaye, whose position at court was that of First Carver. He had two favourite themes: the antiquity of his family and his plans for improving the palace. So great was the hold that the past exercised over him – he confused the various names that the rooms had been given in different reigns, and even in the course of a single reign – that it was often rather difficult to follow his train of thought. The voice of his father, or grandfather, or great-grandfather would speak through him, making him say, alternately and indiscriminately, Cour des Bains when referring to the Cour des Cerfs, Oratory for the Méridienne Room, Wig Room instead of the Thermal Baths Office or Mirror Room . . . In his mind, where the present Royal Wine Cellars Courtyard lay, the Ambassadors' Stairway still rose, and through the white marble of the Royal Chapel, there continued to shimmer the blue-tinted reflections of Thetis's Grotto . . . But, for the moment, his sole preoccupation was the antiquity of his family. The thing that he deplored most about Versailles, the great flaw that obsessed him, namely that *Versailles did not have an entrance worthy of the great palace building*, was presently relegated to second place in his mind.

Monsieur de La Chesnaye harried his victim more and more relentlessly. The medals and ornaments covering his person jingled a shrill musical accompaniment to the litany of his ancestors and their virtues. Then he paused in his recital, as he noticed I was there.

'Ah! Madame Laborde, we were discussing the Noailles family; it seemed to me that their honourable conduct might justly be applauded. The Duchess de Noailles, as a close friend of Madame de Neuilly, First Reader to the Queen, must be well known to you. What is your assessment of her?'

I stammered a reply, embarrassed at having to admit that I did not know her. I had never even seen her, save at a distance. And I was even more ashamed that I did not know Madame de Neuilly either. At Monsieur de La Chesnaye's question, I felt a twinge of mortification. I walked away.

Once again I encountered Monsieur de Feutry, accompanied by Jacob-Nicolas Moreau. Monsieur Moreau's heavy and ever-present satchel was making him lean to one side. This happened to be the side where Monsieur de Feutry was. This position made my friend's remarks look very confidential to an outsider, which in reality they were not.

'Madame has honoured me with her private views of the matter. You know how judicious the Countess de Provence is and how greatly I value her opinions. Well she said to me, and I am quoting literally: "The situation seems to me to bode ill." '

'The deuce! Is that your opinion as well?'

'I said so yesterday evening to Madame Laborde.' (He had just noticed me.) 'I think we are doomed, purely and simply.'

'This is not the first time I have heard you say that.'

'True. Mankind has defied Heaven once too often, and Heaven, in spite of all its forbearance, has finally taken revenge. Conditions were right for punishment, but I did not know what form the punishment would take or that it was so near. Speaking of imminent punishment, Monsieur, I am informed that you have in your possession an . . . interesting document. How shall I say? . . . An opuscule? A pamphlet? Yes. A pamphlet. The 'List of heads that must fall . . .' or some such abomination . . . Could you lend it to me so that I may copy it out and file it in my archives?'

He bowed to Monsieur de Feutry, took leave of me with a wave of his hand, and went back to his fourth-floor room.

'Punishment'; he had uttered the word distinctly, raising his voice a little. This was too loud for a certain Monsieur Lemire, wax warmer, an extremely timid man even in normal times. He wanted us all to lower our voices. So we whispered the pathetic half-sentences that were all we had to offer each other. Little by little a multitude of priests came to swell our ranks. They were quivering and frightened. Their lips were moving constantly, giving passage to a smooth and endless stream of prayers. Their numbers became so great in certain salons that those rooms might well have been mistaken for chapels. I began to pray with them and was shocked to hear a resonant voice coming from the next room, where a man was talking about hunting with hawks ('Hush! Hush!' begged the wax warmer).

'People have a wrong notion of Flemish falconers; they are first-rate. I hunted recently with the Royal Hawking. Its falconers, as you know, are for the most part Flemish or Dutch. They displayed exceptional skill, such as one might seek in vain among falconers coming from the South and yet the Southerners are much admired. The King would have it that the falconers from the North are better. And he is right. Believe me, we can trust His Majesty's judgement. In matters of hawking, Louis XVI is incomparably superior to his predecessors, even Louis XIII.'

'In matters of hawking, to be sure, and for every form of hunting, Louis XVI is a great king.'

The animation in the next room subsided. The murmur of prayers dominated once more. We were left with nothing to distract our minds from the thing it was impossible to name.

Close the gates

We were made still more uneasy when someone suddenly noticed how small our numbers were. And there was still the threat of that troop marching down on us from Paris. How were we to defend ourselves? 'At the very least, the gates ought to stay closed for the day,' suggested a gentleman who informed the company that his name was Liard and that he was a mole catcher. (This gives some idea of how irrelevant the social order and hierarchy had become.)

'Ridiculous,' was the immediate verdict. 'Ridiculous and ill-considered. It would be giving the enemy proof that we are afraid.'

'We are afraid. And for that reason, I say again, let's close the gates.' The mole catcher was not backing down. 'What difference does it make? What's ridiculous about it? When you are attacked, it is not ridiculous to protect yourself. Those gates have got to be closed, the ones that lead on to the Place d'Armes, the ones that are part of the Royal Fence . . . They were closed during the night. We will be running greater risks tomorrow, that is to say, today . . .'

'It may be, when all is said and done, that the idea is not without merit. Closing the gates would be a fundamental act of protection. Not even protection, an act of dissuasion.'

'We are dealing with people whom we have no business persuading or dissuading. One does not reason with savages.'

'What if we threw them some coins? A few gold louis to distract them. They would fight among themselves, and while they were doing that, we would be left in peace. The device has been used many a time.'

'Distract them? The thing to do is give them a sound beating, crush them, grind them. Oh, I would like to get my hands on one of them! That bunch of rogues! Scum, rabble, lackeys, mongrel dogs!'

Just then there was the sound of something falling, and we all jumped. It was only a statuette that someone's elbow had knocked over. The guilty party looked at the damage with no sign of astonishment, said merely, 'Oh, excuse me,' and pushed the pieces away with his sword.

I had the feeling that, before our very eyes and at preternatural speed, the palace was coming apart. On a console table of gilded wood, housing a sculpture representing Astronomy, a large basin of water had been set. A few people had rushed over and were dipping their faces in it or trying to drink directly from the bowl.

The proposal to close the gates prompted further debate. The mole catcher had found a supporter.

'The man is right, why not give orders that the palace gates are to be kept shut? It would not greatly alter the situation, but even so. It would discourage the waverers. Those swine are going to cut our throats, and we'll have done nothing to stop them . . .'

'Keeping the gates shut all day would be unprecedented.'

'You are mistaken, gentlemen, the gates have already been shut once in the middle of the day; that was when Louis XIV was dying . . . An exemplary death. Everything Louis XIV did was exemplary, even his dying. Louis XV pulled himself together just in time to die honourably. But with Louis XIV there was not a hint of weakness. Everything about him was admirable, and his death a high point . . . Overcome at last by suffering, and with all the details of his funeral ceremonies scrupulously organised, the King lay in state. Before he lapsed into unconsciousness, he had uttered the supplication: "Oh, God! Help me to die." Then he opened his eyes again and articulated clearly, speaking not to his confessor but to Madame de Maintenon: "Do you know, madam, it is not at all difficult to die . . ." The King had entered into negotiations with Eternity. That was why he had ordered the gates closed: Versailles had ceased to belong to the kingdom of mortal men.'

'Louis XIV died of gangrene, Louis XV of smallpox . . . how astounding that our last two kings, rather than dying in what one could call a proper way, should have rotted!'

'It's all in the carcass, Your Lordship . . .'

(These words, insolent and offensive, come back to me on sleepless nights. They act on my memory like irritants.)

Close the gates: very well, but who would go out and give orders to that effect? It was for the King to give such commands. Before daybreak. But how could he be reached? It would be best if one of us went instead. The mole catcher volunteered. It was unanimously agreed that, however great the chaos that confronted us might be, a mole catcher could not be the bearer of a royal order. Just when the stalemate appeared hopeless, Jean-François Heurtier spoke up; he was the Palace Architect and Inspector. He had joined the group a moment earlier and now put a speedy end to the discussion.

'It had occurred to me, back on 10 July, to take that precaution, that is, to give some thought to the closing of the gates. I went to see for myself. There are neither keys nor locks. I have ordered new ones to be made, but it will be several weeks before I receive them. That being so, the palace is open, both night and day.'

Dark fatalism now prevailed. Some men checked their pistols – rather as a matter of principle than out of a clear determination to fight: have a set-to with a lot of lackeys, how humiliating! In contrast to this attitude, I heard the final words of a challenge to a duel. I had no need to hear the actual words, I could infer them from the arched backs, the fierce looks, the hands clenched on sword hilts, a kind of opposing electrical current, flowing fraternally but mortally between the two young men.

No one knew what was contained in the announcement that

Field Marshal de Broglie was making at that moment to the members of the War Council. But it was known that he had not gone to bed and had spent the night in consultation. Among us, almost all conversation had stopped. A few prone figures were to be seen, in silhouette, dozing on seats here or there. Others were erect as though on the lookout, but they were as insubstantial as ghosts. You would only have had to touch them or say 'hello' very softly, and they would have vanished. In some places, wall candelabra had been lit, adding an end-of-the-festivities feel to this dawn scene.

In the Royal Apartments, in the antechambers, the small salons, the studies, in the public ceremonial areas as in the most secret places, on the stairways, in the corridors and passageways, behind official doors or hidden entrances, fear was a dense, material presence: a substance that had hardened overnight and now held us immobilised. I wanted to get out, escape. I felt that if I did not do so now, it would never be possible again. I no longer believed that a hostile intrusion was imminent or that we were really about to be surrounded. Perhaps 'they' were approaching, but they were still far off. A new day was dawning. The view in every direction was still wide open. I pushed my way through the assemblage of ghosts – my confederates. I caught another glimpse of Monsieur de La Chesnaye. The shadow of his double nose was swaying back and forth over a most unhappy prudish maiden lady, Adèle-Élisabeth Bichebois, a laceworker, who had strayed into our midst, a basket over her arm.

I had to go outside; I had to breathe.

16 July 1789

DAY

Outdoors, under the windows of the Queen's
Bedchamber: between 5 and 6 a.m.

Outside, I skirted the wing of the palace known as Aile des
Princes. I walked as if I knew where I was going, when in reality
I had not the remotest idea. Over towards the Orangerie I saw a
girl wearing a grumpy expression and with circles of fatigue
under her eyes. She was coming away from the apartments of
His Royal Highness the Count d'Artois. He may have been the
only man, on that night, who found time for an interlude of
pleasure before plunging back into the maelstrom. It was in his
nature, like the fact that he took lessons in tightrope walking in
preference to applying himself to serious studies. I have always
been of two minds where the Count d'Artois is concerned: I felt,
and continue to feel, strenuous moral disapproval, but I could
not help being attracted. So I pointedly turned my steps away
from that low creature, thus showing my contempt and at the
same time refusing to concern myself with the libertine behaviour of the King's brother.

As for deciding which way to walk, no decision had been
required of me. There was only one way my feet could take
me: willy-nilly, I was now under the windows of the Queen's
Bedchamber. From the time I had left her, I had been obsessed
by a single thought: she was packing for departure; she was
abandoning Versailles. Metz was not a pleasure sojourn like
any other, it was a fallback position, before the battle. And
since at that time I did not imagine for a second that the King
could be of a different mind, I assumed the departure of the
royal family was imminent. The royal family accompanied by

the Polignacs, that is – for in my view it was a certainty that if the Queen insisted on the presence of Gabrielle, her *inséparable*, she would also take the whole clan with her, under her protection. I bitterly recalled how Diane de Polignac had spent part of the night going from one group to another, collecting information, exhorting us to have no thought in our mind but the welfare of the King and Queen. Easy for her to lecture others on what they should do, when she knew that, come what may, she would not be separated from the Queen. I, however, would almost certainly not be 'going along' on the journey to Metz; what, then, did 'acting in the best interest of the Queen' mean in my case? Waiting for her? Trying by every possible means to join her in Metz? I looked around me. There was a pale sky. The clouds, moving rapidly, seemed to skim the treetops. A recent rain made the scent of the orange blossoms even stronger and the white of the statues even less lustrous. I gazed upward. What if she was already gone?

In a moment of folly – since in all likelihood she had not yet left the palace but was shut away from view in her Little Apartments, continuing to make her arrangements for departure – I stepped back several paces in the hope that I would catch a glimpse of her. No one in sight, of course. No movement on the other side, no silhouetted figure. I walked away, feeling terribly lost. The stabbing sensation of loneliness that had been with me these last few days became unbelievably intense. And the palace grounds, in all their stunning beauty, turned against me. The prospect of living here without her caused me atrocious, unbearable pain. I sat down at the top of the steps, overlooking the Latona fountain. And suddenly, I could stand it no longer; I stretched out full length on the marble landing and gave way to wracking sobs. I could hear myself crying, and far from trying to exercise restraint, I wished I could cry even harder, I wanted the tears to flow even more abundantly, in torrents: I was dispossessed. The earth had opened beneath my feet. It was going to swallow me up. I did not struggle. Rather, I fell . . . and found myself lying across the stairway, gasping for breath. Then, as in the aftermath of an earthquake, an unfamiliar calm swept over me. I regained a measure of self-control and looked for some water to bathe my face, but Latona was dry. I went to a stone bench opposite the façade and, in a curiously detached way, as though I had been a visitor out for a walk, sat observing the palace from outside.

An eerie silence

The curtains were still drawn: only the ones in the Queen's Bedchamber had been left open. I could easily have imagined that the entire palace was fast asleep. The silence all around was untroubled. That was a surprise. No noise. The tiny vending stalls that sprang up like weeds – outside, against the fences; and inside, the length of the Lower Gallery and on a number of staircases – must, I thought, be closed. I saw no sign of the animated, energetic crowd of barterers, vendors, beggars, visitors, and gawkers who normally began passing through the palace gates at first light. They would jostle the troop of cobble sweepers; and the sweepers, unhurried, conscious of their right to occupy the courtyards, calmly went on with their work. But this morning the cobble sweepers were gone.

Sitting on my stone bench, I was straightening out my clothes as best I could. I smoothed my hair: at that time I wore a chignon, set quite low, with a lock of hair escaping from it to fall over one shoulder. I opened my prayer book. But the silence hanging over Versailles was so unaccustomed that it claimed my attention. The silence intrigued me. It amounted to an enigma.

Let me be clear about something that most people would probably have trouble imagining today: noise was inseparable from Versailles. The sound of Versailles remains a part of me even now. It is a single block compounded of a myriad individual sounds: ritual, military, religious, the changing of the guard and the ringing of the bells, a continuous background of barking, neighing, coach wheels turning, orders being shouted, raised voices at day's end, music being played on all sides in the night, and the endless to-and-fro of servants' footsteps on the wooden floors; all this surrounded by the din, the disorder, the dust of the omnipresent construction projects, never finished and always starting up again, the permanent 'work in progress' that went on night and day: painting, beautifying, making alterations to apartments, adding balconies, relocating stairways, laying ornamental tiles, hanging shutters, repairing chimneys. You stopped to admire a canvas by Watteau or Hubert Robert, and a few steps farther along you tripped over scaffolding and blobs of plaster were flying through the air . . . The noise comes back to me occasionally, perhaps deafening to the outsider, but deep, violent, mysteriously nourishing, vitally necessary to the person living inside it. These revisitations of the sounds of Versailles fill me with delight. I savour them; I pick out the individual themes; I play them back to myself, varying the rhythms and inter-pretations . . .

The silence of this particular morning was made more remark-able by a sudden realisation of another curious phenomenon, besides the absence of visitors: the French Guards had deserted in the night, disappearing as one man. They had followed the example of their comrades in Paris. Gone were the sounds of boots and the click of heels, the arms drills, orders repeated for the changing of the guard, the watchwords and songs that had punctuated my life just as surely as morning Mass and evening prayers. The amazing bustle in and around the palace, the daily metamorphosis from palace to caravanserai, had suddenly ceased, and I was left stupefied. I was still 'in my own home', but in a state of mental confusion; I had lost the living bond between the external hubbub and my inner music, my tonality of soul. I was no longer rendered powerless by the stupor of defeat and the fear of being attacked, as I had been in the middle of the night. Instead, I was panic-stricken at finding myself in an unrecognisable space, a space emptied as though under the threat of a plague; I was terrified at having been transported overnight to a place with a curse on it. I now had a better understanding of why the proposal to keep the gates closed had been so ineffectual: Versailles was open, the opposite of a fortress. Versailles let everybody in. The vendors who offered licentious engravings and publications that they hid in the folds of their capes, the impostors who rented a manservant for the day, disguised him as an ambassador, and attempted to gain an audience with the monarch, passing themselves off as kings of distant islands . . . The schemers, too, the *intrigantes*, women who waited spider-like in the antechambers, along the garden paths, behind the bushes, prepared to do anything that would catch a noble lord in their web . . . There was a time, during more dissolute reigns, when the first person these ladies sought to seduce was the King. Under Louis XVI they had given up trying: as they had no hope of attracting his attention, they lowered their sights. The King was so chaste that if occasionally, on the way from his apartments to the chapel, he addressed a few words to a woman (this did not happen often: in general if he wished to acknowledge someone, he went no further than a curt nod), it had to be an elderly woman . . .

But the human tide of sightseers, adventurers, schemers, coming in wave after endless wave, impelled by need or greed, was only the most visible part of another, less evident, but deeper current, carried by a nameless force. This current was the stream of beggars, and its force lay in the very might of their destitute condition. The beggars were numberless, nameless, relentless. They surrounded the palace on every side. They were driven off and, unfailingly, back they came, dirtier, sicklier, more crippled than before – now humble, now threatening. The palace offered them any number of hiding places where they could lie in wait. Officially they were banned from Versailles, but they paid no attention. They knew they could always count either on a guard being momentarily distracted, or on the darkness that reigned virtually everywhere, the moment you stepped outside the perimeter of the Royal Apartments – a deep, impenetrable darkness, relieved only for a brief instant by a few candles that soon melted, their glimmer a pathetic effort against the boundless shadows of night. (The 'lodgers' disbursed ruinous amounts in their struggle with the dark: there were winter days when they spent as much on candles as they would have done in an entire season had they stayed in their country mansions, where people took the weather as it came and darkness when it fell.) The darkness, though, allowed the beggars to thumb their noses at regulations. For who shall keep Night from entering in?

'One of these times,' Madame de Grasse had complained after being accosted as she left her apartments, by a group of miserable wretches whom her household servants had mercilessly thrashed, 'a beggar will bring the plague into the palace with him.' As for me, I sometimes felt that the plague was near at hand, whenever the usual smells of Versailles (strong smells, of course, but I had come to appreciate them) were augmented by the sickly, sugary odour of rotting flesh. Impossible to eradicate although its source could not be traced, intermittent, this stench would suddenly be there and as suddenly be gone. Gripped by a spasm of nausea, I would close my eyes. A dead body? At Versailles? That was specifically prohibited; there must be no corpse at the palace unless the dead person was a member of the royal family . . . Despite which, yes, there was a dead body . . . I was not the only one to notice it, but no one spoke up . . . And then the stench would dissipate. It was at its worst only for a while . . . And now? Since there was no longer anyone to stop them, would the beggars come swarming into the palace? Had they joined forces with the populace that was marching down upon us? I doubted it; the beggars constituted a distinct populace of their own.

The victors rejoice: about 8 a.m.

Around me, everything was silent and empty, hostile and threatening. I sought refuge in my room. Perhaps I would read awhile, if I was unable to sleep, for I had reached a level of anxiety which made it unlikely I would drop off. That was when I saw them: two doorkeepers, their persons in scandalous disarray. They had thrown their blue cloth jackets on the ground, and there they were, right under the windows of the Queen's Bedchamber, in shirtsleeves, with a bottle of wine set down at their feet, jabbering away to each other. One was straddling a marble statue; the other, his back propped against the statue's base, was putting a makeshift bandage over his hand. The pair were not talking but shouting at each other. I was forced to stop: they were barring the way to my room. I ought to have turned around and used a different doorway. More to the point, I ought to have sent them packing, ordered them out from under the windows of the Queen's Bedchamber, instead of staying there listening to them. There is a horrid fascination, though, in hatred and vulgarity, in the thing that, some day or other, is going to swallow you up.

'Y'know what I did yesterday morning when the Duke de Richelieu came in?'

'No, what?'

'Nothing.'

'You mean you didn't stamp your foot twice while you announced him in your loudest voice: His Excellency the Duke de Richelieu?'

'I didn't let out a peep. The Duke stopped at the entrance to the salon, and waited. Looked at me, he did. I didn't say anything, I tell you.' (He was bellowing, crazed with his own daring, his legs thumping against the statue.) 'Duke and peer he may be, but I didn't do a thing. I didn't move a muscle, I didn't say a word. Anyhow, why announce him? He knows what his name is. I don't care if he *is* an old wreck before his time. A degenerate, a rotten fruit of his father's debauched loins, he still knows his own name. Your name is the last thing you forget. Isn't that right, Boineau?'

'Moinel, stupid. My name is Sylvain Moinel.'

'See? Even *you* remember your name.'

'Don't be so damned smart! Why do you have to poke fun at everybody? Isn't the Duke de Richelieu enough excitement for you? I can send you lots more like him. There's no shortage.'

'Thanks, Boineau, I knew you were one of us.'

Although he had an injured hand wrapped in a bandage, the other man leaped up and hit out at his companion to make him fall. The one astride the statue held on, and was about to hit back, but did not dare. He was inhibited by his partner's injured hand.

'All right, Moinel, it was just my little joke. My own name is Pignon, Chrétien Pignon. I didn't mean any harm. If a man can't have a laugh these days, when will he? Hey! To celebrate the Bastille, and freeing the prisoners, and the processions and all that, my wife and I broke everything in our house. I mean, we smashed *everything*. The bed, the table, clay pot, the tumblers. By the time we were done, there was nothing left but an iron pot, and we bashed that till it was all shrunk up. My wife was the one who threw it at the window so's it split the paper apart.'

'You're lucky to have a wife like that. She's much more fun than mine. That Suzette, she's always going to church and praying. She says turning ourselves into a republic is something that'll have to be atoned for and it's going to take a long time, a really long time. Our children's children will still be paying. What if she's right? It scares me, it really does. Sending our children, and our children's children, to roast in Hell, are *you* prepared to do that?'

'You're about as cheerful as your wife, for God's sake! I never thought I'd see the day! . . . The day I refuse to greet a lord and peer. The day the world turns upside-down. Because that's what a revolution is, after all. You take something, no matter what, and you turn it upside-down.'

'No matter what, eh? In that case, a person might as well take a woman and a strumpet to do what you're talking about. That's it, let's do things in the right order here, let's start by revolutionising a whore! But you haven't told me what reaction you got from the *present* Duke de Richelieu. We have to be precise, you know, because the old man, the *Intendant des Menus Plaisirs* the Marshal, this one's father, was so famous and lasted such a long time that nobody believes the son is now the Duke. There are still some who call him the Duke de Fronsac.'

'Does he set them straight?'

'What do you think? So straight he's all worn out!'

And they both went off in a fit of giggles. The one on the statue slid down off his perch. The other man was rolling on the ground with laughter. I observed their behaviour as one might observe monsters. What metamorphoses were taking possession of this place and the people it harboured? These two, who previously stood as stiff and dumb as pokers in their cloth uniforms and were as inanimate as the doors they tended, were now talking back and forth at the top of their lungs, or lying on the ground, waving their arms and moaning about how it hurt to laugh so hard; but then one of them would repeat, 'He sets them so straight he's all worn out,' and the braying would start again . . .

They cried and wiped their eyes with their shirts. They would start to get up and then collapse. Their laughter was a subtle allusion to the last duel fought by the poor Duke de Richelieu nine years earlier when he was still the Duke de Fronsac. His father's marriage to a young window, at the age of eighty-four, had been the subject of various mocking gibes. Overhearing one of these, the Duke de Fronsac had challenged the scoffer to a duel and killed him.

'I have to admit he was quite a man with the ladies. *Intendant des Menus Plaisirs*, the King's Little Pleasures, as it's officially called. He was that, all right, but the first pleasures he looked after were his own, and they weren't specially little! He married a youngster and still spent his nights chasing after actresses. And d'you know why the Marshal-Duke was such a rake?'

'You're always asking me whether I know or I don't know. It really irritates me. As though you're calling me a dummy every two minutes.'

'Right, so you don't know. No problem, a man can learn, he can improve his knowledge. Well, since you don't know, I'll tell you: the Marshal-Duke was such a rake because of milk baths. When he woke up, while he was drinking his first bottle of champagne, he took a milk bath.'

'You sure it wasn't the other way round?'

'What d'you mean, the other way round?'

'He didn't drink a bowl of milk, while having a champagne bath . . .'

'No. You're not a quick learner, are you? No, seriously, citizen, milk baths help stave off those occasions where a man can't perform.'

'Attacks like that are strictly for the nobs. With ordinary people like us, it doesn't happen. Nature takes its course. But even supposing, let's say a man was really tired . . . It could never happen, but okay, just for the sake of argument, suppos-ing . . . Once you know that, about the milk baths, where does it get you? My wife, who's a wet nurse, is currently suckling six babies. Even if I made them go without, that would never give me enough to have a bath!'

'You're too quick at spotting problems!'

'And what happened to the bath milk after he was through with it? What did he do with it?'

'*He* didn't do anything. But his personal valet took it and sold it, and it poisoned our children. The aristocrats take milk baths and our children die. The same as with the flour. The flour shortage comes from them using it all to make gruel for their cats! Or the houses! People have nowhere to bed down for the night. In winter the ones who are the poorest drop like flies. In the charity shelters they pack them together on straw to sleep. In the hospitals, they put them three or four to a bed. You wake up in the middle of the night, you've got a corpse lying against you, stretched out stiff and cold. I'm not exaggerating!'

'Yes, yes, I know . . .'.

'And meanwhile, *they* own so many châteaux that there are some they've never set foot in; they don't even know where they are, in which province . . . They've inherited them . . . They don't give a tinker's damn about them . . . Can you imagine all those bedrooms, the beds, the big fireplaces, the . . .'

'Like here.'

'And their dogs! You've seen where they keep their dogs! In kennels lined with satin, studded with gold nails. Each one like a gem of a little house. You look at those kennels and all you can think is: Well, I certainly wouldn't mind being one of those dogs; and they get the choice bits of food, too! What a bunch of wastrels, profiteers, bloodsuckers!'

'Hyenas, cankers, bastards! What's more, not all the soldiers in the foreign armies have gone. You can hear German dialect being spoken in the parts of town where working people live. There are Spaniards, too. They're tough customers, those Spaniards. If they're told to wipe us out, they'll do it.'

'The people here in the palace will issue the order for us all to be killed, and not give it a second thought.'

'Not the King! He cares about us. He's good. But *her*; she'd do it without a blink! I command you! I can just hear her shouting, in her own tongue: "Let them be slain, all of them, to the last man!"'

'She has a lot of faults, but it can't be denied that she speaks French. You've heard her, same as me.'

'Yes, but that doesn't matter. I've been reading the newspapers, where it gives the complete programme of the court faction, and it's worse than you think. They want to reduce Paris to starvation, and in order to hasten the city's destruction, they want to place a hundred pieces of artillery at the top of the Butte Montmartre and the same number – a hundred cannon –

up on Belleville, all with their sights trained on the city down below. They're going to fire their cannon and, at the same time, put the city to the sword and the torch and kill the people, until Paris, what's left of it, submits and asks for the National Assembly to be suspended. A diabolical plan. It has Antoinette written all over it.'

They took some time to swig from the bottle and enjoy a better foretaste of what was to come.

'. . . It's fantastic how Austrian she is.'

'Everything about her. Her orange hair, her sharp nose . . .'

'Her carroty hair, her little stick of a nose, like a puppet in a Punch-and-Judy show.'

'Her lips that make you think she's above it all. Her way of holding her head way up, higher than anybody else. We who live at Versailles and see her every day – which is no treat . . .'

'Which *was* no treat. We're not going to hang on here till we grow roots. As soon as I finish my newspaper, I'm away.'

'. . . we've seen her every day, and we can testify: she's just plain Austrian. More all the time.'

'With a mouth that looks ready to spit out whatever goes in.'

'She doesn't spit anything out because she doesn't swallow anything. She doesn't eat. She goes through the motions. That's one more way she deceives the nation.'

'But you've never seen her eat or not eat; you're always on duty at that time on a Sunday.'

'Not me, no, but my brother has seen her not eating. He was determined to give his oldest son a look at the King, as a first-communion present. It's a tradition in our family. Well, I can tell you for certain: the Austrian doesn't eat anything. She drinks the same glass of water from the time the meal starts till it ends. She doesn't really drink: she wets her lips. And instead of eating she moves the same piece of meat around on her plate with the tip of her fork (because, even if she doesn't eat, she has to have a fork, a knife, spoons, the whole caboodle, all made of gold, naturally). She shoves it a bit to the right, a bit to the left, back to the middle. She hesitates over where it should go next. She calls that eating. And what's more, she doesn't take her gloves off at the table . . . can you imagine? She keeps her gloves on *and* uses a fork . . . She takes a hammer to all our good, French ways. She shows no respect for anything French. Before she came along, the King and Queen used to eat in public twice a week. With her here, and I reckon after she goes, it's just once a week, one measly time. You cross the country on foot, for that one chance a week, and she gives you nothing to look at. You've come all that way to watch her eat, and she doesn't eat.'

'They're horrible, those Austrians. The dirtiest, most nit-picking nation of liars you could ever hope to find. Some of their customs are really disgusting. In Austria, when you marry a girl, she's already been deflowered by her brother. The family gets first go, then you. That's how it worked with Antoinette. She'd lost her virginity to her brother Joseph before she came to Louis's bed.'

'Would *you* want to be king?'

'On those terms, no, I would not. If things were different, I might.'

'Everything is the King's, all those beautiful provinces, the forests, the oceans, you, me, the Orangerie, the Grand Stables and the Lesser Stables, everything belongs to him. That must give a person *some* kind of special feeling.'

'But how does he make it *feel* that it belongs to him?'

'Well, when he uses things, he just takes them without asking permission. From anybody. Whatever he decides he wants, he gets. He eats green peas on Easter Day, if he feels like it. And he really eats, that one.'

'He's partial to little peas.'

'Or deputies! . . . '

(The next instant they were lying on the ground again, doubled up with laughter, because of the King's famous slip of the tongue when the Estates General were holding their first meetings. He had said: 'I would enjoy another helping of those *députés*,' instead of 'petits pois'!)

'No . . . The King isn't fussy about his food. He eats almost anything.'

'. . . He eats almost everything. Have you any idea what the menus for his meals are like? The most exquisite dishes and always in vast quantities. Just his everyday fare, picture it, four main courses, twenty side dishes, six joints of meat, fifteen normal desserts, thirty little desserts, a dozen platters of pastry.'

'I don't have to picture it, my brother described it for me: creme fritters with raspberry sauce, chocolate pie, almond tarts, every flavour of sherbet: cantaloupe, lemon, fig, blackberry, pomegranate, and there were Ali Babas, too . . . There's nobody who wouldn't like food as fabulous as that. Just talking about it makes my mouth water. How do you suppose the gentlemen servers manage to keep their hands off?'

'They don't keep them off. I'm sure that the King's serving dishes have been eaten from before they get to their destination. Think about it, it's a long trip from the kitchen . . . the temptation must be strong . . .'

'Result: the King eats things that are already partly eaten.'

'Partly eaten, and cold. You have five hundred people officially in your service, and the food you eat is cold.'

'Five hundred! The Royal Commissary must be pretty big.'

'The Royal Commissary is enormous. When you take into account that the Household Commissary includes the Royal Table-linen Officers, the Corps of Gentlemen Cupbearers, the Officers of the King's Bread-pantry and a whole lot more . . .'

'Our King is an ogre. Only ogres eat on that scale.'

'But he's a *nice* ogre. I like Bailly's motion, to "have, on the ruins of the recently demolished Bastille, a monument erected *to the glory of Louis XVI, friend to his people, friend of liberty*".'

'I like all the motions. The patriotic ones. Motions are a great invention! . . . Still, the King can't eat everything, or use everything. He can't be out horseback-riding and hearing a concert at the Trianon at the same time.'

'He's not actually very keen on music! Except the Saint

Hubert's Day concerts. But the Foreigner inflicts her damned Austrian music on everyone, with that Gluck of hers.'

'He can't ride his three thousand horses all at once.'

'He can if he wants. There's nothing he can't do.'

'You're right. Under normal circumstances, he can do anything. If he touches someone, they're cured; if he's out riding and a condemned man comes his way, the man's life is saved.'

'But then who touches *him*, when *he* gets sick?'

'His witch of a wife. That's why he's careful not to get sick.'

'But he does get sick just the same. She sees to it he gets sick. She's slowly poisoning him. She keeps poison hidden in her rings. She also uses ground glass.'

'A regular Medici!'

'The King has a tougher constitution than the Dauphin did, so the King has survived. Whereas the child succumbed pretty fast. But he died knowing who was responsible. You know what his last words were: "Stand to one side, if you please, so I may have the pleasure of seeing my mother weep." Of course, the wicked stepmother wasn't really weeping; she was pretending. Is there going to be a war?'

'There will be, if he doesn't get rid of the Poisoner.'

'But what could he do with her?'

'They say she'll be exiled, shut up in the fortress at Ham, sent back to Vienna, shipped off to do penal servitude in Santo Domingo, set ashore and abandoned in Guyana, or branded with a red-hot iron the way they did to that poor, sainted de La Mothe woman. The Austrian will be chained up with cartloads of her fellow sluts, dumped on to a vessel, and sent to the island of Tahiti, in among the savages, to be a fisherwoman . . .'

'. . . No, no, she'd enjoy that!'

'They'll make her mend the fishing nets, round the clock. And every time she looks as if she's about to fall asleep, they'll whip her. She'll be forced to keep on plying her mending hook the whole time. She'll have cuts all over her fingers, and when salt gets in them she'll yell with pain. Another possibility is to keep her in Paris and put her through the same torture they used on the Nuremberg Virgin.'

'The Austrian, a virgin? Not likely.'

'The Nuremberg strumpet, more like.'

'The whore!'

'They could also put her in prison at Bicêtre. Or make her sweep the streets of Paris.'

'Sweep the street of Paris! Hold on, now! . . . You're going a bit far . . . But I admit I'd love to see it! The Queen dressed in homespun, with her head shaved, and a broom in her hands. And the Parisians at their windows emptying their shit over her head.'

'In homespun? Why not stark naked, why go on paying for her to have clothes? . . . There's something else people say about her, but this isn't punishment, it's something she is, and it deserves to be punished: they say she's tribadistic. Have you heard it, too? D'you understand what it means?'

'Um, yes, I think so. Tribadistic, lesbian, sort of like Austrian. No difference, really. She's Austrian: she's lesbian. That's how it was with her mother, Austrian, lesbian, same thing.'

The two men were still puzzled. One of them pointed to the newspapers lying on the ground.

'Have you read what's in those?'

'Some of it, not a lot. I don't read fast enough to keep up, these days. I was all right as long as nothing was happening.'

'Give it a try anyway, Moinel.'

He opened a newspaper ('It's printed very small!') and he read, struggling to separate out the syllables:

. . . Motion to withdraw the troops and create a Citizens' Guard. Sire . . . when once we have become alarmed for our freedom, neither curb nor rein can hold us back . . . Sire, we beseech you in the name of this our native land, in the name of your future prosperity and renown: send your soldiers back to the posts from whence your councillors brought them . . . Consider! Why would a king beloved of twenty-five million Frenchmen seek at great expense to surround his throne with a few thousand hastily summoned foreigners? Sire, in the midst of those who call themselves your children, let yourself be guarded only by their love: the representatives of the Nation are called upon to join with you in establishing the pre-eminent rights of royalty on the im-mu-ta-ble foundation of the freedom of the people . . .

Both men were moved to tears. They stood up and embraced one another. They kept repeating, like a magic formula: '. . . on the im-mu-ta-ble foundation of the freedom of the people.'

And all of a sudden, one of them reacted.

'But Moinel, it means we've won! The newspaper is even slower at catching on than you are. Those troops have withdrawn; even if there are a few still hanging around, we'll get them! They're as good as dead. Just the way we'll get *her*, that Messalina!'

And he shook his injured fist at Marie-Antoinette's windows.

I was devastated. It was as though I had aided and abetted them in besmirching the name of the Queen.

For me, a time of distress and confusion;
encounter with a sensible woman; omnipresence
of 'the Queen's unrequited lover'

———————

I must have looked completely lost when a woman in the service
of the late Dauphin came walking toward me. She was trans-
porting a cartful of toys form the château of Meudon, intending
to deposit them in the toy cupboard of the new Dauphin, on the
ground floor of the palace. I was exhausted. Torn between
weariness and shame, I was of a mind to proclaim my woes. I
scarcely knew the woman, but I needed to talk to someone. I
made her the confidante of all my fears, in a rush of chaotic and
contradictory utterances. I told her in the same breath that we
had to save the Queen and that the Queen had gone, that she
had to be protected and that she had fled, that her bedchamber,
indeed all her apartments, were empty. I had personally helped
with her departure, so I knew whereof I spoke . . .

'You read too much, madam,' she said jokingly. 'It is wiser to
confine oneself to what one can actually see. Words are dangerous. They told me so when I was just a little girl, and I am
convinced they were right. I had an uncle who wanted to teach
me to read. My father stood out against it. He said: "I want the
child to be happy." The King and Queen are still at the palace.
Believe me. Each of them is lying peacefully in a royal bedchamber, still asleep. They are recruiting their strength for the day
that is presently breaking. They will need it.'

'How can you be so sure? I stood for a while under the
windows of the Queen's Bedchamber. I saw no sign of life. The
curtains were open as usual, but in the bedchamber nothing was
stirring.'

'And what about that man over there; do you see him? Does
his presence have no significance for you?'

A few yards away, more or less hidden behind a bush, I could see the scarecrow-like outline of a man who was perfectly familiar to me; indeed, I had the impression that I was forever seeing him. Everyone referred to him as 'the Queen's unrequited lover' . . . Yes, I had to agree, his presence was significant: among his other oddities was his insistence on never being very far from where the Queen was. With his body straining in the direction of the place where she happened to be – a place sometimes hidden from his view but whose location, mysteriously, he could always sense – 'the Queen's unrequited lover' stood and waited. His real name was Monsieur de Castelnaux, and in the days when he was of sound mind, he had filled the position of Councillor in the Bordeaux Parliament. But his mania now engrossed him so utterly that it was hard to believe he had ever had a name, a position, and a profession. Among the courtiers, as with Captain de Laroche, though this fellow was more tragic than comic, Monsieur de Castelnaux was a source of great amusement. The sayings of both men were repeated, their speech and manner imitated for fun. That may explain why both of them stand out so clearly in my memory, and why I can quite effortlessly call up the sallow complexion, the wild-eyed facial expression, of the man 'madly' in love with the Queen. Call up, as well, his figure, curiously apt to pass unnoticed because it blended in so easily with the trees and branches, but haunting, too, because it might suddenly come into view anywhere. All one had to do was cross the invisible line of communication established by his monomania, linking him at all times to the Queen.

'The Queen's unrequited lover' was a tall, thin man, his greenish face marked with the scabs of small cuts, which he scratched at, causing them to bleed. Most often, he was silent, preoccupied with his obsession. He was a sinister sight, painful to behold. You found yourself wishing he were somewhere else. At the very least, it would have been a great relief to stop running into him every time you were answering a summons to the Queen's presence. Vain hope: he was always there. Throughout the two evening hours taken up by the Queen's

Games, he stood motionless, facing Her Majesty's Square; at the Royal Chapel, likewise, he chose a seat just below the royal balcony where she could look down and see him; and he never failed to be present at the King's Dinner or the ceremonial Public Repast. When the Queen went to Mademoiselle Montansier's theatre, he sat as close as he could to her *loge*: locked in one position, devouring her with his great imploring eyes, he did not turn away from her for a single moment. One might have hoped for a respite from this baneful individual when leaving the palace to travel elsewhere, but no such thing was granted. For ten years, wherever the court had gone, so too had he. In fact, he went ahead. He would leave for Fontainebleau or Saint-Cloud the day before the court set out; and when the Queen arrived at these various residences, the first person she encountered upon alighting from her carriage was her lugubrious admirer. During the Queen's sojourns at the Petit Trianon, his passion became even further inflamed. He would have a hasty bite to eat with one of the guards, then spend the entire day, even in rainy weather, going round and round the gardens. He walked with long strides, always keeping to the edge of the ditches. He wore the same garments in all weathers: a green jacket and yellow breeches. His waistcoat, which must once have been elegant, was in tatters. Pieces of lining protruded from the jacket. The colours were washed out. His faded clothes showed lighter streaks, giving the impression that water never stopped trickling down him, even when the sun was shining. He held in his hand a plumed hat, whose feathers were frayed almost down to their central shaft. Leaves and twigs caught in his jacket collar. 'The Queen's unrequited lover' had a rented room in the town, but most of the time he spent his nights outside, standing watch beneath the windows of his goddess. It had to be exceptionally cold, or snowing, to make him abandon his post. And I can even remember one winter morning when, in the wan light of day, and while the only things still discernible on the snow-covered surface of the gardens were the black flocks of crows, he had been found stretched out on the frozen ground, just at the foot of the statue of King Louis XV. They had carried him to a sentry box. When he had come back to life, he had known a moment of terror, because from this unfamiliar place he could no longer determine the whereabouts of his adored one.

How had he gone from what could be considered simply as a somewhat excessive royalist fidelity to this utterly unbridled love? Or was madness already incipient in the way he collected everything having the remotest relation to the Queen's existence? Not an engraving, not a printed line appeared without his buying it or copying it over into a large notebook that he called *Journal of Coincidences or Register of Events Ordained by Fate*. By way of an epigraph, he had written on the first page, in huge letters: 'A Large Circle gathered in the Queen's Apartments.' The same sentence recurred several times, but written in a feverish, irregular hand. 'Queen' might take up an entire page. The notebook of 'the unrequited lover' was black, with a thick cardboard cover. The corners of it were worn, and like his clothing, the black of the cover and the ink of the written sentences were smudged, bleached by the inclemencies of the weather.

Most of the time, he was content simply to be there, close to Her side or calculating with unfailing accuracy the exact location of Her presence. At the Petit Trianon, the Queen often met him when she was out walking, alone or with her children. He would bow and turn rigid, as though struck by lightning. After a certain interval, which he required in order to recover from his emotions, he would resume his patrol along the edge of the ditch (he also walked along the Grand Canal, on the very brink). The Queen was by now some distance off; he would gaze after her, still deeply affected by the 'coincidence'. She, for her part, never went out of her way to avoid him and never turned aside when she allowed him to kiss her hand; he would remain bent over, his nostrils pinched, his eyes white, trembling from head to foot. He did not have the strength to stand erect again; a lackey had to help him. The Queen saw to it that this was gently done: 'Do not hurt him,' she ordered. Badly shaken, beside himself, 'the

Queen's unrequited lover' would wag his head this way and that, and try to fend off the impending attack of nerves. Most often, under the effect of Her presence, he succeeded. The attack would come later. Then he could be heard, howling in the woods: *Marie-Antoinette Queen of France and Navarre, Marie-Antoinette Queen of France and Navarre*, and adding, in litany sequence, *Marie-Christine, Marie-Élisabeth, Marie-Amélie, Jeanne-Gabrielle, Marie-Josèphe, Marie-Caroline, sisters to my Queen.* Those who had seen him in that state knew that he gashed his face with his nails and banged his head against the statues – all of which he hated, reviling them as usurping women, filthy trollops, harlots of the open marketplace. But other times, most times, the ceremony of an encounter with Marie-Antoinette went off much more tranquilly. Ecstatic at the miracle that her hand should be in his, he would only murmur, 'My Queen,' and remain kneeling, motionless – for eternity, if he could have had his wish.

The Queen, who was incapable of committing a harsh act, however slight, had thought of a tactful way to escape his unwanted attentions: one day she had given Monsieur de Sèze permission to enter the Trianon, and had then sent word that he was to proceed to Madame Campan's quarters. The First Lady of the Bedchamber had been instructed to brief the celebrated lawyer concerning the obsession of 'the unrequited lover', and then send for 'the lover', so that Monsieur de Sèze could have a private conversation with him. Skilled in handling every sort of case, Monsieur de Sèze spoke to him for almost an hour and made a great impression on his mind – probably because the lawyer used a form of discourse that Monsieur de Castelnaux himself had once used professionally. Convinced, if only for the moment, and restored to his former self, he penned a note, to be conveyed to the Queen, informing her that as she found his continued presence unwelcome, he was withdrawing forthwith to his native province, where he would return to his earlier pursuits. The Queen, much pleased, conveyed the extent of her royal satisfaction to Monsieur de Sèze.

Half an hour after the lawyer's departure, Monsieur de Castelnaux was announced. He had come to say that he retracted what he had written, for he *could not*, simply by willing himself to do so, stop seeing the Queen. This declaration, soberly delivered but accompanied by behaviour suggestive of deadly resolve, had been unpleasant for the Queen. She had smiled at him and signalled for him to be ushered from her presence; and then she had just said: 'Very well, let him pester me, but let him enjoy unhindered the pleasure of being free.' No sooner was the freedom of the gardens restored to him than Monsieur de Castelnaux, marvelling at not being separated from his love, had declaimed his litanies with exceptional enthusiasm. For once, *Marie-Amélie, Jeanne-Gabrielle, Marie-Josèphe, Marie-Caroline, sisters to my Queen!* had rung out like an ode to joy, enriched by *Marie-Thérèse, Béatrice-Charlotte, daughters to my Queen!* But his confusion of the living and the dead had been particularly painful to Marie-Antoinette, for the previous night, as she was returning late to seek her bed, four candles set on her washstand had gone out one after the other, and she could not help interpreting this as a sinister augury.

Monsieur de Castelnaux, absorbed by his inner torment, was not interested in anything else. He was uniformly indifferent to the people at Versailles, except for me, whom he detested almost as much as he did the ladies in the statues. (Because of my duties as reader? Or 'just because', for no reason?)

If he was here, it meant the Queen could not have left. I fully agreed, and this only added to my bewilderment.

'But I don't understand. I *saw* the Queen packing for her journey. If she hasn't left yet, she's about to. It's a matter of hours, minutes. Everything that happens is now dictated by the National Assembly. That's why the Queen is going away. It's simple, isn't it? A person can understand that without being able to read.'

'A person should certainly not lose her composure over such a trifle. The orators with their cries of rage, the register of grievances, pooh! Just so much huffing and puffing. A breath of wind . . . The King and the Queen have no intention of giving ground in the face of something so insubstantial as the National Assembly. The representatives are puppets, marionettes whose strings they pull to suit themselves . . . My poor dear, you really are not at all yourself. Can you have taken so seriously the great opening procession of the Estates-General? Let me tell you what it really was.'

And she came and stood very close to me. It may have been my imagination, but I had the impression that 'the Queen's unrequited lover' was stirring the foliage of the trees.

'The meeting of the Estates-General', she whispered, 'was decided upon by vote, with the sole purpose of providing a diversion for the King's son as he lay dying. The Estates-General in themselves are of no importance; all they contribute is complaints and recriminations. No, the important thing was the procession announcing their opening. That was what the King wanted to give his little boy for a present. The rest doesn't count.'

And with her fingernail she scraped away a grass blade stuck to one of the topazes decorating a wagon that had been the child's.

The Council members file out of their chamber:
10 a.m.

I had been led to think, after the sleepless night when so many of my assumptions had crumbled (not really under the impact of a piece of news but rather in the crucible of a fateful presentiment, as when an epidemic threatens), that normal life – with the rigidly set pattern, the noises and round of activities I had assimilated into my very being – had disappeared. I now thought I must have been mistaken, for when I drew near to the antechamber called the Œil-de-Boeuf – a kind of crossroads for movement within the palace, whose particular function was as a waiting room where the courtiers assembled every morning between nine and ten o'clock – I found it full of people. Those courtiers who enjoyed the privilege of access to the King's Bedchamber were clustered, as close as they could get, around the door. Of the remainder, farther away, some were standing in the Œil-de-Boeuf, others in the room adjoining it, the First Antechamber. They all had their backs to me: all were facing the focal point of their attention, the double doors to the King's Bedchamber, both of which were shut. At any moment, the usher would appear and announce the First Entries to a perfectly silent throng. He would come back an hour later to bring in the Lesser Entries. Everything seemed in order. The two drunken doorkeepers had been discharged and immediately replaced. My confusion of mind was forgotten. I looked for a corner where I could wait at my ease without sitting down. I went and stood behind the press of the crowd, not far from the door that led by a secret passage to the Queen's apartments. I leaned with my back against a window ledge. Yes, things were going better. Those whose business it was had no doubt regained control of the situation at dawn – unless no control had ever been lost, or even imperilled, and all this had been nothing but an immense masquerade, and I, like many another, had let myself be duped . . . but what of the previous day? and the past night? Had reducing us to a state of terror also been part of the masquerade? The Great Royal Masquerade?

The courtiers spoke not a word. With each fresh arrival, a few of them would turn around and, depending on the newcomer's importance, greet him with a slow, full nod, or a barely perceptible bow, or else ignore him altogether; indeed, with the return of daylight, the passion for treating each person according to rank had regained its imperative, and the retrospective embarrassment of having spoken, during the night, with just anyone – of having consorted, probably more than once, with people of no consequence – made the courtiers quite uncomfortable. But by morning light they remembered who they were, and the innate sense of social distances prevailed once more. Yes, they greeted one another, but only after due consideration. These passing waves ruffled the immobility of the group, then petrification would again descend over them all.

I took care to remain pressed against my window. I did not want to mingle with the group, to which I did not belong, and which, moreover, included only a limited number of women. (Their very presence in this place at this hour was anomalous, but I did not dwell on that detail: I was looking for reassurance.) No doubt the other women were back in their apartments, trying to get some rest. I could well have used some rest myself, but I was very anxious to learn more about the Queen's real intentions. I met the searching gaze of Monsieur Palissot de Montenoy, who held in his hand the *Gazette of Court Bereavements*, one of the most eagerly sought-after publications.

Someone came over to speak to him. I was not surprised; Monsieur Palissot de Montenoy was very well liked. He had an insatiable curiosity about people, living and dead alike; and since his curiosity was served by exceptional powers of observation and remarkable deductive skills, he was rightly considered one of the best sources of information about life at court and circles of influence in Paris. His knowledge ran the gamut from the latest piece of gossip to the complexities of diplomatic negotiations. And, unlike Jacob-Nicolas Moreau, who interpreted history within the framework of the Eternal Scheme of Things, the gazetteer of court bereavements, with his predilection for even the smallest details, saw history from the standpoint of a human life. He kept a register of the last words uttered by people who were dying. I had no special sympathy for the gazetteer, but in order to obtain more information, I placed myself within ear-shot. What a surprise! For perhaps the very first time, Monsieur Palissot de Montenoy admitted that he did not know anything special. He knew only what was generally known: that the King had withdrawn the foreign troops. The only difference was that *he* could supply a figure: there were some sixty thousand men involved. But as for the rest – was the King going to yield to the Estates-General or not, over their demands that Breteuil's gov-ernment be dissolved and Necker brought back? – he was as much in the dark as everyone else. (I did notice, though, and with considerable relief, that he made no references to the Queen's travel preparations.) To retrieve his reputation and prove that he did after all have something to tell, the gazetteer of court bereavements announced some very recent demise that he alone had been informed of. But the death that was preying on everyone's mind did not involve one individual. And the questioner, disappointed, left Monsieur Palissot de Montenoy's side. The gazetteer must have felt somewhat vexed. He stood for a few moments with head slightly bent as though beneath the weight of his reflections. But it was not in his nature to be discouraged for long. He raised his head and began once again to scrutinise the people present.

In former times in the Œil-de-Boeuf – that waiting room of a palace that was itself, to its inhabitants, in a sense, nothing more than an immense, labyrinthine monument to Waiting – the existence of so many unresolved enigmas would have given rise to wagers. Bets would have been laid on the chances of

Necker's being recalled. And the stakes, there beneath the fresco representing playing children, might have risen high, quite possibly as high as when people were betting on the sex of the Chevalier d'Eon or the Queen's pregnancies. But on this occasion, in that room with its floor smooth from hundreds and hundreds of feet treading their invisible paths across it again and again, no one dared offer any comment, nor place any bet. Nevertheless, it soon became abundantly clear to me that the atmosphere was thick with gloomy prognostications. The air of irresponsibility that I had breathed with my very first awakening at Versailles, making life there feel so light and airy (perhaps because some superior power – God? the King? court etiquette? – oversaw its continuance), was a thing of the past. My little burst of optimism faltered.

None of the gentlemen present had shaved, or powdered his hair, or even changed his clothes. They were wearing the garments they had been wearing the previous evening (which meant in effect the garments they had worn all night): mourning clothes, as prescribed by etiquette, which, following the death of His Royal Highness Xavier-François, Dauphin of France, forbade the wearing of colours for two and a half months. Since 12 July we had been in the second period of mourning, which dictated, for the men, costumes all of black with black buttons and plain muslin cuffs, black silk stockings and goatskin shoes; shoe buckles and swords would be silver. I saw one man who had not progressed beyond the first period. He continued to wear a sword and shoe buckles of bronze, and cuffs of cambric. On this day, his solecism passed unremarked . . . There was something generally sombre emanating from the deep mourning that draped the entire palace, its every nook and cranny, its smallest panel . . . and something particularly distressing about this group of people in funereal garb, silent, all their attention focused on a closed door. Everyone had noticed the defection of the French Guards. There was no one left to defend the palace except the Swiss Guards. The level of fear had gone up a notch. It could be detected in a nervous tic common to several courtiers: with tousled hair, and a worried look on their faces, they kept straightening their perukes, not looking at what they were doing – just as, so it was said, an aged Marchioness du Deffand, in the dark night of her blindness, had once tied endless bows.

All these dark costumes were being steeped in a strong smell of food. It came from a nook on the left of the doorway to the King's Bedchamber, where Füchs, the Œil-de-Boeuf custodian, was regularly ensconced. At the moment, he was busy cooking his breakfast *tartiflette*. The courtiers were marinating in an odour of onion, cheese, and alcohol that merged with the smell of pea soup, Füchs's regular fare. Füchs, who was rough-mannered, banged his spoon against the cast-iron stove, and swore in his booming voice. Poking up the fire, his face close to his mess tin where a slice of dark bread spread with cheese lay sizzling, he muttered plaintively:

'What use is a spoon when you're making a *tartiflette*? And a pea soup? *No* use. I like to have a spoon, that's all. It's *my* spoon. A man has a right to his little whims, maybe. Use it to eat a mash you can't stomach. Maybe! And even then . . . I wouldn't put my hand in the fire, no sir, but with my *tartiflette* I can be sure! She certainly cooks well on the fire!' Then he returned to the courtiers, whom he was always ready to treat as a bothersome lot. 'What are they waiting around for, anyway? They're all being mighty impolite today. Nothing new about that, but there are more of them and they all look so sober – sober as judges! Has there been more bad news, I wonder? Because lately, it's been bad news all the time. Has the second Dauphin taken sick? Has the King recalled his minister, that Mister Necker? But why is it the French want that man so bad? They all go round shouting *Necker, Necker, Necker,* like a lot of lunatics. They call him their saviour. I know all about that Necker. He comes from my part of the world, Necker does. Well, anyway, from the same country as my father. Nobody in Switzerland wants any part of him. Not so stupid, the Swiss; they let him go with no argument. If he was so wonderful, they'd have made sure to keep him for themselves. *Necker, Necker, Necker* . . . If he was a financial wizard, for instance, filling the coffers as fast as they emptied. Or if he was like the Count de Saint-Germain, a great man who simply *on request* produces as many diamonds as it takes to bail out the royal treasury . . . Then, I could understand people making a big push to hang on to such a rare bird. A magician who didn't need to eat: he used to go to suppers and do nothing but talk. And did he have things to tell! I mean, after all, when you've lived several centuries, the way he had! How many centuries, exactly? Even one is pretty good. But I can't make out why they would fight to keep Necker. A man who, in Switzerland, in his native country, is of no interest to anyone but his own little family. Wherever you look, they don't give a damn about him. Except in France. The French are not an intelligent people. A people of grumblers. But just because you grumble, that doesn't make you intelligent. They're forever shouting: *Down with this!* or *Death to whatsisname!* They're grumblers and they behave like sheep. Unbelievable! And when they change their minds, it's for no good reason, all of a sudden, bang! For the time being, they want Necker, don't ask me why . . . D'you suppose they'll stay there for a long time like that, without moving? They might at least say hello to me! But they never do. They just come walking in here. This certainly isn't my day! If I've gone and split my spoon, when I only got it out by mistake in the first place, I'll raise hell! But what are *they* after? I don't think it's Necker. Maybe they haven't been told. Maybe. They're waiting to go in and see the King, when there's nobody on the other side of that door. No Petty Levee today. And consequently, since after all there is logic in this whole business, no Grand Levee. And that's how it is. What's this, now? They're going to ask me. Isn't the King getting up this morning? Could be. All I know is, my *tartiflette*'s burning. All right, I'll put it aside and try again later. If I don't tell them, I'll have them breathing down my neck till the cows come home. And there are more of them all the time, because others are starting to arrive for the Grand Levee.'

It was true that we were all listening with bated breath to

Füchs's wordy monologue. But our dignity made it quite impossible to ask him questions. Finally, to relieve us of our doubts, or (rather) so we would leave him at peace in his little niche, he said clearly and distinctly that the King, the Queen, Monsieur, His Royal Highness the Count d'Artois, the princes of the blood, and the ministers had been in the Royal Council Chamber since five o'clock that morning.

There was a general rush towards the Grand Gallery. Everyone was anxious to be there when they came out. The bereaved – the troop of mourners with no tears, at this funeral with no procession – reassembled: not, this time, outside the closed door of the King's Bedchamber, but outside the closed door of the Royal Council Chamber. Oh, surely no one would have believed, seeing this pitiful gathering, that these were the same people who, only four days previously, had strutted along the Gallery like so many conquerors!

Sunday 12 July had been a splendid Sunday at court. With Necker dismissed, and Paris submissive, there was no further cause for worry. Jubilation was in the air. There had been other rebellions, and they had always been quelled . . . Everyone was so smugly pleased about peace having been restored. The whole affair had been nothing more than a false alarm. We all felt tremendously comforted by the 11 July coup d'état. The new government hastily appointed to support Baron de Breteuil put everyone's mind at rest. We were a big, happy family once more.

The hum of voices in the palace sounded a joyful note. Conversations were carried on more loudly than usual, and, though the courtiers never referred directly to the recent event, their happiness at the outcome found expression in renewed volubility, laughter, a sparkle in the eye and in ornament alike: diamonds, set against the black of moiré and silk, and coincidentally readmitted for wear at court that very day, gave an effect of supreme elegance. Without prior arrangement, they had all assembled in the Grand Gallery. They walked the length of it again and again, stepping jauntily with head erect, exchanging, as they met one another, enthusiastic remarks about what a fine day it was. Not all these observations had the same wealth of detail as those of Monsieur de Faucheux. Whatever the climate, he was the unrivalled bard of the weather, a position that earned him the King's good graces; though the sovereign's own interest in the weather was confined strictly to statistics for temperature, he was very sympathetic to any conversation that included those figures. But everyone's praise was clearly uttered. Across the face of mirrors picked out in gold, there had passed that day thousands of knowing smiles, thousands of curtseys from twirling gowns, light touches bestowed by velvet-gloved fingertips, gentle physical contacts, swift embraces during which flounces with pearled tucks were caught for a moment on flower-decked lapel points . . . Yes, it had been a splendid Sunday.

In the afternoon, while the King was hunting, I had read aloud, for the Queen and Gabrielle de Polignac, some poems by Louise Labé. Through the dark hangings of the Queen's Bedchamber, the silk of the summer wallpapers was back in bloom. Petals and feathers took wing. They spiralled upward in the orange-tinted light of their private theatre. And I imagined I could hear, during the brief intervals between words, petals and feathers settling in minuscule layers on the canopy over the bed.

A scant few days later, nothing was further from our thoughts than a victory celebration. These were not the same people, or the same demeanour, or the same faces. To me, however, their appearance was by no means strange, for I recognised the look of panic, set on a ground of sleeplessness, that characterised those who waited for me in the sea-green morning hours, trusting I would come and do a bit of reading, so that with the opium of my voice, as Baroness de L'Allée liked to say, I might procure them a brief interval of peace. These faces bearing the mark of defeat were familiar to me; so too was their skill at erasing all trace of wounds with the coming of daylight, although it never ceased to surprise me. But this time the courtiers had stopped

trying to disguise their wan countenances for each others' benefit. Besides, I was in the same sorry state as they were.

We had only just enough time to stand aside before the Council
members filed out. They certainly had not planned that their
reappearance should be public. I saw first, without really identi-
fying them, several brilliant, ornately clad persons, engaged in
very animated, perhaps even vehement discussion. At the centre
of the group, immediately visible, was the Queen, the only
woman. She was conferring with the Prince de Condé. Nearby,
the Prince de Conti was apparently being subjected to a long
speech from Baron de Breteuil. The Baron, who, in his usual
manner, clicked his heels as he walked and banged his cane
against the floor, was loudly proclaiming his anger. At the same
time, I noted that the Count d'Artois was furious as well, and was
being even more vocal about it than the Baron. Purple in the face,
beside himself with rage, he was venting his anger on the King.
Suddenly, in a gesture that struck me as totally insane, he cast
himself down at the King's feet and pleaded: 'We must leave this
place, I tell you; what do I have to do, Sir, to convince you of that
fact? What words must I employ, O my brother, to ask it of you?'

There were mutterings on our side, and only then did they
realise that people were waiting for them to appear, that there
were spectators. It was not a pleasant surprise. The Count
d'Artois got back to his feet. Still angry and shaken, he bowed
to the King and Queen and walked away. He was followed in
short order by the Prince de Condé and the Prince de Conti. I
was standing beside Monsieur Le Paon, who painted battles for
the Prince de Condé. He was anxiously scanning the entire
scene. He said to me: 'Take care; this is no time to get left
behind.' The members of the new government also looked anxious. They were casting timid glances at Baron de Breteuil. I
asked Monsieur Le Paon to tell me their names: he pointed out
the Duke de La Vauguyon, Minister for Foreign Affairs, Monsieur de La Porte, Minister of the Navy, Monsieur de Barentin,
who was still Lord Privy Seal, and Laurent de Villedeuil, who

had retained his post as Minister of the Royal Household. 'At least, that was the situation as of a few hours ago,' he told me.

Once they became aware that people were watching, the figures emerging from the Council Chamber lost all their spontaneity. There was no longer the slightest hint of wrath on any of the faces – there was no expression of any kind. Flattened against the wall (we could retreat no farther), we were smothered in curtseys and bows. It was imperative that we straighten up and scan those masks again, for our fate depended on them.

The King, as always when he was a prey to strong emotion, seemed to be asleep; indeed, perhaps he really was. His heavy, drooping eyelids, the downturned pouting lips, his clumsy, swaying gait, gave him the appearance of a sleepwalker. It was like watching an enormous mass of flesh that might collapse from one moment to the next if he were suddenly roused from his comatose slumber. There was no danger of the Queen being the one to rouse him; though walking at his side, she seemed a thousand leagues away. Too heavily made up, she was a beacon of red. She was looking straight in front of her, paying no heed to the people who were present. Her eyes were swollen. Looking at the royal pair side by side, it occurred to me not for the first time that neither of them had ever yet seen anyone at Versailles. His timidity and her pride prevented them from admitting to the extreme myopia they were both afflicted with. A few stock phrases enabled them to keep up the deception, but the fact was that they could properly distinguish almost nothing; they carried on with their daily activities in a world whose outlines were totally blurred. And this had been the case from the very outset, from the moment following the death of Louis XV, when they had heard the galloping footsteps of courtiers rushing toward the King's Bedchamber. Then, truly united, terrified, they had petitioned: 'O Lord, pray for us . . . We are too young to reign.'

Nearly fifteen years later, on this sombre July morning, they were still young and still terrified. But not united. True, they were side by side, but almost with their backs to one another.

She with a hard, steady gaze. He with his eyes shut . . . Louis XVI gave a convincing impression of a blind king. From the thin slit of pale-blue colour that filtered past his eyelids, no active presence, no sort of alertness could be inferred. Rather the opposite: that minimal reminder of the blue of his eyes confirmed the absence of seeing, of looking outward, confirmed the never explicitly formulated but obstinately desired *No* that he used as a defence against the world. *No*, I will not be king, it is not up to me to be king.

And I found myself remembering what people said about his childhood, that he was only the younger son, and that the Dauphin, the one born to reign, was an exceptional child, an intelligent, charming, imperious, adulated little boy. The Dauphin did want to reign. And he sobbed, howled, expended his last ounces of strength in outbursts of rage, when he grasped the fact that his illness was leading him deathward, that he would not grow up, would never be king. In vain did he become more and more demanding, tormenting those in his service, including the one he could get at with greatest effect: his brother, poor Louis-Auguste, constantly at his bedside. The sick child could feel royalty slipping away from him, and it was royalty he saw flowing out of him in the warm froth of blood that drenched his sheets.

'Why was I not born God?' the Duke of Burgundy – for that was the child's title – sometimes asked. Between haemorrhages, he would prophesy: 'I shall bring England under my yoke, I shall make the King of Prussia my prisoner. I shall do whatever I want . . .' And he would dictate to his brother a sentence to be entered in his 'spiritual diary'. 'Hurry up, then, Berry! Don't stand there looking an utter ass,' the Child-King, almost Child-God, would impatiently exclaim . . . 'Hurry up, then, Berry!' – everything can always be explained, I thought to myself at the time, by the missing link of a dead child.

We made deeper bows and lower curtseys without moving from the spot, and they continued to walk by and ignore us. Finally, without shedding his cloak of painful non-presence, the

King gave a perfunctory bow and quietly vanished. No one paid attention. Everyone knew where he was headed. Half past ten: it was time (the first time of the day, that is, as he made several trips in the course of the day) for him to go and consult a big crystal thermometer hanging in the Apollo Salon, to see what the temperature was. The other Council members were left standing stock-still, as though transfixed by the conflict dividing them. Only the Count de Provence, apparently recovered from his walk of the previous day, was smiling affably; he responded with a line from Horace when Jacob-Nicolas Moreau eagerly asked what had been decided in Council. 'In a manner of speaking: nothing important,' said the King's brother. I noticed that he had very fine, slender hands, and an attractive way of drumming his fingers in the air. Everything in his manner constantly gave the lie to his heaviness of body: speech, style of humour, the way he stood . . . and those graceful hands. 'Nothing that would really alter the course of life here.'

Flattered to receive this confidence, the Historiographer bowed. Monsieur and his group of courtiers moved on. His wife, looking very much alarmed, went toward him. Monsieur put aside his smile and refined manner.

Some of the courtiers gathered in little groups. I heard one man say: 'Nothing has been decided. It was a perfectly ordinary meeting.'

'At five in the morning, with the Queen and the King's brothers present! I would not call that perfectly ordinary.'

The members of the new government had apparently vanished into thin air. Baron de Breteuil had withdrawn from the Gallery, not long after the Count d'Artois. But Marshal de Broglie was still there. A circle had formed around him. At first he was reluctant to speak. Finally he made up his mind and declared quite frankly: 'The disaster is total and complete. The King hesitated a long time, and then reached a decision. He intends to stay. The Breteuil government is dismissed.'

'And is Necker coming back?'

'I don't know. As of now, it is not absolutely certain that he will return.'

A deathly silence greeted these words.

Monsieur de Barentin offered his assessment. He spoke very softly, his hands clasped on his chest, as though he were going to pray, or make a lengthy statement; but he was brief.

'I think, gentlemen, that we must reconcile ourselves to a change of dynasty.'

Marshal de Broglie's next words supported this judgement: 'Louis XVI is no longer free to make his own decisions. He is a hostage of the Revolution.'

These words, delivered so bluntly by a military commander of Marshal de Broglie's standing, echoed like a death knell. The King and his court no longer ruled. My world was crumbling.

I looked around for the Queen. Unbelievably, this scene was taking place in her presence. People were discussing the situation openly; some had gone. They had left the Gallery without waiting for her to leave first. And she seemed unaware of the scandal. Her face was puffy, her shoulders sagged; nothing remained of the elegantly lofty bearing that was naturally hers at court, as she scanned the people now standing before her, one by one. The Princess de Lamballe, who was closest to her, stepped forward, offering a supporting hand. The Princess was hoping for a smile, or some acknowledgement – but a moment later she could not hide her chagrin, for the Queen conspicuously ignored her. It was not the Princess de Lamballe she wanted; not on the Princess's account had she opened her fan, in which a lorgnette was concealed. Oblivious to the fact that people were watching, the Queen stood there, tense, with her face pressed to her fan. No, she could not find the one she sought. She was forced to pursue her inspection, and she did so, with unimaginable persistence. Madame de Lamballe offered her services once again. And for the second time, the Queen rejected them. Haughtily. Adding arrogance to hard-heartedness. Using cruelty to console herself for the pain *she* was suffering.

She continued to scrutinise the assembled group, her eye still glued to her fan. At last she gave it up. Gabrielle de Polignac was not there; the Queen had no reason to linger. She turned her back on us.

I went over to a window and opened it without attracting attention. I did not want to be considered a foolhardy trouble-maker. But everyone was too taken up with unhappy private thoughts to take any notice of me. I leaned out: there, in the morning light, pointed like a magnetic compass toward the place where the Queen was, her 'unrequited lover' waited. He caught sight of me and shouted: 'You, there, the bookworm: don't look at me.'

I hastily pulled back into the room. Out there in the park, the madman walked away.

I felt even more lost, more orphaned, than I had before the Council meeting adjourned. So the Queen was not leaving after all. She must have given up the idea of going to Metz. Jacob-Nicolas Moreau, who was not in favour of the proposed departure, said to me: 'A queen is not an ordinary private citizen. She may not dispose of her person simply as she wishes. It would have been a shocking thing for her to cast herself and her family out upon the highways like that. Suppose they had been attacked along the road, perhaps been injured . . . It might well have happened, for you heard Marshal de Broglie as well as I did: he is no longer in a position to offer them the protection of the army. It's as I told you yesterday; I said then: "We are doomed." The defeat of the court is irreversible.'

'But when she opted for departure, the Queen was refusing to admit that the game was already over. She was ready to take the risks you describe, in order to preserve royalty.'

'The game is over. From here on, greatness lies only in accept-ing divine punishment. The nobles are going to suffer, but they deserve to. They have been selfish and profligate, neglecting every charitable obligation. They have turned a deaf ear to the lamentations of the poor. Now the poor are taking their revenge and justly so. There comes a day when the poor can no longer put up with being poor.'

'This is all happening so suddenly; I'm frightened . . .'

'We should have taken fright sooner. When the Lord smites us, it is never done treacherously. He sends warnings. Remember, almost exactly one year ago, on 13 July 1788, there was that murderous hailstorm . . . God caused the sky to rain pieces of ice, each one the shape and size of a dagger. Remember, my dear Agathe.'

I tried to take his hand in mine. But when I reached out, what I found in my grasp was the handle of his satchel.

In the Grand Gallery, I found that most of the courtiers were gone. I was surprised to see the Marquess de La Suze, standing alone and forgotten. As Grand Marshal of the Royal Household, he held the crucial position in relation to life at Versailles: it was his job to assign living quarters. Monsieur de La Suze was accustomed to being the object of innumerable requests, outrageous flattery and obsequious fawning; and he had developed various strategies for escaping his petitioners. But he had no strategy for dealing with the unprecedented situation of finding himself in a room where no one would come and speak to him. The crowd had dispersed without so much as glancing at him. Monsieur de La Suze did not know what to do with himself. A little prompting, and he would have walked over to chat with me. He pushed aside a curtain and looked idly out over the grounds, simply to conceal his discomfiture. He ought to have gone away like the others but could not bring himself to do so. He was finally rescued from this dilemma when one of his servants requested his attention. The Marquess turned around. A servant! When was the last time anyone had seen a servant? And this was a likeable fellow: his name was Sautemouche, and he had just come back from Paris.

'Well, now, Sautemouche, tell me: how fares it in Paris?' Monsieur de La Suze enquired with a smile.

'Very well indeed, My Lord; everything is proceeding quite

smoothly. The people took control of the Bastille in so orderly and methodical a fashion that it compels admiration. Messieurs de Launay and du Puget were condemned to be beheaded. Their sentence was carried out with no loss of time. Their heads, as had been decided beforehand, were paraded through the streets on the end of a pike.'

Angst . . . I could feel a great weight pressing on my chest, and sweat that was not induced by heat formed in beads from the nape of my neck to the base of my spine. I was having difficulty swallowing . . . as when an insect, inhaled accidentally, swells and struggles in your throat, then subsides, lies still and nests there for ever . . . *Angst* . . . I wiped the sweat from my brow . . . And I remembered a summer at Marly when the current fashion had been to play at 'being afraid' . . . 'Just one more *being afraid*!' the circle of ladies sitting in the rose garden would beg when someone whose voice was already heavy with sleep suggested that perhaps it was time to retire . . . 'Just one more *being afraid*!' I wished I could recapture the smell of roses hanging in the air, the gentle softness. And I could quite perfectly recall a white dress the Queen wore, one night during that summer of *being afraid*. The way she smiled in the shadows . . .

The Queen's anger at the decision not to leave:
11 a.m.

———————

Thursday 16 July. It was entered in my notebook that there would be a reading session, and nothing could have dissuaded me from going. A kind of futile, fanatical desperation held me in its grip. I had not taken time to do my hair properly, or wash, and I had hastily filled my velvet bag with books chosen perfectly at random – but at least I was ready. I had put a navy-blue mobcap over my hair, to conceal the state it was in. I had been wearing the same grey cardigan for days now, and my skirt, which I actually did pause long enough to change, was too light for the temperature outdoors and not suitable for the time of day. Resolutely, I set out. The Queen had given up the idea of leaving. The King had not accepted her initial decision to leave. The sting of his refusal must have left her smarting unbearably. I did not allow myself to dwell on that. One idea, and one idea only, filled my mind: I was going to see her again.

And yes, the Queen was there. Really there. She was on her feet, very agitated, and angrily contemplating the disorder that surrounded her. Three or four of her women, making themselves as small and inconspicuous as they could, were engaged in unpacking baggage that had never been completely packed. The Queen was not saying a word, but it seemed to me that the entire set of rooms was filled with rage. I lost all vestige of self-assurance. I wished I could withdraw from the scene. I cursed myself for the stubborn obstinacy of my own behaviour. As I stood uncertainly, still clinging to my bag with its foolish burden of books, I realised that the Queen had by no means intended to cancel this reading session. (In retrospect, it is clear to me that she had not cancelled it because she had not thought to do so. By this time, according to her plans, she would already be on her way to Metz.)

In the corner where Madame Campan placed me, someone had set the ritual glass of sugared water, to which had been added a dessert: a dish of clotted cream sprinkled with red-currants. I stared in wide-eyed bewilderment at the red berries. I seriously wonder whether I did not mistake them for rubies, somehow left out of the jewel casket. I stood there, trying to understand what they were. Madame Campan, speaking very softly, said that I might begin. My eyes were still riveted on those berries, as though I were spellbound. 'Well, get on with it,' urged Madame Campan. I rummaged blindly in my bag. Nothing I pulled out struck me as being appropriate to the situation. In my weakened state of mind, I humbled myself to the extent of asking Madame Campan: 'What do you consider might be suitable for me to read to Her Majesty?'

And at that moment my mind was overwhelmed with shame: I feel it again as I write; my cheeks burn as hot as they did that day. Madame Campan allowed herself the satisfaction of not answering. She and one of the chambermaids – her sister, Madame Auguié – exchanged a look fraught with significance. My humiliation was complete. I took from the bag, without looking, a volume by the philosopher David Hume, whereupon Madame Campan whispered to me: 'Come, come, Madame Laborde; surely you will not read from a Protestant author!'

Shame redoubled. I felt relegated to the lowest of the low. I had lost all power of judgement. From a Protestant I moved straight on to a Jesuit! That was better, though not exactly outstanding. As for the text itself, my choice was deplorable. I had opened the pages of a travel narrative, a volume of *Interesting and Instructive Letters from the Missions of the Southern Americas*. A letter by Father Cat. I began:

Here is a thing that I found worthy of remark . . . When it rains in the torrid zone, and in particular close to the Equator, after a few hours the rain appears to change into a multitude of little white worms quite similar to those that germinate in cheese. We can be certain that it is not a case of raindrops being transformed into worms. It is much more natural to believe that the rains, which are very warm and unwholesome, simply cause these small creatures to hatch, as the rain in Europe causes the hatching of those caterpillars and other insects that consume our espaliered fruits. Whatever the truth of the matter may be, the captain advised us to set our clothes out to dry. A few individuals refused to do so, but they regretted it soon after, for they found their garments so laden with worms that they had the greatest difficulty in cleaning them . . .

I ought to have closed the book and chosen something else, but I was incapable of coherent behaviour . . . The best I could do was to skip a few pages and arrive at these lines, which are very beautiful, even if they do describe the ways of pagan people:

The Indians bestow upon the moon the name of mother, and honour her as such. When the moon is in eclipse, they may be seen pouring forth from their cabins, uttering terrible cries and howls, and shooting a prodigious number of arrows up into the air to defend the star of night from the dogs that, as they believe, have leapt upon their mother to tear her apart. Concerning lunar eclipses, several Asian peoples, though civilised, have ideas very like those of the savages in America.

It was too late: the downpour of maggots had had its effect. Madame Campan, her face a study in irony, was counting the chemises. She gave instructions to some ironers. Then she turned to the Queen, who had taken off her gloves and was biting a fingernail. The Queen seemed not to have heard anything. She was sitting under a large portrait of her mother, embroidered in cross-stitch, observing with a wrathful eye the comings and goings that surrounded her. At last she spoke a few words to Madame Campan, who in turn hastened to my side: 'It would be much appreciated if you could call a halt to your nonsense.' She then went back to counting chemises.

I tried Monsieur de Marmontel, a man of better breeding, who was neither a Protestant nor a Jesuit. I picked up a volume of his *Moral Tales*, which could be counted on not to contain anything shocking: 'If you remember the Marquess de Lisban, he had one of those coldly perfect faces that say to the beholder *Here I am*, and one of those clumsy vanities of temperament that forever miss the mark. He prided himself on his ability in every sphere and was in fact not very able in any. He would take the floor, call for silence, get the company's attention, and utter a platitude . . .' At the very first words of Marmontel, the Queen had sunk down in her armchair. An attendant had come and moved the footrest closer to her. Losing patience, she had signalled to me to stop.

'I thank you. Your Marquess de Lisban has no appeal for me. I know him all too well. Him and his ilk . . . You will resume your reading later, at which time you will essay some other tale. Do not go away.'

She had said the same thing to me, directly or through an attendant, any number of times in the past. Her 'later', although spoken to the empty air, not to any one person, always bore the stamp of great courtesy. I stood up, took my folding chair, and went off into a corner, book in hand. I was in a recess decorated with a raised motif of ivy and bindweed painted in green lacquer. It was an exquisite nook, but at the time it somehow frightened me. 'Later' got later and later. They had forgotten my existence. It felt as though the leather edge of Marmontel's *Moral Tales*, pressed against the palm of my hand, was going to be permanently embedded there.

When another reading was requested, however, the book edge separated from my flesh in one smooth motion. 'Later' did have a way of getting later and later, but most often it came, eventually. What should I read? Another tale? I did not have any others with me, and this was not the time to go hunting along the bookshelves. A serious work? Well, why not? I considered Antoine Court de Gébelin, an eccentric man of learning whose writings, for reasons I have never fathomed, the Queen enjoyed. But there was no Antoine Court de Gébelin in my bag. Instead, I brought out a *Dictionary of Famous Dogs*, something that, given her love of dogs, might very well have interested the Queen. I hesitated to open Father Pluche's *History of Heaven*: it was so immense in scope that I feared that it might add to her anxiety. Finally, I fell back on the book that I myself was currently reading – one that even today is never far from my bedside. It was a collection of stories by Madame de La Fayette. The volume fell open almost of its own accord at a page in 'The Princess of Montpensier':

One day, as he was returning to Loches by a road with which his retinue were little acquainted, the Duke de Guise, who boasted of knowing the road perfectly, placed himself at the head of his little troop to act as guide; but when he had walked for a time, he lost his way and came to the bank of a small river that even he did not recognise. The whole troop upbraided the Duke de Guise for serving them so ill as leader, and having made a halt in that place, and being as readily disposed to enjoyment as young princes customarily are, they perceived a small boat, at rest in the middle of the river, and as the stream was not of great breadth, they easily descried in the boat three or four women, and among them one who appeared to be of great beauty, magnificently attired, attentively watching two men who were fishing close by. This further adventure brought further joy to the two young princes and all those in their retinue: it seemed to them of such wise as might be found in a novel.

I read on. Everything around me had fallen silent. The Queen was listening. I was sure of that and did not need to see the expression on her countenance. The space where chaos had held sway before I came was becoming limpid and orderly; I refer to the very inner essence of her mind. I read on. There was softness and secret pride in my voice, for that voice had successfully wrought a small miracle: it had freed the Queen from the vice-like hold of rage and regrets. The Queen was abandoning herself to the flow of words, as one does to the notes of music. She was being reborn and I was the instrument of her rebirth. Oh, let this moment go on and on! I thought, and it was as though I held her suspended, in mid-air, or floating upon a river, like the sun-haloed vision of the princess in the story. But when Gabrielle de Polignac was announced, the Queen escaped me. The Queen's serving women vanished. Countess de La Fayette was heard no more. Madame Campan was requested to stay. I stayed as well, for Madame Campan had decided that I could make myself useful (her sister and Madame de Rochereuil were busy somewhere else) by carrying on with the task of putting things away. She had been absorbed by this quiet, painstaking transfer of objects ever since she had been informed that the departure would not take place.

Today: rain, doubts, and my pages scattered over
the floor; then, with the return of sunlight, I am
the guest of the Prince de Ligne
(Vienna, June 1810)

I would do well to put into practice, now, the advice of Monsieur de Montdragon, and clap my hands all by myself in bed. My lace mittens are not enough protection, and woollen ones make my fingers go numb. The feeling of always being cold is aggravated by the pains I am suffering, brought on by a terribly humid month of June – so rainy, muddy, and generally disastrous a month is it that I see no hint of June as the harbinger of summer. *Angst* is present, anguish of the spirit. Recumbent, with eyes shut, weakened because I have lost all desire to take food, I think to myself: Why not just die, why go on waiting hopefully for something, especially the return of fine weather? Besides, what difference can summer weather make? What can it add to your existence? The scent of flowers, blue sky, voices of people outside . . . what good is all that? How is that going to give you back the energy to live?

These pages of mine have fallen on the floor and are scattered over the rug. When I am forced to walk a few steps in my room, not only do I take no care to avoid treading on them; I deliberately stick the tip of my cane into the paper to crumple it, tear it, kill it.

My days are deadly dull. I fall headlong into my nights as into a bottomless pit of sleeplessness. Sometimes when I am feverish, my mind wanders. On two occasions, I have caught myself starting out to say a prayer to the Virgin Mary and suddenly speaking the Queen's name instead: 'O Marie-Antoinette . . .' The second time, I gave a start of surprise when my invocation was repeated by the voice of her mad lover, exploding inside my head. Can it be that in the place where he now is, among the dead, he continues to declaim his litanies, disturbing the souls given over to Eternal Rest, while the Queen, in her goodness, continues to pardon him? The sense of something undefined, that came to me with the snow, I now feel with the rain. Despondency, vast, immense, certainly out of proportion to what is after all merely bad weather, makes tears come to my eyes. I hear the raindrops beating on the courtyard paving stones, in a continuous, regular leitmotif. The recurring theme of vain futility, *vanitas vanitatum*, vanity of vanities . . . That is what I hear in the monotonous sound of the water. Against its bass, in which other noises are lost, the rain swells at times into downpours. It bangs at my windowpanes – because wind intervened, the rain was striking the glass almost at right angles a moment ago – then subsides, sinking back into its truculent, regular mode, designed never to stop; either that or it turns to a fine drizzle, so that when I part my curtains in the morning, they open to reveal a November fog.

Odours of wet hay hang over the streets of Vienna. The Danube overflows its banks, as it does when the winter snows melt. One hears reports of landslides, bridges collapsing. In the poverty-ridden outlying quarters that form a belt around the city, the first deaths in an outbreak of cholera have been recorded. I do not know Paris, for I came directly from my home in the provinces to Versailles – so I don't know whether Paris is a capital city dedicated to the cult of death (I mean as a vocation, not just as a result of some crisis, such as the Reign of Terror). But I know that Vienna is the capital of the Kingdom of Death. If you doubt this, you have only to go for a walk on the Graben and see, in the noisy coming and going of carriages and with all the foot traffic, how you are brought up short by the towering Column of the Plague. You cannot tear yourself away; tentacular and terrifying, the column has seized you . . .

I am slipping. I have lost the summer of fear but am not back in the season of the living. I am adrift, huddled under my eiderdown. I have a sensation of being cast out, expelled. If I could breathe deeply, I am sure everything would be restored to me: I would dwell once again in that ancient, antediluvian world, that world on the other side of the River of Time. The brilliance of the Queen's eyes, looking at me for a moment when I capture her attention, has faded and died. The Princess de Montpensier is just a skeleton now, swaying over the water. And all those faces, so young, so near, with their little curls sticking out from under their white perukes and their ambivalent smiles, have retreated into the darkness whence they sprang. Their powdered foreheads, their red lips, and their white hands, hands made not to grasp and hold but to touch, caress, make airy motions . . . Is that why, when the time came, they immediately let go? From an inability to clutch firmly, to hang on?

There is an anecdote that struck me when I heard it: a young boy of noble birth is authorised to go out alone for the first time. As he is aware of his family's financial woes, he enjoys himself, but is careful not to be too extravagant. Upon his return, he proudly shows his grandfather the money he has not spent. The old man, instead of congratulating him, looks him contemptuously up and down, takes the almost intact purse the lad had been given, opens a window and throws it out . . .

Hands trained in that manner had certainly not learned how to hold fast . . . On the other hand, they did know how to throw away. They were wonderfully skilled at throwing away. And the domestics behaved like their masters. At Versailles, it was incredible what they threw out of the window. Complaints, objections, reprimands, nothing had any effect. At night, I was sometimes awakened by the smashing of glazed verandas. But I, Agathe, never threw anything away, and my hands, unlike theirs, have learned to clutch firmly. How, then, did I so easily become involved with people who did not care deeply enough about anything to grasp it and hold it? *Easily* is not the right word, however. Everything is starting to desert me: words, my desire for words, persistence in applying myself to the task . . . The rain with its frenzied behaviour shows no sign of letting up. Will Vienna, already half demolished, finally drown? I close my eyes.

I sleep without really going to sleep. I live without really being alive . . .

At last, one morning, the sun came back, and I sobbed with relief. I wept with my eyes full of light. And I realised that it was not the waiting for summer that was wearing me down, but the fear that when summer came I might have lost the ability to enjoy it. I was wrong. I can still enjoy it. Late in the evening, sitting at the open window, looking out at a sky that is still bright, at daylight that still lingers, I am happy. And one pleasure especially is renewed: feeling the softness of the air. But in Vienna, the season of mild air is short-lived. The midsummer period is too hot, storm-filled, and exhausting. Mosquitoes come, indeed all sorts of insects, carrying strange diseases. Something not unlike Versailles's muggy spells can occur here, but in Versailles such spells were accompanied by splendid skies; there is nothing like that in Vienna. Instead, sticky weather means pestilence, the plague commemorated in that monument on the Graben; stealthily, it finds its way in, and kills.

I am invited to make a stay at the Prince de Ligne's house in the mountains, at Kaltenberg, as I do each year. It is a delightful place, like all his residences. Delightful in its gaiety, and in the light-hearted pleasure that the Prince brings to whatever he does. And even when he is not doing anything, there is the vibrant feeling that happiness is just moments away. For the coming summer, the Prince has promised me one of his prettiest houses – at any rate, my favourite. He owns nine of these little wooden houses. 'Mine' is right beside a river: it is nicknamed 'the Angler's House', a punning play on the *ligne* with which the angler fishes. In the middle of each of its shutters, a heart-shaped hole has been cut . . .

I waited till October, not to come back home, but to pick up my writing again. During my stay at the Prince's house, there was an accident that distressed me a good deal: a governess in the employ of the Princess de Ligne set fire to her dress. She was very quickly transformed into a human torch. Instead of rendering her assistance, the lackeys that came rushing in thought they were seeing a ghost. They fled, their screams as appalling as those of the unfortunate victim. Nothing else unpleasant occurred to mar our vacation . . . A month in the country, a month of indulging the delusion that we were living in a timeless world, that nothing had taken place, ever . . . The Prince has mastered to perfection the art of forgetting what one does not wish to remember. And the only expression of gratitude he expects from his guests, I believe, is that they follow his example and declare themselves young, heedless, eternally magnificent. I find it difficult.

One afternoon when I was dozing under a tree, he came over and lectured me in the kindliest way: 'It is risky to take naps at our age, it gives the Grim Reaper a hold. And that, my dear, is a concession we must never grant him.' He slid his thumb across his front teeth. (Occasionally, the Prince's manners are atrocious – they are part of his charm! That particular gesture gives him the opportunity to emphasise the fact that he still has teeth.) He moved an armchair and sat down, facing me. 'You are about to tell me that you are tired. But you are not, absolutely not! It is all in your mind, I assure you.' When I insisted, he said: 'Look at me. Do I look tired?' He shook the two gold rings he wore in his ears.) 'And yet I could easily choose to be old; it's entirely up to me. Like the others, I have the necessary qualifications.' That he 'had the qualifications' was a charming way to put it, I thought.

In the Prince de Ligne's household, only French is spoken. Life goes on exactly the way it did in France during the reign of Louis XVI. The same habits, the same manners, the same affectations of speech, even the same fashions. The Prince's current circle of personal acquaintances call him 'Charlie', just as his close friends had done at Versailles. Concessions to the present day are kept to a minimum. When a German expression is inadvertently dropped into the conversation, a shocked silence follows.

'One cannot laugh in German,' said the Prince de Ligne.

'And yet the Queen could laugh. And it was not something she learned to do at Versailles; she learned it here in Vienna, in German.'

That response came from me; it was uttered impulsively and at once regretted, for I do not like to vex the Prince. While I was speaking, I seemed to hear the Queen. She was very close by, and she was laughing. The Prince was reclining on a lounge chair, his eyes blinking up at the sun. 'How exquisite is the scent of the linden blossoms,' he sighed. A servant girl leaned over to raise the cushion at my back. That was when I noticed the Prince's emaciated, crooked legs in their twisted, ill-fitting white stockings; above the red-heeled shoes that he was surely the last remaining person in the whole world to persist in wearing, there were unwanted folds of stocking. He did indeed have the qualifications.

A wave of fatigue swept over me. I continued to hear the Queen's laughter in my ear, mingled with the buzzing of the bees among the lindens. The Prince de Ligne's voice had become inaudible to me. And behind him, the French-style grounds, the broad path leading down to the houses on the shore of the Danube, and the Danube itself, simply ceased to be real. Christine, the Prince de Ligne's daughter, succeeded in piercing the fog, but only for a moment; then she, too, was incorporated into the ghostly horizon that was blurring the outlines of summer. Cherries: suddenly I had a violent craving for cherries. And I wondered: 'Where can I get some? Who can I ask to get them for me?'

As though summoned up by my question, the personages of the Grand Staircase appeared. The men were wearing court dress of the seventeenth century: their perukes covered them from their heads to halfway down their backs. The women had huge panniered dresses. The steps shone brightly. They were new, of white marble. As on previous occasions, what fascinated me about this dream was the motionless stance of the courtiers and the intervals rigorously maintained between one and the next. Also their faces, faces I knew without ever being able to put a definite name to any of them . . . As though they turned up in my life only to hold aloof.

And then, from the topmost point on the staircase, the Queen appeared. She came running down the great marble staircase. No one turned, no one gave a curtsey or bow as she passed. Eyes remained vacant. In contrast, there was something irrepressible about the Queen's vitality. She was not satisfied merely to run: she leapt. And with each leap, from step to step, the cherries she wore as earrings threatened to fly off. A man, a minuscule judge, virtually cloaked in his full-bottomed peruke, offered this observation as she sped by: 'The Queen has the bitter taste of the maenads.'

Who can prompt such dreams? Does the Devil grant us no respite?

I must say, to the Prince's credit, that though he rejects the past, he makes an exception for the Queen: he is the only person here who speaks her name. He is also the only person who regularly goes and meditates by the grave of Gabrielle de Polignac, who died of grief on 5 December 1793, in Vienna. When we are together, and he wants to talk about the Queen, he always starts with: 'Do you remember?' I don't have to answer. Both of us saw a great deal of the Queen, he in ways reflecting his position, I according to my station; his world and mine did not communicate. It would be vulgar of me even to pretend that I am trying to remember. There was, however, one occasion when the Prince evoked something that I, too, could recall. I did not say so, but while he was telling about it, I was picturing the scene very precisely, for I was there.

It was a long time ago, at the very beginning of their friendship; the Queen and Gabrielle were playing the game they called 'watching the fans floating'. They would go and stand on a little bridge in the Trianon hamlet and lean over the water, which, they claimed, was covered with fans. They would describe the colours and lovely attributes of all these fans. Silk ones or paper ones, they floated, fully open. The two friends were always very sad when the fans gradually sank beneath the surface. Following their lead, the Ladies-in-Waiting, the Ladies of the Bedchamber, the crowd of Ladies of the Palace, and the courtiers, pushing to get closer, would look searchingly into the water.

There is a tray of figs on my night table. They are set on leaves, unbelievably sweet-smelling. My Castle of Solitude, my Theatre of Memory, has closed around me. 'Do you remember . . . ?'

In the Queen's Little Apartments;
I am unwillingly present at a meeting between
the Queen and her favourite: 1 p.m.

———————

'Indeed, madam, I had envisioned a rather different welcome, attended by different circumstances.'

The Queen indicated a trunk, a chest, some half-open bags. These things made it virtually impossible to move around, for the rooms were tiny, windproofed with curtains and rugs, filled with bits of furniture, which were in turn covered with portraits, boxes, vases, knick-knacks, baskets of flowers done in mother-of-pearl, ivory, ebony, porcelain, feathers, and silk. But Gabrielle de Polignac, slender and supple, had no difficulty picking her way among the pieces of luggage, luggage that would not be needed after all. In the Queen's eyes it was doubly unwanted, because it was a cruel reminder of her failure. Gabrielle, pale-complexioned, hair hanging loosely around her shoulders, was wearing a green dress. A wide belt accentuated her waist. She was a petite young woman, all soft curves. And it was her softness, and her equable temperament, that had charmed the Queen. The favourite possessed a natural beauty, as well as a freshness of complexion that took on surprising lustre in such a setting as Versailles, where make-up and sophisticated lighting prevailed. Compared to her, the other women at court were like automata, gesturing stiffly, walking mechanically, speaking sharply and imperiously. *Her* voice, in contrast, was soft, and her bearing did not impose. Everyone noticed her, precisely because she made no effort to be noticed. Her light-coloured eyes did not linger on any one person. There was a characteristic elusive quality about Gabrielle, and the paleness of those eyes – made paler still by the contrast with her dark hair – enhanced this 'indefinable' effect.

Her curtsey was so weightless and quick that it was more like the opening measure of a dance. She was about to begin another, but the Queen stood up and took her in her arms. At that moment, everything in the Queen's demeanour made her seem tremulous, as though she might crumble at a touch. The brief lifting of the clouds, the moment of serenity produced by my reading, had passed.

'Oh, but I wanted us to leave! Never have I wanted anything so much, with all my might, and I did not get what I wanted. There is no precedent for the mortification I have suffered.'

She was on the verge of giving way to anger once again, but the presence of her friend so softened her mood that affection and sadness came to the fore instead.

'If the King had agreed, you and I would have been saved. And on our return, I can assure you, the libellous rumours would have ceased, and with them the madness that is overtaking the people of France. The French do not know. They do not understand what is happening to them. They hear others howling, and before they have had a chance to consider, the cry is already inside them, issuing from them. A single cry for the whole country. But a cry of what, exactly?'

Gabrielle de Polignac had no answer, and she did not make the effort to find one. She glanced briefly at a mirror, saw their two faces together, or perhaps just her own, and lightly touched a rose pinned in her hair. She moved her head to be sure that the flower was firmly in place. It was a very slight movement – but it was enough, from the Queen's point of view, to break the chain of cares besetting her and the threat of the outside world. The luggage did not matter now; at most, it was the lingering trace of a passing whim.

The Queen seated her friend at her side, on a chair the same height as her own, an armchair previously used only by the King, when he visited that room. She leaned over towards Gabrielle.

'Oh my dear heart . . . I was so worried . . . I feared they might prevent you from coming to see me, that perhaps you were imprisoned, or ill. Terrible imaginings came to my troubled mind. But you are here, and radiant! . . . How beautiful you are in that green dress, that pale-green dress – sea-green? lime-green?'

'I cannot say, Majesty. I have no aptitude for recognising shades of colour.'

Her dancing eyes, the mock primness of her mouth, and the suggestion of a dimple in her left cheek, made it quite clear that she did not care a fig about shades of colour, and in fact, to be more accurate, that she did not care a fig about anything. But she continued in the same vein, playfully secure in the knowledge that the Queen rarely pursued a single topic of conversation for any length of time, so there was little danger of the joke being carried too far. Moreover, though she did not share the Queen's passion for fabrics, Gabrielle did enjoy discussing fashions. As for the Queen, she threw herself wholeheartedly into these frivolous exchanges.

'Is my dress almond-green, bamboo-shoot-green, jade-green, or young-crocodile-green?'

'You are quite mistaken, my girl' – the Queen laughed – 'it is as far from young-crocodile-green as it is from spinach-green or acid-green . . .'

'. . . or envy-green, which is a hideous green.'

'Vile.'

'A colour not to be trusted.'

'And a sentiment, my gentle dove, that has never come anywhere near your heart. That is why having you at my side is so precious.' (She leaned even closer and stroked Gabrielle's cheek, the one with the suggestion of a dimple.)

'Truly,' the Queen went on, 'it seems to me that envy is the emotion most frequently encountered. Everyone spends all his time coveting the position above the one he holds, and all his actions are driven by that one sentiment: people strive unceasingly to appease their envious desire, but the coveted place is no sooner attained than they become aware of the place above that. Naturally, this casts a shadow over their joy, and so once again they have to sally forth and mount a fresh attack. What a torment it must be: the perpetual need to strive, and the instant spoiling of any satisfaction! But the ambition of courtiers was familiar to me; what I had never given any thought to was the ambition of the people.'

'A whole new avenue of thought, indeed . . .' Gabrielle replied, in a tone of total unconcern.

'Our subjects claim the right to choose who shall lead them. A strange notion indeed! And they think they will love the leader they have chosen . . . but how can one love a master one has not known when he was a child? King Louis XV once described for me a scene from his childhood. It was during the Regency of Philippe d'Orléans, and he was living in the Tuileries Palace. Whenever he went to play on a balcony, above the gardens, word would immediately spread, and the Parisians would come flocking. There they would stay for hours, craning their necks in the hope that they might catch a glimpse of their little king at play. The Parisians . . . How they have changed! You, madam, are not envious in the least, and yet your childhood was not happy. Orphaned very young, with no resources, you had ample reason to envy others their good fortune.'

'Did I? I have not really thought about it,' said Gabrielle de Polignac. (And she brushed aside a lock of hair that hid her forehead, under the rose she wore.)

'Talk to me; the truth is, I hardly know you. And if one day we were to be . . . Tell me more, my dear,' requested the Queen, as though her lips were pressed to this bubbling wellspring of candour and she could never drink her fill.

'Majesty, I am perfectly satisfied with my lot. I believe it was ever thus. It is a trait of my character. But thanks to His Majesty's generosity, my contentment is now beyond measure.'

Gabrielle de Polignac did not seem anxious for the conversation to take a more intimate turn. She did not like talking about herself and doubtless would have preferred to go back to the game of naming colours. Since the Queen insisted, however, she was obliged to say something about her mother, who had died young and for whom she had not grieved. Even when she was still alive, her mother had not been much present. Moreover, Gabrielle's memories of her were scanty. She could vaguely recall a woman of elegant figure, charmingly adorned, saying goodbye to her, that was all . . . The woman bends over the little girl, and before the child has had time to respond in kind, her mother has gone. There is the faint echo of heels along the series of dark rooms in a provincial town house, then nothing.

'When she died, I was relieved that there would be no more of those botched goodbyes: she had finally contrived to leave. My father disappeared as well. But before going off to the South of France to live, he entrusted me to a female cousin of his. It was the same sort of provincial town house, equally vast and gloomy, but almost bare of furniture. That was something I actually liked, all those empty rooms. When I turned fourteen, I went from that cousin's home to be reared by my aunt, Countess d'Andlau, who had a position in the Household of the Countess d'Artois. It was my aunt that married me to Count Jules de Polignac, when I was seventeen. And . . . there is no more to tell, because since then I have known nothing but happiness.'

Gabrielle de Polignac had laughed; so had the Queen, but her laughter lacked conviction.

'Still, it was kind of your mother to think of you whenever she was going away.'

'The only pity is that she never thought of me at other times. But I have no right to blame her: I do not know the woman; I never did.'

They sat in silence, each absorbed by her own reflections, and suddenly a picture, remote in time but quite clear, formed in Gabrielle's mind.

She must have been five or six years old when a chambermaid took her, a child who was left to her own devices for days on end, and set out to make her beautiful. When she had been thoroughly washed, when comb and brush had been carefully applied, they had dressed her in a white dress, put a star in her hair, and especially – this was the marvellous part – they had fastened two large wings on her shoulders. And they had thrust her into an immense ballroom where people were dancing. She had been afraid at first, but everyone had treated her with great consideration, congratulating her, standing aside to let her pass, and taking care not to ruffle her splendid feathers. The ball came to an end. The little girl went for two or three days, walking the corridors with her wings still attached. At last she had encountered her mother, who said to her: 'What, still costumed, mademoiselle? Don't you know that everything comes to an end, even a masked ball?'

'Madam,' she had wept, 'I have no one to take these wings off for me.'

'There, there, Gabrielle, don't fret; I will help you, my little angel . . .'

And it was her mother who had unhooked those wings for her.

'It was at that moment,' Gabrielle de Polignac concluded, 'that I was completely overcome with sadness. Mortal sadness.'

And sadness had now returned. They felt it wrap around them, together.

At one point, their conversation shifted to recent bits of gossip about the Princess de Lamballe, who was reported to be pregnant. In order to scotch these rumours, Louise de Lamballe was constantly riding; as a result, she was worn down with aches and pains.

'She ought to stop. She has a weak back.'

'It hurts even more to be slandered. I believe I caught a glimpse of our dear Lamballe earlier, when we were coming out of the Council Chamber. She did look quite ill. But in that crowd of people waiting anxiously for us to appear, she looked no more haggard than many others. The only one who always has a radiant complexion is you. You are an oasis of light in that desolation of gloomy countenances. And the gloominess is not necessarily out of compassion for me, I might add.'

Gabrielle de Polignac seized this opening to apologise for

daring to set aside the rule about mourning raiment. It was not intended as an act of effrontery, but as a gesture to the Queen, who, in all the black surrounding her, might thus, at least in private, find repose for her eyes and heart in a pastel colour, green, the colour of hope . . .

'I have lost all hope. I am touched, however, that you should have thought of me when you chose the colour of your dress, green, my favourite colour . . . You dressed to please me . . . You are so thoughtful, Gabrielle, so generous. With you near to me, I feel less distressed at the failure of my plans. Less distressed at the horror of the situation. We are going through an unhappy phase. Will we see the outcome? I doubt it. Nevertheless, you are right, one must have hope. I must believe in the colour you are wearing . . . oasis-green . . . almost the colour of this bowl . . .' And she picked up a jade goblet from the mantelpiece, turning it over and over in her hands as she spoke. 'How wonderful that there should be such a thing as colour! God might very well have created a world without colours. He was under no requirement . . . A world without colours . . . But then how would we know where a tree ends and the sky begins? Everything would be indiscriminately merged in white. We would see without marking separation or perceiving limits. It would be restful. Perhaps. Or frightening . . . One unending day of snow . . . Unless, of course, He had created a world all of black, one unending day of night, like the day we are having now.'

The Queen detested black. For her it was the colour of misfortune. But black constantly thrust itself upon her. This, despite Gabrielle and her graceful ways, despite the pale-green folds of Gabrielle's negligee, despite the pleasure they both took in their sessions of aimless, shifting chatter, when idle words elicited more idle words. They so enjoyed talking with one another, the Queen especially, but possibly both of them, that they would spend whole afternoons – and evenings – alone together in the Queen's hamlet at the Trianon, hidden in the grotto, or shut in the little blue-and-gold theatre, Marie-Antoinette's little theatre, her dolls' theatre. They so enjoyed talking together, talking for the sake of talking, that when they actually had something to say to each other, it took them a long time to reach the point. Perhaps, after all, they never did reach it . . . Their pleasure was in the journey, not the arrival . . . But as matters now stood, their leisurely dialogue was a forbidden luxury.

I watched them as they sat there close to each other, the Queen so charmed by her friend that, without realising it, she copied her. All at once, she would fall into the same slow rhythm – not her own usual rhythm – or wrinkle her nose in the same manner, which did not become her at all, though it was very charming on the little upturned nose of Gabrielle de Polignac, an impish nose. Or she would use certain stock phrases the way her friend did, for example, 'It's all the same to me,' an expression of Gabrielle's that infuriated Diane de Polignac – who, declarations in favour of the Philosophes notwithstanding, firmly believed that things and people were *not* all the same. Gabrielle had a conclusive way of using this expression: she would half-close her eyes, and then say, speaking very softly, that it was all the same to her. There was no use insisting, or thinking you could induce her to choose. But spoken by the Queen, 'It's all the same to me' meant something quite different. In fact, it conveyed an opposite sense. She used it to signify that she was sulking, so she would get her own way after all. Another set phrase typical of her friend was heard almost as frequently, a phrase Gabrielle repeated so often that she had raised it almost to the status of a motto: 'What you are telling me is beyond my grasp.' But however far she might go in unconscious imitation of her friend, this was an admission the Queen took good care not to make on her own behalf. When Gabrielle de Polignac said it, she exuded sweetness and light; she hung on your every word; she leaned towards you as if to guide you through your first experience of a lesser being. And you, out of common decency to one who had so innocently confessed her limitations, knew you would have to adjust to her level. She almost felt like laughing (it was implied) at the idea that anyone could have thought her so much more intelligent than she really was, or attributed to her anything remotely resembling quickness of mind. *Very, very far beyond her grasp*.

'What a big place the world is!' the Queen said suddenly. 'I have never even seen the sea,' she added, possibly to force a reaction from Gabrielle, who had been left unmoved by the previous avowal.

'Nor have I. It is a fearful thing, I believe. Very salty, and apt to turn people away from religion.'

'The King saw it, when he went to Cherbourg. I do not know whether he touched it. He did not say anything to me on that score. He showed me on the map how to go there. But I cannot envision anything from a map, whereas from a tree or a flower, everything comes to me quite easily.' (This remark consoled me, very slightly: my having proved incapable of drawing a map was, it seemed, not so terrible after all . . .) 'I need only sit in the shade of my cedar of Lebanon, and it is as though I have travelled to the Orient.'

'The whole world is here at Trianon; why put oneself to the bother of travelling?'

The question was inopportune, as Gabrielle was at once aware, but she could not undo her piece of tactlessness. Instead, it was the Queen who found something to say:

'People travel because they are bored with how things are at home, or to make discoveries or perhaps just to see for themselves. Because things are different when one is there, on the spot . . . But foreigners, the real foreigners, those who come from very far away, however hard they try, cannot make us feel what that other world is like . . . Not that I ever meet any; I have a dread of foreigners. I always think, as I did when someone suggested an interview with Voltaire: What will I say to them?'

'You forget, madam, the visit last summer, in August, of the three envoys from Tipoo-Saëb . . . all of them diminutive, three Lilliputians. When they bent over to bow, the only things still visible were three little turbans . . .'

'Ah, yes, the envoys sent by Tipoo-Saëb, Sultan of Mysore . . . Their arrival posed serious problems of etiquette. Our Presenter of Ambassadors had consulted learned treatises, and found only this: "For extraordinary ambassadors of Muscovy, Turkey, and others on whom the King may wish to impress his greatness, nothing has been set down." The King almost declined to receive them, but he had second thoughts on the matter because there were questions of geography he wanted to ask them.'

'Where is this Mysore? And is it Mysore or the Mysore?'

The Queen spread her hands to say: 'I have no idea . . .' They were odd creatures, those ambassadors; she had looked them over very closely; she had even commissioned wax figures of them to amuse her daughter; nothing availed. Their faces would not stay fixed in her mind; they were too exotic to be remembered. They did not resemble anyone. No comparison could be made. It was like their cooking: it burned your mouth, and that was all.

'Oh, yes, now I think of it, I do vaguely remember the one who presented me with a muslin dress. The first day, all three of them were very correct in their behaviour. The following day, they seemed to have lost all interest. During the tour of the gardens, they were constantly scratching the calves of their legs . . .'

Both ladies laughed.

'. . . For the ten days after that, they lived shut away in their apartments at Trianon, waiting to go back to Mysore . . . to the Mysore.'

'They were like you. Afraid of foreigners.'

'They ought to have been even more afraid of the Sultan. Upon their return, Tipoo-Saëb had them beheaded.'

'Let us take care never to go to Mysore.'

They remained silent. The Queen held out her hand to her friend. And thus they held one another for a very long time, for the longest time, as though there were no crisis now, no pressure, no problem to be urgently discussed . . . There were interruptions, however, messages, brought to the Queen, that she waved aside to be opened later. Nothing could disturb their mutual understanding, their singular way of being together.

'Last night,' she confided to Gabrielle, 'I distinctly heard someone whispering very close to me: "Go ahead, do it now, she's taking her diamonds apart." I felt the breath of an assassin on my neck. Sometimes I wonder whether I am losing my mind, and magnifying the hatred all about me.'

'Yes, Majesty, I think you are indeed magnifying your woes. In your weariness, things look worse to you than they are. And this you must never forget: I shall always be here, at your side, sharing your trials. I shall not desert you in adversity. *We* shall not desert you. You have faithful friends, and grateful.'

Upon hearing these words, the Queen looked long and steadily at the one she called 'her dear heart' and loved accordingly. With her eyes fixed upon her friend with the intensity of despair, she said to her:

'I do not magnify the hatred. On the contrary, I think it is a degree of hate that passes my comprehension. But of one thing I am certain: I have dragged you along with me into its path. Because of me, the people are determined you shall die. The French are demanding your head. In fact, that is what I have been wanting to tell you from the outset: something horrible has happened. A woman has been stabbed, in her carriage. By mistake. The murderers thought it was you. You and I are surrounded. We have been burned in effigy, in Paris. After this, they will not stop at effigies. They want the real individuals, they want us, in the flesh. That is why, dearest Gabrielle, for your safety, and please understand what a wrench this is for me, I most earnestly beg you: leave this place, leave France. Do what I have not been able to do. Take your daughter, and take Diane, and flee. If you do not leave, you will be massacred. You and your family. But you first of all, perhaps even you alone . . . You must move swiftly, before the wave of violence has a chance to break over you.'

The Queen has chosen her words carefully and uttered them with deep feeling. She has dared to make her proposal, which she knows is unacceptable, and is fully expecting that she will have to counter her friend's arguments.

But Gabrielle has heard her out, untroubled. Far from protesting, she leaps at the opportunity. She agrees with the Queen: flight is imperative. It is a painful decision, but one dictated by wisdom. It will in any case be a temporary departure; they will very soon be back . . . Aghast at these calm, dispassionate words, the Queen trembles. Gabrielle can see Marie-Antoinette's lips quivering. It makes her uncomfortable, and she turns her eyes away. The heavy silence becomes intolerable. Just to mollify the Queen, Gabrielle says a few more words, words she thinks are anodyne but that pierce the Queen like so many arrows. At last, and without raising her eyes from contemplation of the tips of her embroidery-covered feet, Gabrielle recites, all in one go, everything they will need for departure, carriages, passports, bills of exchange. Precise names and figures are given. Everything has been thought of. Having delivered her message, Gabrielle looks up. The Queen's mouth is half open, her trembling lips painful to see. She has the imploring look of a woman who has just been struck with a fist. Gabrielle is about to say something more. The Queen enjoins her to silence, then stands up to flee from the spot. Gabrielle rushes after her and begins to moan; but stops at once when the Queen puts an arm round her waist and leans her head on her shoulder. The Queen has recovered all her beauty. And Gabrielle implores her: 'Do not let me abandon you.'

'But it is too late,' the Queen says gently. 'That is precisely what you have done. You have abandoned me.'

Unlike Madame Campan, I was not accustomed to feeling transparent and afflicted with non-existence, in a room containing the Queen. For that reason I was deeply troubled by the scene I am describing, but increasingly unable to do anything whatsoever except listen. I found the situation intolerable, and I was on the alert for a chance to steal away so I could stop hearing, stop seeing. The Duchess de Polignac had withdrawn. Her curtsey had seemed to me somewhat less graceful than when she arrived, but perhaps it was my imagination . . .

The Queen was sobbing, the way children weep, caught in the brutality of unappeasable grief. She was entirely at the mercy of her unhappiness. Madame Campan came to bring smelling salts and to look after her. I had absolutely no idea what I should do now. To make myself look busy, I began pushing a trunk toward a store-room, deliberately making slow work of it: I progressed at a snail's pace, never taking my eyes off Madame Campan, who was endeavouring to soothe and console the Queen. But the Queen, in a sudden outburst, leapt to her feet, seized the jade goblet, and hurled it at a mirror. The room was studded with shards of glass. Madame Campan and I had no choice but to sweep them up, taking great care not to cut ourselves. 'Saints preserve us, what a day!' she complained. 'Sweeping has never been one of my assigned tasks, so far as I know.'

I was a witness to the scene involving Gabrielle de Polignac and the Queen, and were it not for the presence of Madame Campan, I would have thought I had dreamed it . . . as with another scene, several months – years? – earlier. This one took place in the ground-floor music room at the Petit Trianon, and on that occasion, too, there was a second witness, Baron de Besenval. Both of us stood mute, not daring to move. Gabrielle de Polignac was lying on top of the Queen. She held the Queen's outspread arms pinned to the floor. The Queen was struggling beneath her friend's body, trying to dislodge her from her victorious position.

'Say it,' a puffing, breathless Gabrielle was demanding. 'Say it. Say: you win, you are the stronger.'

'I will not. I will never say anything so untrue. You are a cruel person. You use shameless tactics . . .'

And she was overcome with a fit of laughter that rendered her entirely defenceless. But when Gabrielle, in turn convulsed with laughter, relaxed her grip, the Queen freed one of her hands and suddenly reversed the positions.

Baron de Besenval watched them, without laughing. It may have been the awareness of this silent, attentive, male presence that brought their game to an end.

Suddenly sobered, the Queen got up and said: 'That still leaves you as the stronger person, I must admit.'

'I want no part of your pity,' said Gabrielle in languishing tones. 'I beg to be spared Your Majesty's magnanimity.'

'*Magnanimity*,' the Queen repeated carefully, as though she were discovering a new word.

They were both being serious and left the music room without paying any attention to us. Baron de Besenval was clearly dying to follow them. He took a few steps in their direction, but thought better of it. Then he turned to me and insolently, arrogantly, enquired: 'Well, my fine reader, what do you make of that?' I could tell that he would gladly have wreaked vengeance on me for the scornful treatment meted out to him by the two friends; I quietly slipped away.

'You are the stronger' – how true, alas, those words were turning out to be! It was not so much Gabrielle de Polignac's strength that was now in evidence (she was, this time, too, merely the messenger delegated by her husband and Diane), as the Queen's unbelievable weakness in dealing with her: Gabrielle's wishes were no sooner formulated than the Queen could think of nothing but how best to satisfy them . . .

To whom could I turn next, I wondered, and found no answer. I was exhausted and dejected. Honorine, completely taken up by her duties in Madame de La Tour du Pin's household, was nowhere to be seen. Jacob-Nicolas Moreau was presumably at work in his study. Dismally, I abandoned myself to the flow of events. Though schedules might be all awry, some forms of etiquette were still being haphazardly observed. Not that any good would come of it, I thought.

Mass in the royal chapel: 3 p.m.

There was Mass, then lunch. Before that, the King had gone to the Queen's apartments, where she was having her face made up.

At the time of the King's visit (so I was told by Madame Vacher, an attendant whom the Queen held in specially high esteem), nothing very remarkable occurred. The King announced the temperature reading that he had taken late in the morning. He was entirely covered with dust, and a spider's web hung down in front of his waistcoat; the explanation for this was that on leaving the Apollo Room he had walked up to the attic. The Queen made no attempt to hide her exasperation at seeing him in such a state. She could not abide the mania he had for walking about in the palace garrets, she detested what she called his 'prisoner's stroll'. The King, on the other hand, set great store by it, as he did by his walks on the palace roofs. These, along with the periods devoted to hunting, handicrafts, and meals, were probably the only times when he felt shielded from the watchful eyes of the courtiers. But he preferred not to argue, so the quarrel had blown over very quickly. They had then given fresh consideration to the matter of leaving Versailles. The King, who had said no in the Council meeting, wondered whether there was still time to change his mind . . . whereas the Queen, who had hotly defended her plan and been so upset at having to relinquish it, hesitated to go back on the decision that had been reached. The luggage was unpacked, the travel costumes were not ready, no carriage offering the requisite size and comfort was to be found, and as for domestic staff able to accompany them, none had been designated . . . To set out unescorted, on the sly: there was something hasty and improvised about the whole scheme, not consonant with royal dignity. Basically, the King was in agreement: they should stay. But now it was the Queen's turn to wonder aloud, uncertain in her mind, whether leaving was not perhaps their only hope of survival . . . Finally, the King asked a question.

'Tell me, madam, I pray you: does this convey any sense to you? I have learned – it was Monsieur de Noailles who made me privy to this information at my Couchee – that the people want not only bread, but also power. When insanity reaches that point, I am, I confess, completely at a loss. I had hitherto understood power to be a burden of duties and responsibilities that we inherited and that we accepted out of humility, and out of respect for the One who had invested us with that charge. A kind of curse hidden beneath an ermine cloak. Is it possible I have been mistaken? Could there be something desirable about power?'

At Mass, I noticed an extreme languor in the ritual gestures and even in the prayers. The congregation was rather small, and the few who had turned out appeared exhausted. The King and the Queen were models of piety and dignity. As was the Count de Provence, though the Count d'Artois was distracted – but then he often was. The Mass celebrated Camillus de Lellis, a saint the King held in affection on account of his aunts, who were particularly devoted to Saint Camillus. Indeed, with the passing years, the two elderly ladies had come to venerate the founder of the Order of Fathers of a Good Death more and more. They had in their possession sachets containing a few pinches of dust from the stones of the monk's cell. So far, they had not broken into this precious hoard; they were waiting for the day when they were really sick. They might easily have chosen this day, for Louis XV's daughter looked to be suffering extreme fatigue. They could not sleep. They complained that they were surrounded by conspirators and even said they could hear anti-royalist conversations, coming from the mezzanine rooms just above their ground-floor apartments. Which, added Madame Adélaïde, placed them in the front line of fire. 'They' had only to smash the panes of glass, and 'they' would be in the royal aunts' suite of rooms . . .

Incidentally, speaking of 'them', where were 'they' now? The fragile assurance I had felt that morning was gone. Beggars, brigands, madmen – they were coming our way, no doubt about it. They were an army, growing steadily as fresh recruits arrived. Women and children were coming to swell the ranks. They had plundered L'Arsenal and Les Invalides, and certainly did not lack for weapons. Or fury. The market women of La Halle led the march, knives in hand. Once again, the congregation sang *Plaudite Regem manibus*. But this time, nobody applauded.

The King's Luncheon; its sudden and disastrous conclusion: 4 p.m.

Luncheon was served, after a considerable delay. The succession of royal viands had been standing unserved in the stairway for at least two hours. For my part, I was famished, and I was not the only one. But instead of going off with all due haste in search of something to eat, at least a score of the people who had attended Mass also insisted on attending the King's Luncheon. This was a breach of etiquette: firstly because some of us were not normally eligible to take part in this ceremonial repast; and secondly because it was Thursday, the day reserved for the more intimate Petty Luncheon. Hence there was no reason to remain, as we did, all stubbornly lined up facing the rectangular white-linened table at which the King and Queen had taken their places. No reason, except – I speak of course for myself – a kind of silly, childish, superstitious behaviour: from the moment I found out that the Queen had made up her mind to flee, every time she disappeared from view I was afraid I was losing her for ever. As long as I could see her, I was restored, if not to peace of mind, at least to bearable anxiety. The same must have been true for the rest of that meagre band of diners. Like me, they could feel their world collapsing. To see the King or the Queen gave them comfort. No doubt the royal couple sensed this need, for neither one spoke up to request that we leave them in peace. The King could have had his attendants say to us: 'Ladies and gentlemen, this way, if you please.' He refrained from doing so. In any event, at that meal, etiquette was to be violated more than once, and our presence, though irregular, was not the worst . . .

Everything started off well, however. The King and the Queen sat down side by side in the lovely blue-and-gold room where the table had been set. The Almoner in Ordinary, Father

Cornu de La Balivière, blessed the table, and Their Majesties crossed themselves. Then they were handed a damp, scented towel on which they wiped their hands. As far as the Queen was concerned, her participation ended there. She did not drink a drop from the glass of water set before her and did not even pretend to need a plate. As she did not ask for anything, the manservant stationed behind her armchair maintained a total immobility that seemed to redouble her own motionless state and make it more evident. Sad, her eyes downcast, she waited with resignation for the King's appetite to be sated. She knew this would take time, because for him, this was the beginning of a festival of devourment. 'His Majesty's appetite deserves to be remembered by posterity' was a phrase commonly heard at Versailles. And whereas nothing was happening around the Queen, in the King's vicinity there arose a brisk rhythm of comings and goings. A great many palace servants had disappeared, but the Royal Commissary remained faithful.

At the start of the meal, then, everything gave me a feeling of order and permanence. The delay had not been a prelude to disorganisation. The ceremony of the Royal Repast had always been grandiose, and this occasion promised to be no exception. The King's breakfast, it appeared, had been cutlets and savates of veal, gulped down with undignified haste before sunrise so he could attend that dawn meeting of the Royal Council. Uneasy in his mind, and still wavering over the dilemma of whether to go or not, he had demanded more. 'Cutlets and savates of veal amount to very little,' he had said. 'Have them do me some eggs in mustard sauce.' Six, he had added for greater precision. And a bottle and a half of Burgundy wine. But that had been much earlier in the day. Since then, what with the awkward moments and painful emotions aroused, he had worked up a serious appetite. Food trolleys replaced trays, to be replaced in turn by entire tables covered with cooked dishes. The King went on devouring. Entrées, meat dishes, and fish dishes, artful heaps of vegetables. First course, second course, third course. Joint of beef scarlet-rare, rice soup served with fatted pullet, Turkish-style minced wildfowl, water pheasant, skate livers, hashed ram's testes, hares' tongues, mutton sausages, chicken in fat, chicken *blondin*, chicken *vestale*, leek fritters, cauliflower fritters, oceans of green peas. He ate, he drank, he spoke not a word . . . except to request another serving of pigeon, of eel and weever, of crayfish, pig's head, and turkeys' feet: After a time, he stopped talking altogether, and sat half-swooning, his waistcoat and doublet unbuttoned, confining himself to pointing at quivering mounds of white and green jellies, blancmange and celadon eggs, conglomerations of roes, and hare's-ear mushrooms prepared in various ways.

An impeccable gastronomic performance, an improbable refilling of the royal cavity . . . but towards the end, when it was time for the course of sweets and mousses, an incident occurred. There was an inexplicable pause in the proceedings. No one came to remove the dishes. After a lengthy wait, the King decided to send the Chief Cupbearer in Ordinary to make inquiries. The Chief Cupbearer did not come back. So the King sent the Yeoman-Scullery-Cupbearer accompanied by the Cup-bearer Officer of the Commissary. They did not come back either. The King, purple in the face, said something in an under-tone to the Queen, who gave the briefest of answers. Suddenly, like a meteor, there came running in a dishevelled creature copiously daubed with soot. All she was wearing was a filthy skirt and a fichu that left her breasts bare. To me she looked as though she had escaped from the howling, leaping, galloping, flying firedance that, in defiance of the succour brought to man by religion, has spanned the centuries and still serves to summon up witches. Surely she had come straight out of such a coven, with her plateful of impurities held aloft by her fingertips and her great mouth split from ear to ear in a perverse and toothless grin. She went to the King, where he sat waiting with all those serving dishes around him: on one platter a half-gnawed bone stood out, on others a rabbit's head, or a collapsed pyramid of celery soufflé, a few crab shells, a ring of mullet, piles of giblets . . . She slapped down, on to the table in front of him, an iron plate on which had been arranged, in a kind of ridge above a carpet of potato peelings dragged through ashes before-hand, some tufts of animal hair and a dead rat. She burst out laughing and quickly vanished. There was a hubbub in our little gathering. But no one dared to stir. For several seconds the King examined the horrid concluding dish in his menu. Then he stood up; with difficulty, but successfully.

As he had done in the morning after the Council meeting broke up, but walking much less steadily, he repaired to the Apollo Room to ascertain the temperature. The notebook was in its place. But the valet whose task it was to record the figures was gone. There remained the big crystal thermometer hanging from a window. The King leaned right up against the panes to discern the numbers. He was reluctant to record the temperat-ure himself. He did not do so.

The Queen, on leaving the luncheon room, had headed in the direction of her apartments. At first I thought she was indeed going to her own rooms; in reality, she was making for those of Gabrielle de Polignac.

Nowhere in the various salons had the flowers been changed. I was told that the same was true in the Queen's apartments.

I am gripped by Panic: 6 p.m.

So many warning signs had been accumulating, and all of them baleful. I noticed, too, a singular stir and bustle in the palace, but paid no attention. Six o'clock in the evening was when people normally withdrew to their own lodgings, played games, made music, read, and – especially – got dressed for the evening's activities. It was the time when jewelled ornaments circulated among the ladies of fashion, when visiting started, between families, apartments, or different parts of the palace, and maintained a lively pace that would last until midnight and even beyond. More prosaically, in this case, it was the time when I needed to find some supper and went to see if Honorine could oblige. I wanted to talk to her about everything I had witnessed: in particular, the episode of the repugnant dessert had left me badly frightened.

Honorine was available, and she could give me some supper. Monsieur and Madame de La Tour du Pin's apartment boasted an unusual feature: a huge kitchen, equipped with several stoves. Once I had eaten and was feeling the better for it, I started out to share my recent discoveries with my friend, but discovered there was nothing I could say. I felt it would be indiscreet to describe for her what had transpired between the Queen and Gabrielle de Polignac. As for the ending to the King's Luncheon, I feared lest by reporting it I might propagate its evil spell. So instead, it was Honorine who told me the latest news from Paris. We resumed work on the unfinished tapestry. Gradations of green, mosses, ferns, tall forest trees, with some white and brown for a doe near a pond. Embroidery exercises a calming effect on me; it is the daytime equivalent of reciting lists to myself. But now, as I listened to what Honorine had to tell me, the remedy did not work. The Parisians had gone completely wild in victory. At the

Bastille, they had put to death the Swiss Guards and even, in their frenzy, a few prisoners. They were indoctrinating the army, tearing up the cobbled city streets, obtaining weapons everywhere, fabricating bombs, setting fire to the aristocratic Faubourg Saint-Germain. They were running along the ramparts of the city bellowing murderous songs. The Prince de Lambesc, pursued by this maddened horde, had returned with his officers to Versailles.

I pricked my finger and let go of the tapestry. I looked up at the palace grounds, to be struck by an absolutely timeless image: going past the windows, preceded by two footmen, was the ancient, paralytic Duke de Reybaud. As he did at this time every day, weather permitting, he was having himself carried to the Ballroom Bosquet. Ordinarily, Monsieur de Reybaud was half dead. A glimmer of life returned to his lacklustre eyes only when he could contemplate Le Nôtre's masterpiece of landscape gardening. What was it about this thicket of trees that appealed to him? The limpid water trickling over the rockeries, the wellspring coolness of the air, a scene from his past? He was accompanied by his wife, who was a very young girl, and by one of his daughters from a previous marriage, who was an old woman. I was amazed.

'Look,' I said to Honorine, 'over that way, not far from the Hundred-Step Stairway. Look; it's His Grace the Duke de Reybaud. He is completely unaware of the calamitous events taking place around him. He is going ahead with his daily outing as he has done from the beginning of time. Surely he must be accounted more fortunate than any of us.'

'Maybe,' my friend replied (she was now working on the tapestry by herself). 'But being unaware that a thing exists has never prevented that thing from existing. In Paris, the people have seized the Bastille. They are armed. Nothing can stop them now. In Versailles, the National Assembly has scored two victories over the King. He has given up his army and dismissed his ministers. I don't know what is being planned here at the palace. Nothing good, in the opinion of Madame de La Tour du Pin.

The fear we experienced last night has only got worse. No voice is raised here that would suggest the presence of a leader prepared to step forward and instill the court with fresh energy. Monsieur de La Tour du Pin is firmly resolved not to give up the palace, to stay and fight, but there are not many, I fear, who share his determination.'

Outside, the pathetic little procession moved on. At its own pace. Unhurried. And after all, why hurry? They knew where they were going by heart. And the Ballroom Bosquet would always be there waiting for them. An empty place, to those two women and the valets; a place humming with life, filled with sounds of festivities and music, to the old man who could no longer go anywhere except in his memory . . .

Honorine had not convinced me. I still favoured the policy of deliberate refusal to know, provided that we followed it unswervingly. Troublesome matters, so it seemed to me, could be abolished by resorting to *Enough of that* or *Let's think about something else* . . . I was mustering arguments, my gaze was wandering among the treetops, level with the Orangerie terrace . . . Well, but . . . It was *her* again, the misshapen creature, with her red hair and her arms held out stiffly in front of her. She was barely touching the ground. She had presided in the kitchens, and now she was heading into the gardens. She was making for the old Duke's little procession, but veered away before they met.

'It's her! Honorine, it's her, it's Panic, Panic incarnate!'

My cries had come too late; I was now in her power. She was moving with the speed of disaster, her hair soaked in blood, her obscene flesh made even more obscene by her garment that hung in tatters – tatters one might see on the stage of a theatre. She had emerged on to the terrace, hurtled through the clumps of trees at the Water Garden, careered off past the Orangerie towards the Pond des Suisses; she was coming back now, up to the Latona fountain, fulminating, bent on meting out punishment, turning away from the palace, all the while imperiously calling down the wrath of the gods. From Latona, she darted down by way of the Colonnade to the Fountain of Apollo, spun round, her speed increasing tenfold out of frustration at finding a space devoid of humans, came then to the park's northerly section, and crossed it with one mighty swoop, vaguely recognising in her impetuous flight the Enceladus fountain, the Cupids of the Happy Isle, and the broad Neptune basin, created for more propitious hours than these. She did not linger there; enraged at having found no one in her round of the park, she came back on to the terrace to resume possession of the palace. And this time she would not confine herself to the kitchens . . .

The living Panic had charged blindly along her way, with no thought of turning around and looking back to enjoy the fruits of her stormy passage. Thus she had seen nothing of the frightened old man abandoned at the top of the stairway. At the first air current fanned up by Panic in her mad course, the menservants had fled. One of them had nearly been crushed under a carriage that suddenly swept by at a gallop. The Duke's wife, almost as nimble as the two rascally servants, had hitched up her dress to mid-thigh, and reached the statue of the Sphinx Child in a few quick strides. His daughter, too, had left the old man's side, but, being rheumatic and hoary with age, she was limping along far behind. Panic does not take time; her sphere of influence is a hole in time, into which she flings everyone that she snatches up along her path.

She has understood in a flash: there is no one out in the palace grounds. The place she must come back to, the place where she must do her work, is the palace itself. There, unlike in the park, there were victims in abundance, victims by the dozen, by the hundred, for the asking; she could start with me; I was hers, body and soul. Her hair, dripping with blood, had brushed against me. It had not left a stain, not even a mark, but in the overly fine fabric of my summer skirt there was a red dot, as when an extraneous thread gets into the weaving to produce a flaw.

Honorine and her words of common sense were forgotten. I

began to run every which way, up the staircases and down, retracing my steps suddenly, opening a door. I lost all notion of where I was. I wanted to be made of glass so I could shatter. I wanted to be the goblet that the Queen had shattered. So I could be reduced to nothing.

Over the next few hours, I was aware of Panic only from the ravages she left in her wake. She stopped being seen 'in person' – seen by me, that is, for Versailles was so vast that one could readily imagine her to be operating in other spheres. One thing is certain: she was committing her rampages in conjunction with the people and their rebellion. The people had Panic working for them, we had her working against us: that, at least, is what I believed at the time, for I realised later that Panic was acting *equally* on both sides, but in the enclosed, defenceless, trapped space of Versailles, such an overview could not possibly be achieved . . . The hellish, unbelievable fact, that the populace was strong enough to attack the Bastille and succeed in bringing it down, remained a kind of barrier preventing my mind from going any further. (In a similar vein, Count de Ségur would later write: 'That fit of madness which, even now, describing it, I still have difficulty believing . . .'). Repeatedly I told myself: 'It was a natural, not a supernatural event. The Parisians found weapons, the citadel was poorly defended, they took it by storm. There were enough of them, they had enough rifles and cannons to carry the day.' This, though very painful, was logical. But logical reasoning had no effect. I could see them hurling their defiance heavenward, and it was the heavens that came crashing down, in the thunderous roar of the Bastille's collapsing towers. The people had stormed Heaven, and Heaven had fallen. It was said that since 14 July they had been labouring day and night at demolishing the Bastille. An accursed worksite! People were gathering up the stones, packing them on their backs, and going out into the provinces to sell them! Pedlars selling the ruins of Heaven. They claimed to be furnishing proof! Frankly, to me the whole affair was unthinkable. I tried to think about something else, no matter what, to take my mind off it, but I kept coming back to that. I could no longer think of anything but that . . . and ended up not thinking at all. Here was another way in which Panic operated: not just putting everyone to flight, but putting into everyone's mind a thing it could not imagine; substituting, for the mind's intelligence, a whirlwind.

I came and went, came and went, a creature near to madness. I had ceased to recognise people and places. I was stopping in front of paintings and talking to the people in them. Occasionally I would laugh and cover my eyes with my hands. I was talking to myself out loud. But Panic loosened her grip. A more powerful force had intervened.

From my life at court and my constant preoccupation with the Queen, I had developed, along with the art of never missing an opportunity to gaze upon her, the more subtle art of sensing her nearness before I saw her. All at once I would know that she was not far off, that she was about to appear.

What's that you say? You knew? Knew, how? From an unexpected surge of warmth, an exquisite moment of weakness, a pounding of the heart. Others, physically present around me, would blur and move farther away. They became a vague, indistinct background against which, suddenly (for the signs telling of her imminent appearance in no way diminished the suddenness of her arrival), she stood out.

And thus it chanced that at this moment, coming magically into view, there she was.

We were on the ground floor, in a corridor with entrance doors to several of the apartments occupied by her friends. The Queen, when I saw her, was facing away from me. She was alone, holding a candlestick. She was standing at one of the doors. She was politely and humbly asking to be admitted. After a moment of waiting, she tried again at the lodgings of other friends. At each door, she was greeted by the same silence. Then she lost patience, became indignant, began to utter loud reproaches. But her voice dropped when, on reaching out to give one of the doors a shake, she realised that it was padlocked. As were others. With padlocks hastily installed, more or less everywhere along the corridor, on those white-and-gold doors, like locks on gardeners' huts.

The Queen had two manners of walking that I knew well: her official manner, rather slow and solemn and making her look larger; and her private one, very brisk, but showing the curves of her body and with a slight swaying of the hips that made you want to sing. What I had never seen before was this heavy gait, a sagging of the shoulders, and an uncertainty, a kind of stupor that inhibited her movements. A walk that betokened misfortune, betokened the discovery that there was an additional degree to her unhappiness. She had thought she could turn to friends for support to help her bear the estrangement of Gabrielle de Polignac, but the friends were not responding. For the first time, the roles were reversed: she was asking something of them. She needed them.

The Queen had never experienced the dark side of these corridors, salons and private studies. She had never in her life come up against a closed door. She had never opened a door, for that matter, never touched a door. There was a lost, wandering quality to her progress as she came back towards her own apartments. Like me a moment earlier, she gave the impression of not knowing exactly where she was. Her pace was rapid, but she stopped at intervals. She seemed to be in fear of some danger, lurking very nearby and ready to pounce on her. She turned slightly, but could not escape. She had just entered the Salon de la Guerre. She held her candlestick high, cautiously casting light into a corner or behind a screen. She could have gone to the King's rooms to ask for protection, but she did the opposite: she turned away from him. At that moment, a breath of air put her candle out. She stood motionless, stiff, facing the impassable threshold of the Grand Gallery. There was no longer any guard to announce *The Queen*. Not a single courtier to react to such an announcement. Her presence caused no stir. Everything hung upon the movement she could not bring herself to make. She put a foot forward, and drew back. She was terrified as she faced that chasm of shadow. She knew she must make the leap, find the courage to walk forward by herself, between rows of mirrors with no images.

I can still hear the sound of her dress brushing across the inlaid floor, I can see her ring-laden hands holding open the high double doors. I can feel her irregular, terrified breathing. Before her, undulating, beckoning, and treacherous, like a body of water opaquely concealing its bottomless depths, there stretches the Hall of Mirrors.

She has lost the ability to walk. Alone, she cannot walk.

I tell myself: she won't do it. She will not have the courage to do it. And in my disordered mind, the Queen is no different from that paralytic, the old Duke de Reybaud, left by himself in his chair.

I close my eyes.

I weep for her, for them.

'All is lost,' my friend had said. He was right. All was lost, irremediably lost.

The Historiographer of France is entrusted by the
King with a sacred mission – the drafting of a
'Pastoral Letter': 7 p.m.

'The Queen is alone,' I said, as I walked into Jacob-Nicolas
Moreau's study.

'The privilege of greatness, my dear.'

His tone of voice surprised me.

'You don't understand what I'm saying. She is alone in front
of closed doors. She is hurting her hands trying to open padlocks. She is alone at the entrance to the Grand Gallery.'

'Everything you are telling me is unimaginable and shocking.
And many other things are, I suspect, in store, that will be
equally unimaginable and shocking, horrors beyond imagining,
unless . . .'

'You said it before, and now I'm convinced: we are doomed;
the day of punishment is upon us.'

'I did say it, but possibly there is a way to avoid the worst, and
suspend the punishment.'

'By force of arms?'

'No, the King is prepared to make every concession in order
to avoid civil war. All his actions stem from that one policy. He
does not want to see killing take place among his children. He
swore that no drop of French blood would be shed through any
fault of his. He is having recourse to prayer. The country is
seething with unrest. The people have been won over and are
beside themselves with rage. The real question is to ascertain
whether there is still a chance for them to come back to their
senses and return to the love of God.'

'I dare say . . . but it seems to me you are considering the
matter with a confidence you entirely lacked, not so long since.'

'That's because in the interval I have been honoured with a

commission from the King. A charge so deeply moving and so characteristic of his great goodness that my only fear is of not measuring up to the task. That would be worse than anything. But if I contrived, were it only in part, to meet His Majesty's expectations, then the spirit of discord might diminish, and the Revolution, which, as its name suggests, is a circular motion, might bring us back to a time of obedience. The people will be cured of this state of combustion, which must surely be hard to live with, and from which, if the truth were known, they long to be freed. They will be cured and the nobility saved, saved from its own cynicism and hard-heartedness. We are experiencing an illness of the soul, to which no one has proved completely immune. A return to godliness of spirit is the only remedy.'

'The King had already honoured you with an explicit commission, before the Estates-General convened.'

'. . . Last February, my *French Monarchical Constitution Expounded and Defended*. It did not enjoy the success I had hoped for. Did my diction lack vitality, did my reasoning need to be more tightly argued?' (Here I protested.) 'I do not know; I shall rework it when time permits. What I do realise now with certainty, is that aside from my weaknesses as a writer, the basic error lay in treating my subject on a political plane, when in fact the problem is a religious one. Politics is the enemy's ground. Ours is faith. I must find the words that can bring an end to the state of non-belief presently gripping the French people, the noxious scepticism poisoning their minds. I must find words that will strike down "the wicked in all their effrontery", to use His Majesty's sublime expression.'

'And what form will your composition take? Does it have a title?' I asked timidly.

'His majesty has commissioned from me a "Pastoral Letter Relating to Instruction for Parish Priests". It will be sent to all the bishops in the kingdom for publication in their respective dioceses.'

'But how wonderful! This means that it is up to you to change the course of history.'

Monsieur Moreau was quivering with the excitement of it all. He sensed the critical importance of this piece of writing and how vital it was that mediocrity of any kind be excluded. That was why, though he was by nature a reserved man, he could not resist the desire to read me the opening lines. Holding his pen in one hand, and his written pages in the other, he began: 'Pastoral instruction requiring public prayers to be offered, in accordance with the request from Louis XVI to all French Bishops, for the granting of divine light to guide the National Assembly, and for an end to the troubles already threatening France.'

Just from his reading of the title, I was deeply moved. I could hear it echoing in the sacred precincts of a church, delivered from a raised pulpit. I had no doubts of its power to sway. I could see the whole of France on its knees.

'You are too generous, madam,' said the Historiographer playfully, but he continued, his voice betraying even greater emotion.

You are aware of the acts of rebellion and banditry that have been perpetrated in the Capital City. If this spirit of sedition should chance to reach the confines of your Diocese or spread into those confines, you will, I am persuaded, place in its path every obstacle that your zeal, your attachment to My Person and most of all the Holy Religion whose Minister you are, cannot fail to suggest. The upholding of public order is a Gospel law as it is a law to the State; and whatever disturbs that order is criminal in the eyes of God and man alike.

It was a splendid text. Splendid and convincing. I had admired his *French Monarchical Constitution Expounded and Defended*, but his 'Pastoral Letter' was beyond compare. With this new opus, written at this moment of religious crisis and national emergency, his talent had realised its full potential. Jacob-Nicolas Moreau could not sit still. He paced back and forth between his various pieces of non-matching furniture, picking his way along the narrow trenches reserved for walking, in what little space remained between the piles of books. His oratorical enthusiasm did not prevent him from carefully respecting the piles. He threaded his way through the labyrinth formed by towers of paper, declaiming as he went: 'It is important that you be accurately informed as to the causes and consequences of the riots in Paris. These causes and consequences, revealed by you to the populations of your various Dioceses, will effectively preserve them from sedition, preventing them from being either its victims or its accomplices. Revolt has been fomented by men coming from outside, and infiltrating the parishes they wished to subvert. These depraved men . . .'

But he stopped short. He rushed to the door and double-locked it. He stayed with his back against the door, arms outspread.

'Listen,' he said to me, 'don't you hear?'

My reaction was stupid: I tried to step out and see what was happening.

'Don't go out of the room. They're here. They're inside the palace.'

We stayed for a few minutes with our ears pressed to the door. The sounds of Versailles were familiar to me, but this one was new.

'Are they pulling cannon?'

Jacob-Nicolas Moreau had softly withdrawn the key so he could look through the keyhole. What he had seen left him flabbergasted. He straightened up.

'We can go out. There is no danger.'

Indeed, there was little to be feared from the shameful band who were trying to be as discreet as they could and achieving exactly the opposite effect. The courtiers were moving out, and it was abundantly clear that they were quite unused to what this entailed. In truth, it would be hard to imagine a more unlikely, awkward group, or anyone less skilled in the handling of furniture, luggage, and packages that gaped open because they were not properly tied. These people were leaving Versailles as speedily as they could; and for the few who were fleeing empty-handed with just one idea in mind – to leap on a horse and make for foreign soil – there were many more, the majority, in fact, who were re-enacting the King's indecisive behaviour on a smaller scale. They wanted to leave, as fast as possible and without attracting notice, but baulked at the prospect of travelling without their creature comforts. Perhaps, too, the thought occurred that if they were rushing off pell-mell into an unknown land, they might be glad one day to have the option of selling the rosewood console table, the marble statuette, the Sèvres umbrella stand, the sapphire-inlaid clock, or whatever object it was that they held absurdly hugged in their arms until, either so as to move faster or because they had just cracked their treasure in two by banging into a door, they simply left it there on the spot. Not without regret: some of them actually turned and came back to pick up the abandoned item, which in many cases had been a gift from the King or the Queen. I heard arguments and recriminations. And, as there were no children at Versailles, the courtiers were going away without them, confident that the wet nurse who had begun to suckle them would continue to do so. Or else the courtiers completely forgot them. Reverting to savagery, for they could feel rebel hands around their throats, dragging them away to be hanged from the nearest lamp-post, some of these noble parents did not even remember having procreated.

A lady was walking with slow steps. Her husband was striding ahead. Struck by a sudden thought, she set down the hatbox she was carrying in her arms, and asked: 'What are we going to do about Henriette?'

'To what Henriette does Your Ladyship refer?'

'Our daughter, Your Lordship.'

'I beg you will not confuse all these problems one with the other. It happens there is an immediate one. The people are a tangible threat. They are drawing near. They intend to kill us. They *are going to* kill us. Our names are on lists. Perhaps as early as tomorrow, Versailles will have been reduced to a heap of ruins, with bodies scattered about: nothing else will remain of the last French court. Do you quite understand, madam?' (He was expressing himself with grandiloquence and speaking too loudly, addressing his wife as though he were at one end of a feudal castle and she at the other.) 'Is that the fate you desire? To die here? If so, I give you leave, I do not force you to follow me, but do not seek to delay me with trivial queries. And I would point out to you that Henriette is not our only child. You appear to take very lightly, madam, the matter of Achille, Modeste, Sosthène, and Bénédicte.'

The lady abandoned her hatbox by a wall, almost at my feet. And thus disencumbered of her baggage and her maternal solicitude, she could move on at the same rate as her husband.

The awkward feature of the affair was the accumulation of bags, trunks, chests, and bundles that were being dragged along and had very quickly, in that narrow corridor, begun to block the passage.

The people who were leaving with baggage are the ones I remember most vividly, because they looked so ridiculous as they struggled past. Because of the mixture of haste and waste, and their rather touching incompetence, thus exposed for anyone to see. By the very manner of their fleeing, they were forgetting what was due to their rank. Perhaps that explained the shame they felt: it was not the flight, but the fact of being forced to flee in this disgraceful fashion – without a presentable travel costume, the objection the Queen had raised a few hours earlier in relation to herself. Many, however, rendered even more distraught by the sense of urgency, were departing empty-handed. It seemed to them that their lives were hanging by a thread, that to linger was to perish, victims of a collective massacre. I think that was when the latest of many malign rumours reached us: it was said that the underground passages at Versailles were stuffed with explosives. The palace was going to blow up at any moment. Over the previous few days, the same fear had had the Parisians terrorised and helpless: they were convinced that the royalists had planted bombs and Paris was about to be wiped out.

Panic took hold of me again.

'My dear, you must keep your wits about you. If we are on the point of being blown up, we are too late to prevent it. We will be dead a few seconds from now. Or else we already are. Let us put aside this rumour and return to my apartments. I will read you the next part of my "Pastoral Letter".'

'Some of them are leaving without any baggage, without a change of clothing, without the basic necessities. Could they be intending to return in a few days? That would explain why they are not taking anything with them.'

'How could I possibly have the answer to your question? Who knows? But perhaps it's as you say . . . We shall soon see them returning . . . those who escape the wrathful fury of the rebels. The others, well . . . As for us, no purpose is served by continuing to stand in the path of the herd, where we could easily come to grief. Someone might do us a mischief, and we've already learned all we need to know about human ingratitude.'

Just then, as though to supply him with additional proof, he spied a man in the act of pulling a small painting off the wall: a *Still Life with Asparagus*. Jacob-Nicolas Moreau could not help intervening.

'Monsieur Moreau,' said the culprit, speaking with the greatest arrogance, 'you are a good, decent writer, a respectable scholar, a remarkable librarian, and an unrivalled observer of human behaviour, but I invite you to take your remonstrances and stuff them up your arse. You can mention that in your notebooks for the edification of posterity.'

I would have liked to come to the insulted man's defence, but he persuaded me to hold my tongue. 'Let it be; I'm used to it. My undertakings are generally greeted with nothing but derision and disdain.' Then, after a pause, 'The scoundrel did not mention my abilities as a historiographer.'

Those who were running away chose the least conspicuous routes. Most of them went by way of the inner courtyards. There is a very old rule of courtesy that states the following precept: 'When visiting, one must be at pains, upon leaving a group, to make one's exit as discreetly as possible. It should be an object to spare the hostess the awkwardness of a formal leave-taking. For that reason, one often seizes a moment when others are arriving.' In a manner of speaking, if one judges solely by outward behaviour, those words describe exactly what was happening here. The courtiers were leaving as discreetly as possible. They were making it an object to spare the lady of the house the awkwardness of a leave-taking. They were even putting into practice a courteous little device sanctioned by custom: slipping quietly out, under cover of the noise made by those who were coming in. Except that their actions were no longer dictated by courtesy . . .

Panic ignores pauses; she does not consider rank, nor does she distinguish between a casual *au revoir* and a final *adieu*. For her there are only solutions or obstacles. And it happened that obstacles, unforeseen ones, were about to emerge.

The Historiographer now had the strength of a man imbued with a mission. His position was safe, unassailable. (And he maintained the same serenity, of the kind that stands above events, until the day he was incarcerated at Les Récollets prison in the town of Versailles, in 1793. Then, as a precaution, he asked his wife to burn any papers of his that might compromise him; she, in her anxiety to comply, threw all his manuscripts, including his journal, on to the fire.) The calmness of his demeanour had the effect of shutting me out. Not in any harsh way, but I simply could not rise to – much less maintain – his level of certainty and resolve. I could pray, in the shadows, and ask for help. The voice of God did not speak in me, certainly not for the sacred purpose of reaching out through me to touch the heart of France. I have to confess that in me the voice was barely audible. I could no longer recognise my world in the wreckage of those hours. Details caught my attention. Fragments that I was unable to set into a whole picture. I was too close or too far removed. Was it a result of having lived constantly with books, or in the paradise of gold and flowers called Versailles? In the palace libraries nothing came to break up the neat line of books; the very doors gave the illusion that you were part of the library. This sheltered enclosure had now been violated.

That earlier scene, of the Queen knocking at her friends' doors, replayed itself over and over in my mind. She calls out to them. Then she perceives that their doors are shut with padlocks. She sways, is on the verge of fainting. She tries to steady herself by grasping the padlocks. She scrapes her hands on them . . . Her fingers laden with rings, her hands holding apart the double doors to the Grand Gallery, are grazed and scratched.

There remains that 'shining' of hers, a light that never goes out. 'What you are trying to describe is her goodness,' says the Prince de Ligne, when I use such vague expressions.

They were fleeing. They were barely taking time to fasten the straps on their baggage. They were leaving everything behind – everything and nothing. Those cramped, tiny rooms they had fought so hard to obtain were nothing now but places where they changed their raiment. Four times a day. Without having had the least suspicion of what was coming, they found themselves living under the roof of a vanquished king, linked to a party that had been annihilated. They wanted to put as much distance as they could between themselves and that defeat, so as not to be swallowed up in the catastrophe. They were deserting, with no regard for their hosts. But perhaps it was not as simple as this: some of them may have had minds more divided than their behaviour suggested.

That man there, for instance: he is in riding dress and carries a bag, but as he passes through the King's Bedchamber, he does not fail to make a genuflection in front of His Majesty's bed.

Everywhere except in the steady accumulation of sentences comprising the 'Pastoral Letter', disorder mounted. The volume of noise was increasing. Chaos was gaining ground. I learned that the vestry of the Royal Chapel was being used as a camp. There were people occupying the confessionals. I beg your pardon? What's that you say? A camp? I rushed to see. But well before I reached the vestry I realised that new elements were coming into play. There was tremendous congestion at the doors, those leading to the grounds as well as those facing the town. Oddly enough, the palace of Versailles – which to me was the epitome of danger, the deadly trap, the place that was liable to blow up at any moment, the place that was beyond any doubt going to be assailed and destroyed – did not appear in that light to everyone. To me, if there was one word that summed up Versailles, it was vulnerability. For the past two days, we had been confronted with our complete lack of defensive means. In the last analysis, this lack had been our sole object of contemplation through all that sleepless night. It had been like something out of a bad dream: the realisation that Versailles's only protections were its curtains, its wall hangings, and its shutters. This was a house of cards, a palace of cards, collapsing noiselessly at the first breath of hostility. To stay was to get killed; that, uncoded, was the message conveyed by the wild migration I was now witnessing. Well, this deadfall, this mouse-trap was suddenly being invaded by a multitude of individuals who were *seeking* refuge at Versailles, 'in these parts', as though, once within its gates, in the other world tangibly represented by the palace, they were entering an inviolable space.

I wrote 'multitude'; I am overstating. Their overwrought condition, the look they had, of people with the Devil on their tail, made me think they were more numerous than they in fact were. Compared to the exodus of the 'lodgers', the refugees were in a minority, but in their greedy desire to put in at the safe haven they had steered for, they were every bit as frenzied as the people running away. I could tell from their bearing and attire that the newcomers were of noble birth. They were arriving for the most part as families, and sometimes with a few servants, faithful souls who, seeing their master set off on this desperate venture, had clung to his coat-tails or else been carried along in spite of themselves from force of habit. These servants, though passive, increased the number of newcomers and made it even more difficult to move around. The people arriving and the ones leaving collided, had confrontations, stood their ground, pushed, and were pushed back with equal firmness, both sides fully determined not to give an inch.

Suddenly, under pressure from farther back in the crowd, someone's resistance would yield. Over the unlucky person's body a group of deserters would stream out or a few refugees would surge in. The new arrivals, once they got past the bottle-neck and had the illusion of finally being safe, were inclined to be communicative. They dropped into comfortable chairs that other people's arms were just about to heave up out of the way. They wanted to tell their story. And since the time for con-voluted speech and apt turns of phrase was long gone, they launched wild-eyed straight into tales of châteaux in flames, looting, and manhunts. Count de Grisac, a Representative of the Nobility to the Estates-General, had been returning home to his demesne in the province of Limousin. He had been recog-nised by his farm labourers as he turned into the road that led to the little village. Hatred flared! They brandished their pitchforks as they shouted: 'String him up! We're going to hang you high, Your Lordship! We're going to bust you open, bleed you like a stuck pig! We're going to get you, we'll tear your heart out, we'll have your guts to weave our baskets.'

' "We'll have your guts to weave our baskets"? Did they really say that?' asked a young woman wearing an immense hat. She was bending over a wicker trunk that she was trying to shut with a dog leash and did not turn around to put her question.

'Well, yes, in their local dialect, of course.'

Two palace servants who were crossing the salon arm in arm, striking the floor very noisily with their heels, burst into loud laughter. Walking noisily was, I suppose, one of the lessons in the new *Directions to Servants* by the Irish Protestant Jonathan Swift; farther away, moreover, I noticed other domestics con-scientiously breaking one of the feet on every chair. The Count had a baby face and protruding eyes. The sound of the servants' laughter made him uncontrollably angry; with his fist raised, he threw himself upon the two louts, who caught him from either side and neutralised him with a few punches. He came to rest on the floor, not far from the lady with the trunk. She went through the motions of tucking her skirt more tightly to her body, as though to emphasise the boundaries of her personal dignity, as well as the fact that the misadventures of the fallen Count were no concern of hers. The Count, though thoroughly battered and still lying there, could not stop talking. His face no longer displayed any kind of emotion, while his mouth continued to speak.

'Little Pierrot, the tenant farmer's son, a lad who has played with my children, managed to clamber up on to the footboard and break the carriage window. I know the child very well; why, I can't think of anyone I know better than young Pierrot, he's the one, little Pierrot's the one who on the anniversary of my birth date always comes and sings me a poem, made up by my villagers specially to please me, for they're clever people, y'know, they're not a bunch of boobies, not at all . . .'

The lady had shut her trunk. She stood up and tried to slip out through the door, but once again it was badly blocked with people. At first she tried to push her trunk along bit by bit. Faced with the negative result, she made no further attempt to push it and waited for the surge of movement to carry it through. But nothing was moving. Suddenly changing her strategy, she considered a window whose lower edge was level with a mezzanine a few stairs up. She withdrew from the group of people petitioning to leave by way of the door and asked me to help her jump out and then throw her trunk out to her. I drew open for her a panel of the honey-coloured curtains that hid the window, and she jumped. There was a crash, followed by tears.

They all wanted to tell their story and convince themselves that they really were still alive. From these tales I inferred that while there were some people who were arriving from far away, from big houses on country estates – and who had barely avoided perishing in burning buildings or being gutted by their farm people – many others were coming from no farther afield than Paris, or places even closer.

There was one woman who had only come from nearby Ville-d'Avray and had had the merest brush with danger, but because she spoke in a loud voice and was red-faced and voluminous, she nevertheless contrived to interest one and all in her epic narrative. She was the widow of a Farmer-General of Royal Taxes and, since the death of her husband, she had ceased to keep abreast of political events. Hence she had been stunned, on the morning of 14 July, when an express messenger had arrived from Paris and handed her a note to the effect that Paris was in the throes of upheaval and a troop of rebels had set out in the night to lay hands on her and her neighbour – Monsieur Thierry, the King's Personal Valet – and carry them forcibly away. Monsieur Thierry, who was a more plausible candidate than herself for being carried away, had taken to his heels without asking for details, so that she had found herself alone with her daughter. Agony! That's what she had endured, sheer agony! It was written right there on that paper: they intended to carry her off and burn her house down. Prompt action was called for. She had taken with her, besides her daughter, only one servant woman, and left all the other domestics where they were. The three women had started to bury the good plate, but finally, unequal to the task, had left orders with some of the servants to do it for them. ('You can imagine how well my instructions will be followed!') Agony! It had been nothing less than agony! The only money she had brought away was five thousand livres and a pocketbook of valuable papers . . . It wasn't much to manage on for several days; it was too much, if she started to think about robbers.

Well, now, the fact was that during the entire journey she had thought of nothing *but* robbers. When they reached Versailles, the torment had got to the limit of what a person could bear. For one thing, where were they supposed to sleep? Three women, including a fearfully squint-eyed servant . . . On the first night, that wretch of a Jeannon had led them to a hovel, and the next day, before vanishing into the blue, she had led them to a den of thieves. This was what things had come to. This was where that slattern of a Jeannon had taken them. Everything in that pigsty was on the side of the rebels: the camp beds, the filth, the bedbugs. Look, just look . . . She stuck out her chin – not, in her case, an attractive feature.

People were starting to wish they could interrupt her. But the stream of words resumed. In the course of the journey there had been a hundred moments when she was sure she was going to die. Every time she had encountered two or three country people in a group, or a merchant had doffed his hat to her, she was sure they were going to kill her. And she was still convinced it was so. Nothing could rid her mind of that notion: they were out to kill her.

'But the fact is they spared you. You did *not* die,' I said, because I did not care for the way this woman, in the throes of her 'agony', clung to me, squeezed my hands, and treated me in exactly the way one might mangle a handkerchief or twist one's dress in a fit of despair.

My observation was taken as a piece of insolence. The new arrivals, who throughout all her lamentations had shown no sympathy for the Farmer-General's widow, were suddenly in league with her. They loathed our view of the situation – it betrayed the attitude, in their eyes, of a privileged, protected group. *We* had stayed snug in the palace. *We* did not know what was happening out there. If proof were needed, it lay in our readiness to flee, to choose the attacks of highwaymen over the comfort of our indolent existence in the lap of luxury. Whereas *they* had seen how things were. *They* had the right to state an opinion. *We* were to keep our opinions to ourselves and help them. That was all they expected of us.

I said no more. The lady let go of my hands. Her daughter fanned her and settled her comfortably so she could give her full attention to the terrible adventure of a nobly born Rep-resentative. He began by expressing agreement with the lady's point of view. The roads were indeed dangerous and the pea-sants armed. The most frightful events, however, were taking place in the capital city, seat of the insurrection and source of the torrent of violence threatening the entire country. Unlike the lady, who was still extremely upset and had not stopped weep-ing and wailing, the Representative had initially shown a certain cool detachment, as though he were giving a well-prepared public speech. But with his very first words, his confidence deserted him. He could only stammer out a few phrases, to the effect that the populace had stopped the coach he had hired to come back from the Assembly. After that, everything had hap-pened very quickly: he had been taken to City Hall through a crowd of armed people. On the Place de la Grève, where criminals were executed, they had shown him the black-clad body of a decapitated man, and said: 'See that? That's Monsieur de Launay. What's left of Monsieur de Launay. Take a good look, because in a little while you'll be just like him.'

The man was shaking, speaking incoherently. The sabre that takes your head off in one sweeping blow, the hands tightening around your neck to strangle you, the rope being slipped over your head: to them, these things were tangible and concrete. They made it clear that they considered us soft, out of touch with reality. They were eager to tell their stories, partly to reassure themselves, and also to persuade us not to venture out, to stay where we were, safe. It was of no avail. The recital of all those horrors did not stop those about to flee from wanting to flee; nor did it even discourage the incomers from taking to the road again, later that night.

Panic was jubilant. She had us all in her power. She was manipulating us just as she liked. Once more, savagery was rising to the surface. Despite having been warned of what would happen to them out there, the departing palace dwellers were frantic to go.

Their behaviour no longer showed any consideration for rank, sex, or age. A snarling court dandy used his knee to block the path of a venerable old man. A haughty dowager found herself swept aside by a little Burgundian woman, screaming, but showing no inclination to turn around and go back: 'My parents were taken hostage and their female companion murdered before my very eyes.' A peer of the realm had the experience of being collared by a bourgeois nobody, who under normal circumstances would never have dared look him in the eye. All this was brought about partly by sheer numbers, but also, and especially, by the power of revelation that was driving the courtiers out from the palace with tremendous force, a reversal of the force of inertia which for years had kept them passionately chained to the place, unable to stay away.

The new arrivals had met horror, face-on. They could bear witness to the fact that, despite what some people were obstinately repeating, the insurrection had spread beyond the capital city; but unlike the terror-stricken crew of Versailles who were abandoning ship, they had not heard the mast snapping off or felt the deck slide out from under their feet to slope steeply down toward the abyss; they had not seen the waves part, upon the announcement that the King had sacrificed his armies and his government ministers, to swallow up centuries of dynasty.

That morning the court had surrendered once and for all. The defeat had become a fact; deep inside them, the deserters knew it was so. That defeat had released them from their code of honour and left them no recourse other than flight.

In the midst of so much disorder I had difficulty moving from one spot to another. The palace, as Monsieur de La Chesnaye was fond of pointing out, did not have an entrance worthy of its splendour. Just now, it would have been more relevant to say it did not have an exit . . .

There was the noisy sound of a window being opened. A woman wearing a high, fluted bonnet leaned out to hang a caged parrot from one of the shutters. The bird was shocked into silence.

People were abandoning birds in their cages; they were forgetting they had children; they were casting aside, so as not to add one more burden to their expedition, the little black slaves who carried Milady's parasol. These hapless youngsters would die of cold the following winter, and perhaps as they stood wide-eyed and motionless, they already apprehended their own fate. The dogs, too, could smell betrayal in the air and were barking as they do when death is present; they went dashing away down the corridors and surged in packs up the staircases.

My confusion of mind became worse and worse. People were telling me to leave. People were pleading with me to stay. I was hearing vivid descriptions of the carnage out there. I was being reminded that 'they' would soon be here. The gallop of a horse in the courtyard brought my heart into my mouth. The Queen, it was reported, had gone down to the Dauphin's apartments. She was obsessively anxious about him. This did imply, though, that she had managed to cross the Grand Gallery alone. Unless she had gone around it, which I was inclined to think she must have done. I was mistaken.

The Queen had once admitted to her friend 'you are the stronger' – but the opposite was now true.

I walked through the so-called Madame Sophie Library and went soundlessly into her lavender-blue room, the bathing room of her new apartment on the ground floor. I thought at first it was empty, for I did not immediately see the Queen, lying on the day bed. She was wrapped in a white satin dressing gown, under a canopy hung with midnight-blue. The bed was high, narrow, and angled towards windows looking on to the Marble Courtyard. To escape inquisitive eyes, the Queen had had a hedge of flowers planted in the courtyard, and a cherry tree as well. The windows were closed, but the curtains had been left open, for they were really not needed owing to the interlacing of foliage and flowers, which swayed outside and made a muffled sound as of stealthy footsteps.

The Queen was lying on her side. She had her back turned to me. She seemed huge, with very long legs tapering from broad hips to extraordinarily slender ankles. I thought this must be the first time I had seen her hips, for that part of the body is usually concealed by the fullness of a woman's skirts. And just as I tried not to breathe, on those occasions when I smelled her jasmine-scented hair salve, because that would have invaded her unimaginable privacy, so this time I tried not to look at her. I made a conscious effort to turn my eyes away from that alluring body stretched out in the blue-tinged half-light. I looked steadily at the window where dark shadows stirred. Then I brought my gaze back to her. She was not sleeping. With a fingertip, she was following the outline of swans and seashells decorating the wainscot. She was giving it her complete attention, just the way she had so often become utterly absorbed in contemplating her *Notebook of Ladies' Attire*. But now it was rather as though she were deciphering a new alphabet.

'Put your books down, madam; I have at my bedside what I wish to hear you read.'

She had turned over as she spoke and was pointing to a little table, where a bundle of letters lay stuffed into a pocketbook. An impression of strength and certainty emanated from the Queen. And though she lay quite still, I felt a strange sort of weightlessness and a spiralling movement bearing me upward. All fear of disturbing her privacy had vanished. I went and picked up the letters and handed them to her. She chose unhesitatingly. The letters were arranged in an order that she knew by heart. The Queen smiled at me. It was like being in the presence of a loving, peaceable giantess. I kissed her hand. She smiled at me again, a smile more kindly yet. The air was preternaturally light. I went to sit at a small table where four lit candles had been set. I began.

'Madame and dearest daughter, I spent the whole of yesterday more in France than in Austria, and went back in my mind over all the happy time that is now long past. Even to remember it is a consolation; I am very glad that your little girl, whom you describe as such a sweet child, is recovering her health, and glad also for all you have told me about how matters stand between you and the King. We must hope for a good outcome. I confess I did not know with certainty that . . .' (here I spoke more slowly, being unsure whether I ought to read *everything* aloud, but she urged me to do so) '. . . you and he did not sleep together; I suspected it. I can find no fault with what you tell me; it strikes me as perfectly valid, but I would have liked you to sleep German style, more on account of a certain intimacy that results from being together.

'I am very pleased that you intend resuming all the public ceremonial at Versailles: I know at first hand just how boring and meaningless these rituals are; but believe me, if they are not observed, the ill consequences that follow run much deeper than the little vexations of the ceremonial, especially where you are, in a nation so quick to take offence. Like you, I had very much hoped that winter would bring an end to the Emperor's travels; but he is fully occupied with preparations for journeying to the Netherlands in early March and remaining abroad all summer. These absences increase every year, and my worries and anxieties are increased as well, and at my age I could well do with support and consolation, and I am losing all those whom I love, one after another; I am sorely afflicted . . .'

The Queen had sat partly upright against the head of the bed, with that same wonderful suppleness and visible lengthening of herself. She repeated the words for her own benefit: 'I am losing all those whom I love, one after another . . . Vienna, 3 November 1780.'

These past few weeks, I had so often found her weeping and despondent that I expected to see her tears come. Instead, she remained perfectly in control of herself, even conveying a suggestion of some mysterious inner rapture. She leaned back, propping one shoulder against the blue wall with its motif of swans and seashells. And once again I was overwhelmed by the feeling I had experienced the very first time she had appeared before my wondering eyes: she mingled with the rest of us out of a kindly disposition and from goodness of heart; in reality, she belonged to a different order of magnitude and moved in a different sphere, that of the statues in the palace grounds and the goddesses emerging from the ornamental ponds. Long and white, with one hand pushing back her hair, she floated before my eyes. And her voice that drew me to her, a voice that asked me to be even closer to her, was repeating, softly but with no hesitancy:

'I am losing all those whom I love, and I am afflicted. But I shall not let my affliction get the better of me. I shall follow, in this as in all things, the example of my mother the Empress.' And she added, without any transition, as if she were just discovering the finish on her bathing-room walls and the repeating motif that decorated them: 'The King is very fond of swans, as I am.'

The next thing she asked me to read was not another letter

from Marie-Thérèse of Austria, but the 'Rule to Be Read Every Month' that her mother had given into her care when she left Vienna as a girl. She recited it from memory, keeping time with my reading, and she restored Austrian stresses to some of the words. Her voice no longer had the least trace of softness; harsh and aged, the voice was compelling because it was terrifying. I was maddened with fright. I clung to the table and did not finish reading the text. The flames rose very high. And in the shadows where the Queen was, I could no longer distinguish anything.

But that deep voice went on without me: 'You will take time to meditate as often as you can during the day, especially at Holy Mass. I trust you will hear Mass, and be edified by it, every day, and even more than once on holy days and Sundays, if that is the custom at your court. As much as I wish you to occupy your time with prayer and instructive reading, I would not by any means have you follow or seek to introduce practices other than what is customary in France; you must not make particular claims or cite as an example how things are done here, nor ask that our usages be imitated there; on the contrary, you must participate without reserve in whatever the Court is accustomed to do. Go, if possible, after dinner, and especially each Sunday, to Vespers and Evensong. I do not know whether the custom in France is to toll the angelus; but do not fail to meditate at that time, if not in public, at least in your heart. The same holds for the evening period or whenever your steps take you past a church or a cross, without, however, performing any outward action but those in common use. That need not prevent your heart from retiring within itself and offering inward prayers, God's presence being the sole means to that end on every occasion; your matchless father possessed this ability to perfection. When entering churches, let yourself in the first instance be filled with the greatest respect and do not give way to your curiosity, which causes the mind to be distracted. All eyes will be upon you, so do nothing that may give rise to rumour or be grounds for scandal. Be pious, respectful, unassuming and submissive. But most of all, pious. Lastly, let me say, to sum up, and in the sure knowledge that if you do not stray from this admonition, nothing regrettable will come to pass: as much as you can, my dear daughter, be on your knees, at prayer . . .'

And then, her ordinary speaking tones – 'Come now, it is time they dressed me' – dispelled the command bridging the centuries: a mother's voice, a dead person's voice that never falters. I cannot say the voice disappeared; I knew it was there now and for always, but it would never again make itself heard.

'I must assemble my good friends the de Polignac family and impress on them the necessity to leave. Their kind hearts will not let them obey. As for you, Madame Laborde, I have a request to make of you as well, and I hope that in the kindness of *your* heart you will not demur. If I remember rightly, you assured me the day before yesterday that you would journey far, very far, to please me. Well, this is not the time to go back on your word. Make the journey; leave this place. You will be included in the escape of the Duke and Duchess de Polignac. And as the Duchess is unfortunately too famous and is wrongly held in disrepute, I must beg you to don her clothing and occupy her seat in the carriage. She, in turn, will disguise herself as a townswoman, a simple lady companion or even a servant. What matters is either that she should pass unnoticed; or, if by mischance your group were stopped by men of the National Guard, that Madame de Polignac should escape with her life.'

It was almost nine o'clock in the evening. I had barely time to fetch a few things before the darkness swallowed me up.

People were fleeing; others were arriving. The ones arriving bore the marks of insults and blows on their countenances. There was a great difference between terror at the prospect of a hostile attack and actually casting oneself into the enemy's clutches.

I went back to my room. I wanted to take with me the things I cared most deeply about. But as I looked around, misty-eyed, at what had been the setting for my personal life through all those years, everything in it seemed to me equally precious. I could not save the little white marble vase unless I also took the straw-yellow paper background against which my successive bouquets of flowers had been shown to advantage. I wanted the mirror, because it was the first one I had owned and I had never gone to stand in front of it without feeling a shiver of sinfulness. I wanted the embroidered bedspread that had been with me since boarding-school days, so worn in places as to be transparent.

Lastly, or rather firstly, I wanted to keep my room.

My Bedroom of the Perfect Sleep.

My private Office of the Setting and the Rising Sun.

At once my Library and my Bathing Room.

My Boudoir of Conversations.

My white-and-rainbow-coloured room. My room.

I had been so taken with it that on certain evenings, I had actually preferred it to the finest shows on the stage of the palace Opera House. In my room, I could be delightfully relaxed. There I prepared my readings for the Queen, I read, I dreamed, I recited my lists. Through its attic window, I followed the metamorphoses of the clouds. Within its walls, precisely because the space was so constricted, I felt safe, out of reach. This contentment had saved me from the frenzy of moving out that had the courtiers running distractedly here and there.

I liked to hear, from where I lay still asleep in my bed, the thump of pitchers being set down in the hallways, the sound of army drills out in the courtyard.

I also liked, when only half awake, to pick up a book, read a few pages, and fall back asleep. Often it was Honorine who came and woke me up. We would start our day by laughing, before we spoke.

My bedspread was frayed and threadbare, reflecting the volume of sleep it had known in my company. It was imprinted, but invisibly to other eyes than mine, with the thousand and one outlines of my world of dreams.

I would not leave my bedspread behind. Not the bedspread, and not the candlestick . . .

What about my books? I started by filling my velvet bag with books, but that made it heavy and there was no room left for clothes. I lifted the bag to test its weight. I hesitated. I was well aware that for this scrambling journey on which the Queen was dispatching me, my presence had to be weightless. I abandoned the books. I took only a few pieces of clothing that I rolled up in a shawl.

Into my bag I put two hats, slippers and a pair of ankle boots. I would find whatever else I needed when we got there.

Got where?

I went to say goodbye to Jacob-Nicolas Moreau. He opened his door to me, with the air of someone whose mind is not entirely on what he is doing. Convinced of the greatness and gravity of his task, he had been working unremittingly at his discourse.

'Oh, my dear friend!' was all I could say. And I dissolved in tears.

He took me in his arms. I could not find the words to explain why I was leaving. I was not fleeing on account of fear but from a sense of duty. I was simply obeying. But even at the time, I was being pulled in two directions, I was torn. I could have and I should have avoided receiving such an order, or found some way not to comply. Moreover, since what I was being asked to do was to take someone else's place and pass myself off as that other person, my role was interchangeable. It did not matter a great deal whether it was me . . . I was being too quick to obey, I ought to have stopped for a moment's reflection. But I was beyond the point of rational reflection, I was being carried along at a speed and by passions that were foreign to me . . . Instead of admitting to my scruples, I preferred to enquire about the 'Pastoral Letter to the Bishops of France'.

'I have reread what I have written, and without being as enthusiastic as you are, I must admit that I am not entirely dissatisfied. The flow of my periods shows a sense of style, the expositions are forcefully developed, and overall, these few pages are infused with genuine fervour. To be quite exact, these *two* pages. There lies the problem. And I must confess to you that I am extremely worried. I have very little time in which to carry out this mission. I have been working too hard. The seventh volume of my *History of France* has left me worn out. My pen, these days, is soon wearied. Can the pace be sustained? My pen will need to be swift and its arguments unanswerable. It must take the brigands and their propaganda unawares. The hour is early still, and I have a long night's work ahead of me and a good supply of candles, but I am beginning to lack for energy. My pen wants rest.'

'Then give it some rest, and tomorrow . . .'

'Ah! Tomorrow! But what will tomorrow bring, Agathe, my dear? Where will you be?'

With my heavy shawl and my bedspread in one hand, my bulging velvet bag in the other, I stopped short, taken aback by the question. I tried once more to picture the world outside Versailles. No picture formed in my mind.

Versailles was my life. And as with my life, I had never really imagined what its last day might be. Or even that there would be a last day, with a morning, an afternoon, an evening, and then a night with nothing on the other side – nothing familiar, at any rate.

Flight; I am frightened in the underground
passages; the message received by mistake:
10 p.m. to midnight

'It is true, and for this we give thanks to Divine Providence:
among the inhabitants of our Kingdom, only a minority have
joined the band of rebels. Those who have not stifled the cry of
conscience, and who sense the full importance of maintaining
order and respecting authority, would blush to join a revolt
whose instigators are behaving as criminally towards God as
towards men.' Hurrying along to the apartments of Diane de
Polignac, I continued to recite the last words of the 'Pastoral
Letter' over and over again – it was a way of staying with my
good friend a little longer, keeping up my fortitude, and warding
off the evil spirit of Diane. Diane called God 'the Great Juggler'
and connived with him in feats of skill and acrobatics. She was
always finding new stunts to perform and made no distinction
between juggling and magic tricks: a ball she threw in the air
might take wing and fly away as a dove.

At Versailles, even in normal times, people were afraid of
Diane. I had caught sight of her, prowling around, throughout
a whole stretch of the night. Her public declarations of fidelity to
King and Crown, her admonitions, when compared to the petti-
ness of my own thoughts, had filled me with shame. Then she
had vanished and no more had been seen of her during the day.
But I had not found it very difficult to guess at Diane's true
preoccupation, behind this public display. It certainly did not
involve altruism, nor the slightest hint of noble sentiment. Contrary to what she would have had us believe, the safety of the
royal family was not a consideration for her. In fact, by the night
of 14 July, she must already have been planning to flee. Her fine
speech was intended to avert a general migration: if she was to

225

obtain the Queen's full support, it was in Diane's interest that her departure be an exception – unless, of course, she had been acting out the little sacrifice scene for the sheer pleasure of deceiving others. Diane was guided by a single principle: do whatever was best for herself. She served just one cause: her own; but she served that cause with rare talent and rapacity. And now, suddenly, I found myself in the same boat as that monster. I was supposed to save myself from being shipwrecked, by embarking on her disreputable little tub.

The large salon that I entered was a scene of feverish activity; but where the palace presented at every turn the image of total disorder, headlong flight or chaotic gatherings, here one had the impression that the people present had *not* been taken by surprise, that they were prepared, so to speak, for any eventuality, including this one.

Six or seven people were gathered there. Diane's usual headquarters staff: Count de Vaudreuil, the Duke de Polignac, the Duke de Coigny, and Father Cornu de La Balivière, Almoner in Ordinary to the King, who had become a member of this tight little circle through his passion for gaming. There was also Gabrielle de Polignac. She lay on a sofa, listless, her face hidden by a fan. At her side, her daughter Madame de Gramont was looking sadly at a newborn son from whom she would have to be parted. For the observer with a complete view of this *tableau vivant*, Gabrielle de Polignac and her daughter represented an enclave of inertia and melancholy, in stark contrast to the other characters, at whose centre stood Diane, very much in command.

'I would rather die here and now than end up in a watering resort!'

Peremptory as always, Diane de Polignac leaned slightly back and crossed her arms. Her hard features, the authoritarian attitude, that uncivil manner of speaking . . . I could only shrink timidly back. Her short hands with their stubby fingers were like parts of a machine for distributing slaps in the face. She was very liberal with these, and if her domestic staff thought twice before approaching her, it was from fear, not respect. They handed things to her at arm's length, while turning their bodies away a little, ready to dodge. Their vigilance did not prevent those twin paddles from coming down on them with terrible precision and violence, leaving them bruised and convinced that the blows emanated from a diabolical power. There was something of that sort in her nature.

'Spa!' yelped Diane. 'You want to send us to Spa! There is nothing so mortifying as staying in a watering resort. Those places smell of mildew and rotten egg. You are at the mercy of a lot of beastly doctors. There are some I know who have no compunctions about undressing you.'

Count de Vaudreuil sniggered. Along with the Duke de Polignac, he was examining several habits cut from dark cloth, such as merchants wear. The priest, standing at a billiard table and concentrating on his shot, was at the same time considering the matter of desirable destinations. The suggestion of a watering resort must have come from him.

'I shall not leave Versailles, where it is not the custom to thwart my wishes, in order to fall under the jurisdiction of a bunch of doctors. I shall no more go to Spa than to Plombières or Vichy. The only people to be met with at such places are fools who think they are dying. They persecute one with the account of their physiological disorders. They can age you ten years in the space of an hour. They have no conversation and to be regularly in their company is quite intolerable.'

'And yet I remember a stay at Bath . . .' protested the Duke de Guiche.

'Be quiet, Mimi. I was referring to the danger posed by doctors and by doctors' clients who fancy themselves ill, to say nothing of how disagreeable it is to be surrounded by whores and adventurers. The most vulgar members of society pullulate in towns where people come to take the waters. Not to mention the waters themselves, which are poisonous. In short, Reverend Father, Spa is out.'

The priest bowed. He was a fine-looking man in the prime of life. A great hunter and unrepentant gambler, he had been known to rise from the gaming table and go directly to the altar where he said early Mass. Parishioners taking Holy Communion, and watching him dexterously manipulate the host, had complained that it was like watching a player cut a deck of cards.

'The precise destination does not matter a damn. What matters is getting well away from here. Putting a frontier between the cannibals and us. Any frontier. If need be, we will throw them a bone so they will have something to get their teeth into.'

I shivered inwardly; and the uneasiness I felt, at casting my lot in with this godless, lawless band, became more pronounced.

'I have attended to the basic problem, finding a carriage and horses. Now we must think how we are to be dressed. Let us bear in mind that, even if Gabrielle is the person most threatened, we are all in danger.'

Diane went and sat in an armchair, which she filled as though it were a throne. Being accustomed to organising the daily activities of her family and associates, she had no difficulty organising their exile. All at once, there were sounds of banging from a nearby apartment, accompanied by calls for help.

'Go and see,' ordered Diane. In the past – she did not yet fully understand that it was indeed past – she had only to toss out an order, casually, and there would always be someone to do her bidding. But this time no one budged. The command had dissolved into the air, and the din, whatever its source, got louder. Diane dropped the papers she was busy examining, looked around, saw only relatives, people of her own blood and rank, people whose lives she was in the habit of running but whom one did not order to 'go and see'. Then she spied me, in a corner, clutching my bundle. 'Oh. Would you be so good, Madam . . .'

I let the noise guide me. When I reached the door that was being pierced with cries and pounded till it shook, I heard: 'Rondon de La Tour, you damned useless count! Let me out of here, for God's sake! It's me, La Joie, your valet. You forgot me, you bastard! You take off and leave your drudge behind, just like that. Here I am, sweating over the *Horoscope Set at Naught*. I'm churning out lines of Alexandrine poetry. I'm slaving away. I'm knocking myself out:

O lady, 'twas in vain that once I courted you,
And told you of my love, and spoke as lovers do.
My loins once yearned for you, though this I durst not tell,
And thought by subtle means to let you know full well.
Alas, my feeble cries, you, lady, chose to spurn;
My incense and my heart alike you left to burn.
But time has wrought its change; a maid you are no more,
Yet fresh and fit for love, and lovely as before.

'Beautiful, hey? Hey? HEY?' (He was throwing his full weight into it.) 'Could *you* have written that? Not bloody likely! NO! NO! NO! And yet it's by you. It'll be written by you. You just have to sign it and they'll all say Rondon de La Tour has just dished us up a real little masterpiece. The *Horoscope Set at Naught* is a monument of the literary art. Listen, Rondon, you whore-monger, you've let me down. You degenerate son-of-a-bitch. Why d'you disappear like that, you pox-ridden count? Of course I'll give you a good thrashing when you come to let me loose, but that's not why you bolted. Something really horrible is going on . . . There's a scary silence in the miserable rooms around here. As if the wardens have had their throats cut or something. Help! Help!' The door gave way. And under it, carried by his own impetus, Count Rondon's personal valet came crashing down. He was silent at last, for the table to which he was chained had fallen on him.

Diane gave the incident not one second of her attention, and the members of her entourage were equally unconcerned. Mean-while, Switzerland had been settled upon as the destination. As always happened when there was a serious decision involved, Diane de Polignac's strategic intelligence and practical common sense had infected her clan. Every member was busily occupied with the departure. The priest was digging around in a trunk: I can remember that red trunk in great detail, sitting directly beneath a portrait of Madame Adélaïde as a very young woman – Louis XV's daughter was posed for the artist in full court dress.

Diane had donned a man's costume, something a townsman would wear, dark-coloured, and perfectly moulded to her squat figure. I looked curiously at the calves of her legs, heavily muscled, their vigorous curves showing clearly under the cotton stockings. She took my glance for one of admiration and gave me in return one of those quick, brilliant smiles that she could produce at will, smiles that, coupled with her intelligence, were the key to her ascendancy over other people. That male costume restored her to her true nature. The dress, which lay where it had fallen at her feet, became a garment that had given her an assumed identity. She pushed it away with the toe of her boot. And I said to myself that in her head she had already treated Versailles the same way she was treating the dress; that in the few moments it took to have her stays unlaced, she had thrown all the years of her life at the Court of France into the dustbin. Which is why she was striding impatiently up and down in the large salon of her apartment, now transformed into an actor's dressing room in which the members of her company, unwilling candidates for exile, were fussing around.

Monsieur de Vaudreuil was gloomily contemplating the cloak in which he would be required to muffle himself. 'Paris mud, the latest shade,' he joked. 'Well, if they are hounding us out of the country, at least we can say we were sporting their colours.' Monsieur de Polignac, his fingers caught in the embroidery around the buttonholes on his waistcoat, was in no mood for laughter. With one violent tug, he snapped the silk cords. 'What now?' he asked, ridding himself of the waistcoat and pointing to an ornate lace shirt.

'That's not a shirt a merchant would wear,' said Diane de Polignac, exasperated by the blunder. Alone of the group, she could hear the approaching footsteps of a populace crying out for vengeance. She alone was truly persuaded that the pamphlets did not lie.

Alongside their fear, intensified by lack of experience, the Polignac clan also felt the sort of excitement that was generated by rehearsing a play. Father de La Balivière also wanted to wear a disguise. He suggested he might travel as a nun.

'Very suitable,' remarked Diane.

Monsieur de Vaudreuil had bared his pale torso, with its sunken chest; perched on high-heeled shoes, he was strutting back and forth in front of a mirror, trying to coax Diane into the performance, pulling her by the hand. Then he went down on his knees before her, as one expressing adoration.

'You're impossible,' she said, but she was tempted.

He stood up and whispered a few words to Father de La Balivière, who went away and came back with bottles of champagne. The foam spurted out and splashed over us. The priest's cassock was soaked. Goblets were produced. 'A celebration of the restoration of the goddess Fortune,' proclaimed Monsieur de Vaudreuil. In the twinkling of an eye he had donned his merchant costume, but he had rouged his pockmarked cheeks and placed a wolf-mask over his eyes.

'Let us honour the goddess Fortune; it is critically important that we do so. The goddess is not to be trifled with.' They were recovering a certain gaiety of spirit, and I could read in the faces and gestures of those three men the same desire to laugh, to touch, to reveal, as well as the regret that at once ensued whenever they recalled their need to put all that sort of thing aside and depart. But each time, the desire resurfaced to act out just one more comedy, just for a few minutes, just so they could laugh.

A table was dragged into the middle of the room to serve as a stage. They covered it with a red carpet. They tried to take Diane's throne from her, but she brandished her sword at them. They settled for a less imposing armchair, which was placed onstage. Gabrielle de Polignac sat down in it, partly recumbent, her arms on the elbow rests, her head thrown back. Facing her, Destiny, Monsieur de Vaudreuil, took up her position. The actor was smiling. Fortune, Gabrielle de Polignac, was gradually supposed to revive – while Adversity, Father de La Balivière, already stooped and bent when the scene opened, caught between Destiny and Fortune, became progressively more sickly, shook with spasms, and finally stretched out stiff and stark on the ground. Standing upright once more, ready to step over the body of Adversity, whose smile was trying so hard to be triumphant that it was starting to look downright nasty, Gabrielle moved like a sleepwalker. Fuddled by champagne, she continued to hold out her goblet and others continued to fill it up for her. Leaning her head on Destiny's chest, she said: 'What is the news? Why must there always be new news?'

Encouraged by Destiny, Gabrielle de Polignac was pitting her nonchalance against Occurrence. Monsieur de Vaudreuil, musing over the absence of Renown, was winding one of his curls around his finger. At that moment the Queen came into the room. We did not have to look at her to know her reaction. Before she had opened her mouth to speak, the enormity of her pain and condemnation smote us like a blow.

'Please, do not stop. It makes a touching scene. Both of you are playing it to perfection.'

It was not so much what she was saying that turned us to stone as the fact that she had entered without being announced. Stunned, incredulous, we stood there looking at her. Diane was the first to collect her wits. Leaving the stage, Gabrielle ran across the room to cast herself at the Queen's feet.

The Queen was moved. She said, speaking clearly but very gently: 'Your departure must be thought of. I am sure it will be only temporary. Soon you will come back to me, but for the moment, I beg of you, make haste.'

The Queen bent down to Gabrielle and raised her to her feet. 'Let me help you, madam.' In a deathly silence, she removed her friend's pale-green dress with her own hands, began to slip a petticoat over Gabrielle's head, and even tried to pull stockings on to the other woman's legs. She was the one on her knees now, at Gabrielle's feet. Her face was firm and resolute. She was driven by a kind of energy and precision born of despair. Gabrielle, all white-faced and unresisting, with the fragile nakedness of a little girl, wept soundlessly.

The Queen, with the impulse for perfection that took hold of her the moment clothing was involved, had reached the stage of covering her friend's shoulders with a fichu, when a thunderous voice announced the arrival of the King. It was the same voice that had shouted: 'Gentlemen, the King,' when the Royal Council emerged from its meeting. The voice's owner must have been replacing the regular Usher. We were profuse with our curtseys and bows. By the time we had done with our reverences, the King was in the middle of the room, holding several passports in his hand, which he proffered to Gabrielle de Polignac. But she, unaware, confused, swept away by the force of a newly discovered grief, did not see them, could not see anything. Her eyes were swimming with tears; tears were streaming down her cheeks, to be lost in dark stains on the garnet-coloured fichu. And the Queen, facing her, still wore that statuesque expression – an expression verging on the non-human, or human only in the intensity of the eyes, as they concentrated on seeing, so as never to forget, the person she was about to lose.

The King's presence had at once been subordinated to the Queen's, as was usual whenever he shared a physical space with her. Whether in love or in fright, she was the person he turned to for all his needs. This meant that any gestures or words of his, intended for other people, were completely robbed of their value. So it was that when he held out the passports, he did so with genuine emotion, but his feelings did not extend beyond the range expected on an official occasion. Since Gabrielle de

Polignac failed to react, the King, uncertain of himself, turned to her husband. The Duke de Polignac was appropriately responsive and lavish with words of thanks. The polite duet of courteous phrases was duly sung.

Meanwhile, Diane had quickly seized the passports and the bills of exchange. Overlooked in my corner, I put on the dress, a very elegant one, that was to disguise me as a person of rank. At that moment a clamour, so violent that it seemed to be rising from very close by, split the air. It was a shout, a howl; we were transfixed. Taken completely aback, we looked at each other. The clamour grew even louder, ungoverned, mighty. The King, vainly seeking a courteous phrase in response to one from the Duke de Polignac, said simply: 'It's the Representatives. They have just been apprised of my orders summoning Necker back. Tomorrow I shall go to Paris.'

The King said no more and remained with his head slightly bent, in a protective stance that he often adopted. The Queen stood beside him. She was looking steadily at us. Suddenly she shivered, turned very pale, and said: 'Come. It is past the time.' The King gave us his blessing, while she, turning so she almost faced a window, so that she was silhouetted clearly against the leafy shade of the gardens, said in a harsh voice, oddly jarred by an accent long since buried: 'Adieu. I bring bad luck to those I love.'

Scarcely had we left the Gallery, along corridors we had trodden many a time ('Noailles Street', people called it), than, after a few routinely used detours, we lost our way. 'My name is Daedalus, builder of mazes,' jeered Monsieur de Vaudreuil, but the desire to play-act was gone. During the course of that day, the palace had lost its familiar appearance, as, bit by bit, it was emptied of the characters who peopled it and cut off from the rituals and routines that gave it life. True, it was no less impressive than before, but it was no longer a miracle of luxury and refinement, nor the grandiose spectacle that had captivated me from the first moment and of which I myself was a part – something I came to understand later, from the lightness of my body and the weightlessness of my footsteps. Now, the palace was impressive as the empty shell left by a disastrous occurrence. Of course, we were making some attempt at caution. We hugged the walls. We took care not to bump into furniture, not to knock over vases or statues. We spoke in low voices, and then only to pass vital information. The map we had available was of the underground passages. Reaching the entrance to them did not, so it had seemed to us, pose much of a problem. This confidence was a little shaken by our first mistake, which took us into a dark corridor leading nowhere. But Monsieur de Vaudreuil was so quick to change direction that the mistake passed almost unnoticed. We were proceeding in such a tight group, stepping so furtively, so hurriedly, that we were bound to awaken at least some distrust in anyone that chanced to be coming the other way.

At the same time, though, the general bearing of the group was dignified. Spontaneously, with a reflex conditioned by the unwritten rule that you never assumed you were safe from observation at Versailles, the clan had been prepared to make a brave show from the moment they stepped out of the apartment into the beginnings of danger. Gabrielle de Polignac, still lost in her grief, had run a hand through her hair. She was reluctant to be seen in servant's garb. Diane had stood more erect. I could sense, there in the dark, her eagerness to receive the marks of deference to which she was accustomed. Through the length and breadth of the country, their names were cursed; there was a price on their heads; they were fleeing an imminent and deadly peril. But at this moment, they were still sustained by their pride as courtiers, pride bolstered by the nearness of rooms and physical objects that had reflected their glory for so long. They did not require lighting to recognise that glory: all these great rooms singing the praises of Louis XIV and his victories had served as a setting for their own triumphs, too. How could they be expected, overnight, to stop thinking of themselves as masters of the world? Surely there was still opportunity for scheming and intrigue. They were still the lords and masters, even if, simply as a concession, they had decided to abandon their stronghold. They were increasingly convinced that such a view was correct. It almost made running away a clever piece of strategy on their part.

For the moment, however, minutes counted, and Monsieur de Vaudreuil was now hopelessly lost. The Duke de Polignac was no help. The group was becoming discouraged. All trace of courtly pride was gone from their demeanour. They were deserters running across open ground in enemy territory. 'Where *is* that wretched exit?' exclaimed Diane. She took the situation in hand. We must split up and leave the palace individually. She told us more than once where we were to meet, and each of us faded away out of sight of the others.

Before I had time to understand how I came to be there, I was in an underground passage. A vague, pale light made it just possible for me to creep along. Blocks of stone jutted out from the walls, and several times I narrowly avoided knocking myself unconscious. Very quickly, it became difficult to breathe. Something cold and clammy floated in the air and made your heart want to stop. But what was especially horrible was the swarms of rats running between my legs. 'Watch out for patrolling guards with their dogs,' Diane had said as she sent me down below ground level. Inwardly, I was praying to meet such a patrol. Let them arrest me, let them do anything to me, so long as they saved me from the rats.

I had instructions, but I did not follow them correctly, and instead of fetching up, as I expected to do, level with a private entrance to the Théâtre de Madame de Montansier, I came out of the passage into a stable. Someone else was already there.

I stayed hidden in the shadows. I could make out two men having some sort of confrontation. They had raced simultaneously over to where a horse was tethered. It was a fine-looking animal, with a gleaming coat. Fidgety and nervous, it was pawing the ground and lashing out with its feet. The two men were quite dissimilar. One, in court dress, was making a great effort to control his impatience. He was prepared to negotiate. He wanted the horse, certainly, but he wanted it legitimately. The other, massively built, wrapped in a black cloak, with a hat pulled down over his eyes, was not saying a word.

'Sir,' argued the man in silken raiment, 'I have no doubt that it was I who saw him first. Not by much, I grant you. And yet, that lead, those few seconds, in the present situation, a very confused, disagreeable situation, I will allow, should weigh with you.'

No reply came from the man wrapped in black. He reacted no more than would a gatepost with a blanket over it. The eloquent one, all frills and furbelows, and obviously dressed for some special occasion, was determined to convince his rival that he was in the right. He was not a horse thief.

'I do not know how it comes about that my coach, which I left in the Cour du Louvre, has vanished into thin air: I absolutely must return home and I am ill-equipped to do so unless I have this horse. I was to meet Baron de Breteuil, an old friend, a man whose punctuality . . .'

The looming hulk exploded into action. The hand that the man in black was keeping out of sight under his cloak suddenly appeared, wielding a club, and delivered a blow. I heard a sickening sound. The courteous man had crumpled, his head smashed to a pulp.

I was, it turned out, very close to our appointed meeting place. When I arrived, my companions and two six-horse *berlinesr* were waiting. The Countess de Polastron, the Marchioness de Poulpry, and the Marchioness de Lage de Volude had joined the group. The planned escape included them. There was the occasional renewed outburst of shouting to mark the recall of Necker.

'Good,' someone said. 'They are busy being enthusiastic and they'll be that much less vigilant.'

Monsieur de Vaudreuil left us. He was to depart with the

Count d'Artois, another man fleeing in the dead of night, as well as the Duke de Bourbon, the Princes de Condé and de Conti, the Castries, the Coignys, the Prince d'Hénin, Count de Grailly, and all the members of the government. I felt stiff and awkward in my aristocratic attire. I was unpleasantly thirsty: my mouth felt dry and bitter, my throat was like cardboard. I ventured to ask for something to drink. 'Later,' answered Diane, and herded us into one of the carriages. She herself climbed up onto the driver's seat, beside the coachman. I had seen him only from behind, but the word 'Maybe,' uttered in a kind of belch, dispelled any lingering doubt: it was Füchs.

Gabrielle and her daughter sat on bracket seats. Monsieur de Polignac and the priest ensconced themselves at the back, with packages on their knees and at their feet. I took the seat that was due to my station, according to the role I had been assigned to play. I settled in by a window. As the carriage began to move, I thought I could hear, during a momentary lull, between bursts of distant shouting over Necker, a snatch of litany being howled . . . *Marie-Amélie, Marie-Anne, Marie-Caroline, Marie-Antoinette, my Queen* . . . the names came floating toward us, distorted, propelled by the raucous voice of Monsieur de Castelnaux, that pathetic voice compounded of love and madness.

Monsieur de Polignac produced a pistol: 'If I catch sight of that fellow, I shall shoot him dead.'

It was not till we had gone a considerable distance farther, and fear of pursuit held all of us silent and tense, that we were overtaken by a horseman travelling at a gallop. The window was partly open. I was about to close it when, without even slackening his pace, the man threw a small roll of something, which I caught in my hand. It was a message, on a single sheet of paper with a gold ring around it. I slid the ring off, and read:

'O most loving of friends, adieu. A dreadful word, adieu, but it cannot be helped. I have only strength enough to send you this kiss. Marie-Antoinette.'

I held the missive out to Gabrielle de Polignac, sitting very small in front of me, her silent tears flowing in a frighteningly steady stream – as though from some external wellspring that had got lodged inside her, with which she would have to live from this day forth.

Vienna, January 1811

I can remember our joy at the moment when we crossed the Swiss border. We were saved. *They* were on the other side. They could no longer harm us. We all hugged and kissed. The German regiment that had escorted us for the last several hours went on its way. Its soldiers did not know why they had come to France, and likewise did not know why they were leaving again – a strange expedition, with no combat and no enemy . . .

And what about me; did *I* know what I was doing there? We had barely done with our hugging and our cries of joy when I began to see everything as from a great distance. I saw the exhausted horses trembling where they stood in a glow of sweat; our carriage, grotesquely overladen with baggage; and little people who had got down from it and were running excitedly back and forth. They were going from one to another, exchanging fervent embraces. From my remote vantage point, their movements looked incoherent and unintelligible. Füchs had not stirred from his seat: 'Maybe' . . . Round about us were only meadows: very green, beautiful, lush; just like the ones around the Menagerie, indeed, except for the silence and the empty space. The sky was grey, almost white. I had crossed the border, the one separating life from empty space.

The Polignacs were using as a guide the directions shown in their letters of exchange. The needle of their compass pointed steadily in one direction: money. The driving force of our era, as Diane often said. She liked the era that was just beginning at least as much as she did the previous one – probably more, for the new era was following a vibrant course and its horizons were vast. A world at war suited Diane's temperament. To me, upheaval and void are synonymous, and killing makes a rather bland ingredient for adding spice to life, which is why those who start cannot stop.

We crossed Switzerland, then sojourned in Italy – in Rome – because it was convenient. It was a floating kind of existence. We did not really alight in these chance sanctuaries. We set up improvised camps in disused palaces. With Diane in our midst and thanks to her genius for expediency, exile took on the appearance of a refinement to the art of gracious living. Her trials had made her even more authoritarian – and more vicious – and given her a breadth of view that enabled her, even as she pondered a treatise by D'Alembert, to obtain subsidies from the Pope, the King of England, and the Emperor of Austria. At her side fluttered the Duke de Polignac and Count de Vaudreuil.

Meanwhile, Gabrielle wept. It was tacitly understood that this was an affectation: elegant, no doubt, but rather wearying over time. I shared that opinion. Moreover, I myself was so sad that the sadness of another, even if it was Gabrielle de Polignac, had no power to move me. I read constantly and only for my own benefit. The unending, silent monologue of words from so many diverse stories was all it took to convince me that I myself did not have a story. Lost in this state of non-existence, I did not even attempt to understand why we left Rome for Vienna, where we have remained. But once we were in Vienna, the bond implied in 'we' came undone. The Prince de Ligne took me under his protection; I ceased to be dependent on the Polignacs. It came as a relief. I continued to see them, but on a basis of social visits, no longer as their client.

For the first time in many years – since the time when I lived at Versailles, in fact – I am finding winter beneficial. The cold, outdoors, is fierce. The city, the ruins of the city, are frozen into a solid block. The branches of the trees, coated in a layer of ice, sparkle with the slightest ray of sunlight. 'The city is shining,' a neighbour says to me. And she repeats, wonderingly, 'Der Frost'. 'I'll go and look,' I tell her, though I am quite convinced I will not feel able to do so. But that does not bother me. I'm very comfortable where I am. I lack for nothing. With all the curtains drawn, my fire lit, and blankets and eiderdowns heaped up over me, I lie perfectly still. There is only my hand moving smoothly over the page; that and, set against a background of pale flames, a succession of scenes, in the present – all equally in the present.

I have described things in an orderly manner where order there was none. I have introduced logical sequence into events I was obsessed with, whereas the memories came at me in an avalanche, chaotic and devastating. I have acted as though the calendar was right. As of course it is, even if I find that terribly painful to admit.

Branches snap off under the weight of their coating of ice. The forests are torn apart. Great cracks appear in the walls. In the houses, no fire is adequate to warm the air. Even people with fireplaces big enough to sleep in are no better off than their neighbours. When I breathe out, a mist escapes from my lips; and to warm my hands, I have to bury them in the bedcovers until they are ready to resume their insect-like progress across the page.

We are into January. Soon it will be time for the Queen's grand ceremonial balls, as the Prince de Ligne never fails to remind us . . . The Queen's grand ceremonial balls . . . It is difficult, after all these years, to appreciate the importance of that event, the magic of those words. That it would soon be time for the Queen's grand formal balls was palpable weeks ahead. Everyone was conscious of it; the entire population of the palace was in a state of commotion, even the numerous individuals who were not involved. The moil and toil of preparations could be inferred partly from the increased number of earnest consultations, but it was also marked by the frenetic coming and going of the child pageboys. They hurried from one apartment to another, carrying messages back and forth, enchanted to be their young selves in their short perukes and their official attire with the shiny ornaments. From their little, round, mocking faces came the perfume of unfettered joy, associated in my mind with essence of lilac, the preferred scent of the Queen's pages. Her pageboys, moreover, were always the ones most in evidence. They were everywhere to be seen, in their red velvet livery with the gold braid. Laughing, quick-moving, they slipped through the crowd. To them, everything was a game. They had transformed the ban on running into a source of amusement, devising a special gait which alternated one ordinary step with two gliding steps. Depending on the urgency of the message, the waxiness of the floor, and the lesser or greater press of people, this gliding step, which was easily lengthened, could take them across a salon in one continuous movement . . . The child pageboys plied the waters of Versailles in every direction, confident of the ship that bore them, unaware of the vast ocean surrounding us. Whether delivering a love-letter or a notification of exile, they brought the same joy to their task.

One image continues to symbolise for me how happy those child pageboys were, how actively aware of their good fortune. *They* had access to the Queen's formal balls, where they were wonderfully apt at presenting sorbets or escorting the ladies back to their chairs. As I, on the other hand, was not eligible to attend, and as I loved oranges more than anything, young de Bigny would arrange to meet me by the ballroom doors at dawn, bringing me a supply of the splendid fruit. He kept his promise, but I would regularly find him asleep on the steps, the pockets of his page's habit bulging to bursting point. I would carefully take the oranges and put them in my bag, then voluptuously peel one and bite into it on my way over to the Great Hall for my cup of coffee. Here and there, in carriages left standing for the night, I would see couples intertwined.

Other signs, too, heralded the approach of the Grand Balls. Dressmaker Rose Bertin would have daily appointments with Marie-Antoinette. They worked together and their collaborative efforts were soon embodied in marvellous dresses. Without being able to observe the dresses in detail, one could form an impression of how they would look, from seeing them through the wide strips of taffeta that covered them. The taffeta gave them the appearance of ghosts, or lost human shapes hunting for the magic spell that would give them back their stolen lives. The Queen's new dresses, which were not officially supposed to be shown until the balls for which they had been created, travelled in that veiled manner, at all hours, through corridors, boudoirs, salons large and small. Standing instructions from the Queen, who was probably concerned lest they be damaged in certain particularly narrow hallways, dictated that the dresses were not taken from place to place by circuitous routes. There was no saying, then, when those dressmaker's dummies might trundle into view. Rattling and hollow, they took up a great deal of space and were an obstruction to anyone walking the halls. I secretly called them 'the white phantoms'. People moved out of their way to let them pass, but with obvious ill-will. I never saw any other reaction to their 'presence'. And though the general feeling was one of amusement, during the few seconds it took for the precious wardrobe to go by, there was an exasperated expression on people's faces. Then everything picked up again where it left off, as though nothing had happened.

I, on the other hand, cherished a special affection for the Queen's 'white phantoms'. I enjoyed positioning myself in their wake, and trotting along after them in the space through which they had forced their way, so that it was suddenly available for walking. Dreamy and contented, I would follow them as far as I could, on their way back up to the Queen's apartments. I would linger a moment after the doors had closed, to savour the luxury and gentle softness emanating from those rooms . . . My only experience of the Queen's formal balls, then, was following their phantoms and, thanks to the kindness of a pageboy, eating a few oranges. It is not very much, yet it is everything . . .